WATCH IT BURN

WATCH IT BURN

CARRIE MAGILLEN

and

STEPHEN TAYLOR

Little Robin
PRESS

First published in Great Britain by
Little Robin Press Ltd, 2025
This paperback edition, 2025

A CIP catalogue record of this book is available from the British Library

e-Book ISBN: 978-1-913692-21-6
Paperback ISBN: 978-1-913692-22-3
Hardback ISBN: 978-1-913692-23-0
Audiobook ISBN: 978-1-913692-24-7

Little Robin Press Ltd
Kemp House, 128 City Road
London EC1V 2NX
United Kingdom

For Emma

*For leaving Stephen in his man cave for hours, for trusting
Carrie with a huge proportion of that time during the writing
of this book, and for coming up with the perfect title.*

You're a superstar!

CHAPTER ONE

PAUL

Have I got time? I glance at the dashboard clock. It's already 11am and I said I'd be there first thing. She can wait. I'll need a coffee if I'm going to listen to her bending my ear all day. I'll tell her the store didn't have the sink she wanted and I had to drive out of town to get it. I'll hint that if she hadn't changed her mind so many bloody times the job would have been finished yesterday. Then she'll feel like shit for whining about me showing up late.

On the passenger seat, my phone rings. Dexter Tanning's name shouts out of the screen at me. I ignore it for the second time this morning. He's going to blow a gasket like he always does. I'm supposed to be at his latest purchase, painting the walls ready for the kitchen fitters to put the carcasses in on Wednesday. But when this woman called on Friday wanting her boot room renovated, I figured I'd get it done over the weekend. I would have, too, if she wasn't such an indecisive old bitch. Dex'll calm down. I'll do his bloody kitchen overnight if I have to.

Starbucks lies ahead with a parking space conveniently empty outside. God, I need that coffee.

I indicate, and prepare to bump the wheels of my transit van up the kerb before dropping them down to park without having to reverse in. I'm just about to turn when the shiny new BMW X5 in front darts into my space without indicating. A thirty-something, middle-class, permatanned yoga chick turns off her engine and laughs with her friend in the passenger seat.

She's oblivious to me, I'm just an invisible lowlife in a white van.

The whirlwind builds in my head. Annoyance turns to anger, anger to fury, and I fight the urge to ram her car, break bones, knock the teeth out of that perfect look-down-her-nose face.

I say nothing, just drive past, my expression emotionless. Forgettable.

By the time I find a parking space, the rage has subsided. Calm again, I rummage through the trough in the dash until my fingers curl around the flick-knife I use for work. Tucking it into my paint-covered overalls, I slip out of my van.

The blonde yoga chick enters Starbucks, her friend hidden from view in front of her. Crouching down by her car, I pretend to tie my shoelaces. No one's looking as I press the button on the knife. The blade clicks reassuringly into place a second before I punch it through the wall of the BMW's rear tyre.

There it is: the release of tension. Order restored. Justice done.

A flicker of a smile dissolves as I tail the women into Starbucks. They're two ahead in the queue. The blonde's ponytail swishes from side to side as she talks. 'Brooke,' she says overenthusiastically to the barista. Fresh from the gym, she's dressed from head to toe in branded Lycra. Her curves wiggle suggestively for all to see, controlling every male eye in the room.

The whirlwind in my head starts up again and my fist clenches. I fight the rage before it consumes me, forcing my hand open and relaxing my face. Moving a step closer to the counter, I imagine seizing that control from her: arms tied behind her back, stripped of Lycra, her own underwear stuffed in her mouth. My hands on her throat squeezing just enough to cause panic as I take her from—

'What can I get you?'

The swell in my jeans subsides as the barista's interruption steals the mood from me, the event hidden under my baggy overalls.

'Large Americano to take away.'

'What's the name?' His pen hovers over the takeout cup.

'Paul.'

Collecting her drink, Brooke glances my way, looking right through me as if I don't exist. When she moves aside, she reveals her friend still waiting for her order.

My mouth falls open as my body turns cold, her name frozen on my lips.

No...no.

It can't be.

You're dead. You're fucking dead.

Yet, she's standing right here, waiting for a coffee as if nothing ever happened. As if *we* never happened. And it's only now, in this very moment, that I realise I never actually saw her die. I just assumed. It seemed inevitable, but somehow... Instinctively my hand goes to my cheek as I recall the touch of her lips setting a fire beneath my skin.

She got out.

Escaped...and then she left me behind.

No – that's impossible. She loved me. She loved me as much as I loved her, I've never doubted that for a second. Not then, nor for a single moment since, in all these years.

She would *never* have left me.

Her eyes wander aimlessly as she waits for the barista to finish preparing her drink. But she must feel the burn of my intense stare because she turns to look at me. Cheeks flushed, she smiles.

I take a step towards her, about to ask her where she's been all these years, why she stayed away, but then I'm distracted by the barista's loud call.

'Millie?'

She looks up, beams at him – too pleasantly for my liking – and takes her cup.

Millie. She must be using another name. Women do that in coffee shops, don't they? Give out a fake name.

'Thank you,' she says, with lips that are just as sweet but a voice that's entirely different.

It's not her.

It's not fucking her.

I struggle to make sense of the realisation. Not feeling the way other people feel, I don't recognise this unwelcome emotion. Devastation? Relief?

Both.

Holding her takeout cup, she glances at me as she glides past, casting her gaze downwards, coyly. She's just as beautiful as I remember: honey-brown hair down to her full breasts, sparkling blue-green eyes. The curve of small hips that invite me to—

'Paul!' shouts the barista.

I ignore him and watch her leave, savour the movement of her body. Only when the door closes behind her do I finally tear myself away and stride to the counter to collect my order.

As I step out on to the street, heading for my van, I'm determined not to look back as Brooke curses over her flat tyre. But then her friend speaks again, and her voice stops me in my tracks. I can't help myself – I have to hear it one more time to be absolutely sure.

It's definitely not her, this Millie...her voice is higher, softer.

I don't understand the abstract concepts people often speak of: happiness, humour, emotional connection. Never have. But I've learned to mimic. I've learned it well. Spinning the wheel of characters at my disposal, I fix on a veneer of soft features, kind eyes and a friendly manner.

'You two alright?'

'I've got a flat.'

'Oh...that's annoying. Er...look, if you've got a spare, I can change it for you.'

'Would you? God, you're a lifesaver.' Brooke flutters her eyelids, finally noticing me for the first time because she wants something from me.

Smiling, I move towards the back of her BMW, imagining my hands around her throat again. 'It's no problem. I'm Paul, by the way.'

'Brooke.' She's all charm and come-on eyes. 'And this is Millie.'

Don't stare at her. Don't stare.

'Can you pop the boot?' I walk by close enough to smell the clean scent of Millie's perfumed deodorant. I risk eye contact, connect with those blue-green eyes for a fleeting moment then flash her a charming grin.

Millie can't help but return it.

I place my cup on the roof of the car and open the hatch. Pushing their gym bags to the back so I can lift up the board and get to the spare tyre and jack, I notice the nearest one isn't zipped up all the way. Inside, a pink purse rests on a lilac towel. The bag is Nike.

Glancing through the back of the car, I clock Millie's outline through the driver's side window. Fuck, what a body. Toned, strong. She's dressed head to toe in pink Lycra. Nike Lycra. Brooke is in black. Pink's obviously more Millie's taste than Brooke's, so it must be her purse. Maybe it'll have a driving licence, an address.

'Are you from around here?' I drop the tyre on the pavement and set the jack in place.

'Not far,' Brooke answers. She's keeping it vague. She doesn't trust me.

While I change the tyre, Brooke talks loudly on her phone and Millie stays near the front of the car, sipping from her coffee cup. But out of the corner of my eye I catch her giving me the occasional glance.

'All done.' I drop the flat and jack in the boot and close it before grabbing my drink, careful to maintain that warm smile and those kind eyes.

'Thank you so much,' Brooke says, 'er...?'

'Paul. And it was no problem. Nice to meet you.'

'Well...thanks again, Paul.'

'Thank you,' Millie adds.

Heading for my van without looking back, I climb into the driver's seat and reach into my overalls for the pink purse.

I flip through the cards, find the driving licence and pull it out. But, when I flick it up in front of me, Brooke Fletcher's name stares back at me.

Fuck! Fuck! Fuck!

My face contorts as I punch the dashboard over and over. Then I pull the knife from my pocket and stab it through the picture of Brooke, pinning it to the dash. Staring at the plastic card, breathing heavily, I lock the rage back down inside. When it finally eases and I'm calm again, I realise the licence still has a use.

She's her friend, this slut. She knows how to find her.

Out of the passenger window, Brooke's BMW sails past and, too busy chatting, neither of them looks my way. But I track Millie's form until the car disappears into flowing traffic.

Fuck...she looks so much like her.

She could be her.

She *will* be her.

CHAPTER TWO

MILLIE

'That was sweet.' I slug back the last mouthful of coffee and exchange the empty cup for my sports bottle in the centre console; I love coffee, but it's a vice I wash away with cucumber water.

'I guess.'

'What do you mean, you guess? He didn't have to help us; we could have been stranded there.'

'Not for long. I have breakdown cover.'

'Wow. Could you *be* more ungrateful?'

'I'm not ungrateful,' Brooke says. 'I'm glad he helped us. I just – I don't know... I mean, sure, he was good-looking, but there was something creepy about him.'

'He wasn't creepy! He was really nice...and pretty sexy. I liked his smile, that cute tiny scar he has under his bottom lip like a dimple. He reminded me of James a little. A lot, actually.'

'He didn't look anything *like* James. James is sweet. Paul was creepy.'

'You're so harsh.'

I'm not surprised by Brooke's reaction. She's like this with all men – all people, actually. I try not to let it bother me, but I often find myself springing to defend everyone even when they don't need it. The majority of Brooke's knives go straight in the back and advocacies fall on deaf ears, so I'm not sure why I bother. I guess it's for my own peace of mind; I need to say out loud what I know in my heart: that I don't agree with her.

Brooke's not really my type. Not like my other friends, who are all really nice. Not that she's not nice – sometimes. She's just...brutal. She thinks she's super-honest and forth-right, and that those are admirable qualities, but, in reality, she doesn't know the difference between candid and cruel.

She's not really my friend; her brother is. He's my best friend and client rolled into one. And if Shawn hadn't recommended my yoga classes to her, I doubt Brooke and I would even be acquaintances. She inserted herself into the middle of our friendship and now makes out to Shawn that she's closer to me than he is and knows me better than he does. I'm the ribbon tied to the rope in their tug of war.

The moment Brooke found out she had to drive past my house to get home – a fact she wheedled out of me on the second day – she insisted on picking me up and dropping me off for every class and I couldn't say no. Not for want of trying. But it's hard to say no to Brooke. Impossible, actually.

Brooke says, 'Well, it doesn't matter whether you thought the tyre guy—'

'Paul.'

'Paul...' she raises an eyebrow with a hint of distaste '...was attractive—'

'You were the one who said he was good-looking; I just agreed with you.'

'Well, it's irrelevant anyway, because you have James and he's a lot nicer. And if James doesn't work out, there's always Shawn.'

'Shut up – he's my best friend, and even—'

'I thought *I* was your best friend.'

'Of course, you are too, but that's not the point. Shawn... he doesn't think of me that way.'

Brooke blurts out a laugh.

'Anyway, we have a date tomorrow night, so—'

'You and Shawn?'

I huff with exasperation. 'Me and *James*. Shawn and I are destined to be best friends and nothing's gonna change that.'

Brooke would love it if I dated her brother, but the idea of her as a sister-in-law. Nope!

The radio has been churning out pop songs all the way to the leisure centre and back and I can't handle any more of Brooke's lead vocal to a chorus of shallow, repetitive tunes. A side effect of being raised by your grandmother is a love for old music. When I'm alone in my car it's all playlists from the '30s and '40s, but Brooke refuses to give them a chance so, regardless of which of us is at the wheel, it's always her music or nothing.

I reach for the knob. 'Can I turn this off?'

'I guess. But you really need to get with the programme. I hope you aren't playing your shit to James every time you go out. Talk about a dick-deflator!' She bursts into song. '*Ah, sweet mystery of life, at last I've found theeeee...*'

'Oh, piss off. How do you even remember that?'

'Are you kidding? It plays in your car every time your iPhone connects. I can't get that shit out of my head.'

'If you had any taste in music at all, you'd realise it was a masterpiece.'

She snorts then drawls out a long, 'Sooooo…are you ready for the big reveal?'

'What big reveal?'

'The first time he gets to see your sweater-stretchers.'

'Sweater-stretchers?! If you mean my breasts, it's not like we haven't done anything. We *have* made out!'

'Yeah, but there's making out and there's *making out*. You've kept him waiting, what, three months? All that pent-up anticipation. It's like letting a dog sniff a bone and then keeping it out of paw's reach; he must be chomping at the bit by now.'

'Am I the bone or the dog in this scenario?'

'The bone, obviously. All I'm saying is, expectation is at an all-time high; you'd better make an effort if he's finally gonna meet your cat.'

In the middle of drinking from my sports bottle, I snort water through my nose and almost spit it on her windscreen. I want to say that whether or not James is going to 'meet my cat' is none of her business, but if I push back too hard on Brooke she gets pissy and doesn't speak to me for days. She doesn't show up to collect me and, if she does, she won't say a word all the way to yoga. So, I do what I always do and just answer her.

'I don't know…maybe. I'm thinking about it. I'll have to see how the evening goes. Perhaps he won't want to sleep with me.'

'Yeah, right! All he'll be thinking is, *about bloody time*!'

'No, he won't. He's not like that. He's a good guy – at least I think he is. He knows I've been through a lot with previous boyfriends, Rob especially, and the last thing I've wanted to do is to jump into bed with another man who isn't going to stick around.'

'Who cares if they stick around? Half the time I'm glad when they leave. Then I don't have to talk to them.'

'Well, for some of us relationships aren't all about sex. Some of us like a little conversation, a little romance. Honestly, if James doesn't work out, I think I'll swear off men for life and become a nun or something.'

'God forbid!'

'I mean it, Brooke – they're like little boys. Only instead of chasing you around the playground and shoving a hand up your skirt, they're taking you to restaurants and copping a feel in the cab home. And the minute they get what they want, they're off.'

'You know *why*, don't you? Why they get out so quick?'

'Because I'm crap in bed?'

She laughs. 'No... Well, maybe you are, but for most blokes any hole's a goal, so I doubt it.'

'Let me have it, then. What's your theory?'

'It's because you're *The One*. The girl next door, the perfect wife, the till-death-us-do-part Cinderella. No guy is going to risk hanging around with you after the first fuck, just in case he falls in love with you. If that happens, it's marriage, kids, and all that stuff they're just not ready for. And, let's face it, that they'll never be ready for.'

'So how come it doesn't happen to you? You don't get dumped after the first shag, but you want marriage and kids just as much as I do.'

Brooke side-eyes me. 'Yeah, but I'd never tell a guy that. And I don't look the type. Men take one look at me and think, *she'll be fun for a while*. I'm the six-months-of-fun, dump-her-when-I'm-done chick. But not you. It takes them three months to get you in the sack and by then their wallet's empty and they're utterly exhausted. The fun's over.'

'Gee, thanks!'

'No, I don't mean that. I mean they daren't stick around any longer because, for a girl like you, three months is already a bigger commitment than they signed up for. And when you finally give it up, they *just know* that for you sex means love.'

I flop back in the seat. 'So why don't they just buy themselves blow-up dolls? No expensive dates, no conversation, no attention required outside of the bedroom. They can go back to their mates, watch the football and down eight cans of lager. Why even bother with women?'

'Because the chase is the best part, and blow-up dolls don't run too fast.'

'I hope you're wrong. I hope James is different. Because, if he does a ding-dong dash like the rest of them, I mean it – I really will swear off men for life.'

'Your problem is that you hold out for too long. And you place too much emphasis on sex. If you got it out of the way on the first date and they ran for the hills, you'd have only wasted one night with a loser, instead of months and months.' After a moment or two she glances at me, taking her eyes off the road for a little too long. 'You like this one, don't you?'

I can't help smiling. 'You know, I think I do.'

'So, have you had a wax? Bought new underwear?'

'No! Where would I find the time for that when I'm training all day?'

'Jesus. If you're gonna give it up, you could make a bit of effort. At least shower and shave.'

'Ew! You really think I need to be told *that*?! You really think I'm gonna train clients all day then go on a date with a hairy, sweaty fanny?'

Once again I'm sharing intimate details with Brooke that I'd rather keep to myself. It's not that I'm a really private person, or someone who minds joking about intimate things; it's just that there's something about Brooke that makes me cautious. She's been coming to my yoga classes for five years now, three times a week, but there's still this gap between us. Although I suspect I'm the only one who notices the yawning crevasse. I think it's because we're so different. She's diamond-tough and equally beautiful. She likes expensive things, wealthy men, and she never has a hair out of place. I don't have the energy for all that. And when it comes to men I just like them kind. James is kind.

'What are you gonna wear?' she asks.

'The strappy black dress.'

'That stretchy thing that comes down to your shins?'

'Yeah. It's comfy. It's my go-to date dress. Not too sexy, not too scruffy.'

'*Not too sexy* is right. Why don't I drive you back to mine? You can borrow something.'

'Thanks, but I'm fine in my little black dress.'

'Are you gonna wear those awful Skechers too?'

'Yes! I am going to wear the *awful* Skechers. They look cute with the dress, and I can walk in them.'

'They do *not* look cute. They look like boys' shoes.' Brooke pulls up outside my house. 'Go on, get out. You're embarrassing.'

'Thanks for the lift. See you Wednesday?'

'Yep. Wednesday.'

I grab my empty coffee cup from the console and my sports bag from her boot. Then I poke my head back through the passenger window. 'You at least gonna wish me luck for tomorrow?'

'You don't need it. You're fuckin' awesome. Knock 'im dead.'

[illegible]

CHAPTER THREE

PAUL

'Right, I'm off now, Mrs Clarke. I'll be back in the morning to grout the tiles, eight o'clock sharp, okay?'

This job should have been finished yesterday and now I have to come back tomorrow as well because, after I'd mixed up the whole bag of bloody grout, she decided she didn't like the colour. Now I want to tell her what I really think about that. Instead, I fake a patient tone and smile while picturing smashing the vase on the hall table into the side of her whining face. I imagine her lying on the carpet in a pool of blood and cheap plastic flowers.

'Okay, no problem, Paul. I'll see you in the morning.' She's fooled by my charming demeanour. Dumb bitch.

I smile one final time before turning away. Purpose served, my face falls into a blank canvas as I head out to my van.

Sitting in the driver's seat, I stare at Brooke's driving licence, still pinned to the dash by my flick-knife.

You've been here before, Paul, you nearly got caught. You should pull the knife out and throw that licence away.

But I have to find her.

Skye.

I leave the knife where it is, start the engine, and pull away. As I drive out of Epping, my eyes flip from the road to the licence and back every few minutes. Leaving the affluence behind, I pull up outside my shitty third-floor flat in the far-less-affluent part of Loughton.

Fingers curled around the handle, I yank the knife from the dash and slide the licence off its tip before folding the blade away and slipping them both into my pocket.

The decision's made, actions and reactions calculated. Brooke knows where Sk...Millie lives, and I have to see her again.

The course is set.

I'll go after dark.

'Paul! Where the fuck have you been?'

Without thinking, I click the knife open inside my overalls pocket and run my eyes along the row of flats. There are too many open windows, televisions flickering in living rooms. On the patch of grass that runs along the side of the building, kids play football in front of the *No Ball Games* sign.

'I've been calling you for two days!'

I know the voice that's stopped me from heading upstairs to my flat, recognise his frustrated anger, and adjust my expression before I turn.

'Tomorrow afternoon, Dex. I promise. Look, I've got a set of keys. The radiators'll be fitted and the walls painted before the kitchen fitters come on Wednesday morning.'

I raise my voice an octave while rolling my shoulders forward to look smaller. It gives Dexter a sense of control to tell me off like a naughty schoolboy. In reality, I'm not remotely bothered by him. He's a bulldog without any bite. The whirlwind doesn't cloud my mind. There's no anger. Dexter's a self-made man. School of hard knocks. He's just being himself. An alpha male being an alpha male. No bullshit. Not like the Brookes of this world: users, manipulators, who twist men around their fingers.

Dex calms down. 'Alright... Tomorrow afternoon, yeah? And you'll let the kitchen guys in Wednesday morning?'

'Without fail. I'll be there.'

'Okay; the builders'll be there Wednesday as well. The cement truck's coming at nine to pour the concrete for the extension foundations.'

'No problem, I won't let you down.'

Dexter leaves, happy with his performance. I've already disregarded him. My face returned to its blank canvas, I straighten up and climb the steps to the third floor. Inside my pocket, I fold the flick-knife away.

Dex has no idea how close he came to meeting a *real* alpha male.

As I unlock my flat, my eyes dart up. The barely visible slice of cardboard is still wedged between the door and its frame. My personal space is safe, sterile, secure.

The cardboard flutters to the floor and I pick it up from the inside doormat, lean across to the computer table and place it carefully next to my keys before shutting the door.

The ritual begins.

The curtains are closed, always closed. Standing perfectly still, I slow my breathing and listen to the sounds of the building. The fridge hums in the kitchen. A faint, rhythmic bass plays in the flat next door. Nothing alien, nothing that shouldn't be here.

Without moving off the mat, I turn on the light and empty my pockets on to my work desk: Brooke's driving licence and a wodge of notes from a previous cash job. Then I slide out of my paint-covered work trainers and rest them neatly side by side on the mat. Stripping off my overalls, I fold them into a perfect square and place them on top of the trainers ready for tomorrow's work day.

Now I can enter the room, small and square, devoid of furniture or personal objects. Occupying the centre of the room is an adjustable bench, surrounded by steel barbells, cast-iron weights and dumbbells. In the far corner, a pull-up bar is fixed to the wall and a punchbag hangs from the ceiling.

There's no TV; I have no interest in that kind of entertainment.

I'm straight into the chair, turning on my computer, watching the three screens in front of me burst into life.

Once the machine completes its boot-up tasks, I open Google Maps on the left screen and type in Brooke's address from her licence. A street map of Epping drops a pin on her location while I open Instant Street View on the middle screen and copy her address into there. The camera view flips to a road on an estate with big homes and neat gardens. Moving along the street, I zoom in to read the house numbers until I locate Brooke's.

The estate is new, with some homes still being built in the final phase. I Google the developers and scroll through several hits until I find a map of the plots and house types. Brooke's is a Richmond. A little more searching finds a PDF of the sales sheet. The picture on the front matches the street view and the floorplans show the upstairs and downstairs layouts.

New estates use Euro Cylinder locks, five- or six-pin barrels. Two, maybe three minutes to pick. From the bottom drawer of my computer desk, I select a Euro Cylinder from an assortment of locks and clamp it in the jaws of a small vice that I've secured to the desk. Then I roll out my leather pouch of lock-picks and select one.

It's a few hours until dark.

Practice makes perfect.

CHAPTER FOUR

MILLIE

The conversation with Brooke plays on my mind while I prep my home gym for Shawn. He'll be here soon. He'll put my wandering thoughts to rest – he always does, he has a knack for it.

I've known Shawn for more than a decade. He was a client at Brandon Hope, the gym I used to work at before setting up on my own. When I left, he followed me, said he couldn't bear the idea of starting with a new trainer. It meant the world to me that he trusted me enough to be my first client, and insisted on paying the same rate, which made no sense: this is no swanky corporate gym. Now, after all these years, he's not just a client; he's my closest friend.

I wish I could run the yoga classes from here as well instead of paying for the studio at the leisure centre, but my home gym is too small. It's still set up from my session last night, and Shawn needs a specialised configuration. Before his motorcycle accident he was surprisingly strong for his slender frame and could bench-press a hundred kilos. But, since fracturing his spine and breaking half a dozen other bones, he's back to beginner level.

I introduced him to weightlifting with chains because they're easier for him. They match the body's strength curve. When you lower the bar to the chest – the hardest bio-mechanical position in a bench-press – the chains hit the ground, and the weight gets lighter. And when you raise the bar – the easiest biomechanical movement with the mo-mentum of a bench-press – the links come off the floor and the weight gets heavier. It means he can bench-press or squat more weight without putting too much pressure on his damaged body.

I squeeze the retaining clips and slide them off the bar before removing the two ten-kilo weights I was bench-pressing last night. I can bench a lot more, but I don't want to build any more muscle than I already have. When I had dreams of competing professionally, I used to push myself to my limits and could bench more than my body weight. I could power-clean – a single accelerated lift from floor to shoulders – sixty-five kilos and deadlift a hundred. Those dreams evaporated when Nanny died; I regretted every hour I'd spent training instead of being with her.

Now, I have nothing to prove.

A lot of guys I train insist on bulking up with protein shakes while bench-pressing far more than they should, just to prove how tough they are. Very gently, I try to persuade them that real strength is on the inside – you know, wax on, wax off and all that – but they're only interested in whether they look good in a tight T-shirt. I wonder if, at ninety years old, they'll lie wizened on their deathbeds thinking, *thank God I spent all that time in the gym*. There's so much wasted life inside these four walls. If I didn't have to be in here to earn a living, I'd be out there, hiking in the woods or wild-swimming in the rivers.

James has dropped hints about me going with him on his next photoshoot. And I'd be lying if I didn't admit that the Chilean coastline topped off with a live-aboard in Antarctica sounds incredible...but perhaps a little too incredible for me. I could do with a break – I haven't been on holiday in years, money's just too tight. I only wish he were going somewhere a little less daunting: Portugal, Spain... But I guess there aren't many penguins or orcas to photograph in Spain. They have monkeys in Gibraltar; why can't he take pictures of those? Probably because every man and his dog is doing that.

I'd never used weightlifting chains – never needed them before Shawn's accident – and I had to watch dozens of YouTube videos to make sure I got the set-up right. But I've got to grips with them now.

Starting with two five-kilo leader chains, I slide their sleeve-like collars on to each end of the barbell. Bolts in the collars bite down on the bar to lock them in place. It's handy that I don't need a wrench to tighten them; each bolt has a solid metal T-bar – a horizontal rod that pokes through a hole in the bolt – that acts like a handle you can turn. Not that I don't own a wrench – I do. I also own a tail pipe cutter, a power chisel, a shingle froe and a host of other bizarre tools you've probably never heard of. Grandad was obsessed by tools, and I've kept every one of them as if they're heirlooms he left me. I have no idea what most of them are for and I don't remember Grandad doing any DIY; Nanny used to fix everything.

Once the lighter leader chains are in place, I move on to the heavy-hitters: four twelve-kilo lifting chains folded in half, two on each side. Shawn thinks that with all that weight combined he's benching close to sixty kilos; he has yet to notice that the lifting chains are linked to the leader chains so low down that half of them stays on the floor even when his arms are fully extended. I know it's naughty of me not to set him straight – a lie by omission is still a lie – and I feel a pang of guilt as I twist the locking nut on the quick link. But I have his best interests at heart when he's benching less than he thinks he is.

He's always waxing lyrical about the chains, saying they're one of the reasons he'd never train with anyone else because I think about every client's individual needs. I research methods that get the fastest results, and invest in bespoke kit for their situation. A lot of gyms get by with standard gear and that's fine, but it doesn't maximise their clients' workout time. I don't want mine wasting any more of their lives in here than they have to.

Shawn had a glint in his eye when he asked why I'd bought the chains. I didn't want him getting the wrong idea, thinking I treat him differently, so I told him he wasn't the only client that needed them and they were a good investment.

It wasn't true.

The truth is, I can't bear to see him in pain, struggling. The chains were expensive and they're a bit of a faff, but they'll speed up his recovery. Seeing him back to his old self will make all this worthwhile. I guess I do treat him differently, but why wouldn't I? He's my best friend.

I manage to keep a straight face when we move from the bench to squats, just about. Shawn has the most amazing bum and it's hard not to stare at it while standing close enough to spot his lifts.

I swear to God, even when he's standing upright you could rest a tray of gin cocktails on his backside. I have to keep a smile under wraps when I'm studying his stance and form. That feels unfaithful to James, but there's no harm in checking out another man's body. It's hard not to in my job; I'm paid to make sure they've got the best. And I'm sure James checks out other women; we're only human.

Shawn and I do engage in harmless flirting occasionally, but neither of us would take it any further. We wouldn't risk our friendship, and he knows I'm seeing James now. When I was single, Shawn had a long-term partner he'd been seeing for years, but she left him a few months after his motorcycle accident. She couldn't cope with how much help he needed or how frustrated he got at being unable to walk or do anything for himself. By the time he recovered from the heartbreak, I'd just met James.

'You're butt-winking,' I say. 'Widen your stance just a little; it'll help you get a deeper squat and keep a neutral spine.'

He does as he's told.

'Can I ask you something?' The moment the words are out, I wonder if he's the right person to give advice on this or if I even want it.

'Sure,' he says. 'As long as it's, "Are you ready for me to add another chain?" My cousin could lift this and he's six.'

'Was your cousin in a motorbike accident? No...I'm not going to ask if you're ready for another chain because you aren't. So stop behaving like a cranky six-year-old and do as you're told.'

'Yes, Mum.'

I watch as he takes the next squat.

'Better. But turn your toes out a little, about thirty degrees, that'll help with the retroversion.'

'What were you gonna ask me?'

'Oh... It's silly really. It's just something Brooke said on the way back from yoga today.' If I am going to ask Shawn for dating advice, it's easier to say to the back of his head. 'I have this date with James tomorrow night and I'm thinking...you know...maybe it's time.'

Shawn puffs. 'You mean you haven't already?'

'No. I didn't want him to turn out to be another Rob.'

'Ah, yes. Mr Rob "eats, shoots and leaves" Walker.'

'I should have known as soon as he told me his surname.'

He lets out a strangled laugh and it's obvious he's tiring but I don't say *I told you so*. 'Well, I'm no dating guru but what's the question?'

'Brooke asked if I'd got a wax and bought new undies. And she said I shouldn't wear my black dress and Skechers. She seemed genuinely horrified. Like, if I don't get waxed from eyebrows to toes, buy a new dress and get my nails done, I'm a lazy skank. But I can't take a whole day off work just to get ready for a date.'

'Since when do you care what Brooke thinks?'

'I don't. It's just...do men *really* care about all that stuff?'

'Some do. But you know Brooke. I love her an' all but when it comes to men she's as clever as bait. If a guy's only interested in stilettos and how far down your cleavage he can see, what does that tell you about him?'

'Good point.'

'Do you mean that black dress that comes up to your neck with the strappy thing down your back?'

'I only have one black dress. So, yes, that one.'

'Ignore Brooke. You look great in that.'

'Even with the Skechers?'

'Especially with the Skechers.'

'Thanks... I was planning on watching the finale of *The Handmaid's Tale* before the date, which only leaves me an hour to get ready.'

'Plucking eyebrows or watching TV? That's a tough one.'

'My point exactly. That's a good stance – does it feel okay?'

'Fine,' Shawn puffs again. 'It just feels weird with the chains. And I'm used to squatting a lot more.'

'When you can handle that weight and talk without getting breathless, I'll add another chain.'

'Spoilsport... So, you like this guy...this James? You think he's the one?'

'He could be. But you know my track record. I don't turn frogs into princes with one kiss, I turn sensitive guys into psychopaths with one shag. It's my gift.'

'Wow...you must really be something in the sack! But hey, if he turns out to be another Rob, we'll plot some humiliating revenge; that'll make you feel better.'

'Will we, now?'

'Sure. What are friends for?'

I stop laughing when I notice him struggling to push out of the squat. With a hand on each side of the bar, I gently assist his lift while getting ready to step back in case he needs to bail. I could take the weight from him and drop it on the rack, but he wouldn't want that. It would make him feel weak – crazy as that is after a serious accident – and I'd rather he bailed.

'You know...' out of breath, Shawn drops the bar on the rack '...if this one turns out to be another arsewipe, maybe you should take a break from dating. Hang with your friends instead.'

'Any particular friends in mind?'

Shawn winks.

'I doubt James'll turn out to be another arsewipe – but speaking of arses, I think it's time we gave the cheek–s a rest. Butt on the mat, mister. Seated chain-pulls.' I point at the floor as if it's an order.

CHAPTER FIVE

PAUL

I've driven past the house twice. There's no car on the drive, no lights on in the house and no alarm box or cameras. I circle out of the estate, turning back on to the main road before taking the next left into an older estate next to hers.

Turning around so the driver's side faces a bush, I pull up in the darkest space between two street lamps. I park that way around because the van has a new side door, and half the signwriting is missing. Some stupid kid on a pizza delivery bike ran into it a few weeks ago, and I haven't had time to get the signage redone. It makes the van look odd: memorable.

I check the road and houses on my side before looking out of the passenger window across the park. I can see right across to the edge of her estate on the other side. Then I check the rear-view mirror. There's no one in front and no one behind.

When I get out, I flick my hood up and head across the expanse of grass: a dark shape, dressed in black, walking at a normal speed. Forgettable to anyone who might glance in my direction.

At the corner of the park, I cross a playground. Twin halogen floodlights, on a tall post in the middle, throw a strong circular glow over the slides and climbing equipment. Two youths sit on swings while another stands behind them; all three look my way. The light over their heads shines down on their baseball caps, casting their faces into shadow. I don't look back. Not through fear or apprehension; they are simply of no interest.

My feet touch a smooth tarmac footpath as I enter her estate. The street is empty, the curtains closed inside the homes on either side. I approach Brooke's house. There's still no car on the drive or lights on inside so I duck down the path to the rear of the property and move to the back door.

Crouching in the gloom, I pick the lock by touch. Latex-gloved hands feel the last pin drop into place in one minute, forty seconds. Only five seconds longer than my last practice at home, but then I wasn't doing it blind.

When I push the handle down gently, the latch pulls cleanly into the door. Then I move into the unlit kitchen without making a sound, closing the door behind me with the lightest of touches. Standing motionless, I listen to the sounds of the house.

Two minutes pass.

Nothing.

Certain now that the house is empty, I turn the kitchen light on. I never use a torch. Torchlight is suspicious. Its movement if seen from outside draws attention, whereas a light turning on is just that: normal, expected.

Women are sixty per cent more likely than men to write things down: addresses, phone numbers, reminders on scraps of paper or calendars. They give birthday presents, cards, gifts to cheer each other up. Men keep numbers stored in their phones to contact each other, nothing more. They don't send cards or presents for birthdays and Christmas unless they have to. Usually for sexual favours from girl-friends or to keep the wife quiet; the exchange unspoken but expected.

First, I notice a spare set of house keys in a dish on the kitchen worktop. Then I check the calendar that hangs on the side of a cabinet above. There are scribbles here and there, Millie's name mentioned for yoga on Mondays, Wednesdays and Fridays. Nothing of much use.

I move on to the drawers. Most people have a drawer in their kitchen for notes, tape, string, and takeaway leaflets. That drawer's quickly found but it doesn't contain any infor-mation about Millie.

Crossing the kitchen, I head into the hall. There's no sign of a man in this house. Brooke's coats are on the rack by the door, her day shoes beneath. I get my hopes up at the sight of a narrow phone table under the stairs, its drawer offering the promise of an address book, but the promise is broken. It contains no more than scraps of paper and junk mail.

A small office at the rear of the lounge also turns up nothing, and the laptop is predictably password-locked.

I should leave, be patient, come back on Friday and follow Brooke to yoga, follow her to Millie. Resolving to do that, I turn off the lights one by one as I make my way back towards the kitchen. But at the bottom of the stairs I pause and look up towards the slut's bedroom.

I *should* leave.

But I don't.

Through the frosted-glass panel to the side of the front door, I'm just a shadow moving in the orange glow of a street-lamp. I climb the stairs, and, as I draw level with the first-floor landing, pairs of stilettos strewn across the carpet meet my eyes.

I stop and take a measured breath.

An image plays through my head: Brooke's stockinged feet sliding into each shoe as she laughs and looks my way, giving me just enough eye contact to ensure I'm on the hook.

I move into the bedroom, halting the whirlwind in my head before it has a chance to build.

The bedroom faces the rear of the house, overlooking the park, so I put the light on without fear of being seen from the road through the open curtains. The bedroom's untidy, unclean. The clothes on the floor and the beauty products spilled across the dresser make me anxious and twitchy.

I check the drawers but find nothing to lead me to Millie.

I've gone too far. It's time to go.

Stepping carefully around the clothes, I reach for the light switch. As my hand hovers over it, I glance down into the laundry basket by my feet. Jeans and a jumper rest on top, covering all but a glimpse of black lace beneath. Hooking a finger into the lace, my latex-covered fingers deny me the feeling of soft fabric as I tease it free.

Already hard, I bring her knickers to my face and inhale deeply: soap, sweat, her sex. I imagine throwing her on the bed, face down, my hand pushing hard on the back of her head to drown out her cries in the pillow as I force myself inside her.

The unmistakable sound of keys sliding into a lock destroys the image.

I shoot an arm out and flick the light off before taking a step back into the darkness. Perfectly still, I wait in the doorway, watching through a small gap in the banisters. Brooke switches on the hall light, then closes the front door behind her.

Alone.

The kitchen light comes on and I move silently out of the bedroom. A cupboard opens then closes, a glass chinks on the counter, and there's the distinctive suck of a fridge.

Can I make it to the front door before she comes out?

Treading carefully around the shoes on the landing, I move to the top step. Realising I still have her knickers in my hand, I shove them into my pocket, ready to move lightly, quickly down the stairs.

I've only lifted one foot to start my descent when Brooke walks into view, turns off the hall light and snaps on the landing light. Directly above her, I stand in plain sight. Then she disappears under the stairs. There's the beep of the answerphone as she checks for messages and by the time she comes back out, I'm already gone, having backed soundlessly into the bedroom.

Toe to heel, I roll my steps to avoid any creaky floorboards. Breathing shallowly, I move to the wardrobe and pull open the louvred door with a slight creak. With it halfway open, I wait. If she goes through to the lounge and turns on the television, I won't have to shut myself in there.

I listen.

Fuck. She's coming up the stairs. I have no choice.

Hoping her footsteps will mask the sound, I push her dresses to one side and slip into shadow.

The door slams shut, and I'm trapped in the dark. Then the key turns and pulls out of the lock. It's a sound I've heard more times than I can remember.

It's pitch black in here. Stuffy. Hard to breathe.

I want to scream at her to let me out, but I don't make a sound.

He's home early.

From the bedroom door, he glances in the direction of the wardrobe. The only thing visible is one grey-green eye lit by a tiny circle of amber travelling through the keyhole from the streetlight outside.

Brooke turns on the bedroom light and the harsh glare snaps me back to the present. I suck in a breath, compose myself and watch. The slats in the wardrobe door angle downwards and, from the highest one, Brooke is visible from the waist down.

Tossing her phone on to the bed, she strips out of her dress and lays it on the duvet before sliding down her stockings. I manage to concentrate on the problem at hand until she peels them off her manicured feet. Then the image of using them, still-warm, to tie her hands behind her back intensifies...even more when she slips out of her underwear. Clenching my fists, I dig my nails into my palms to keep the present in focus.

Brooke puts on silky pyjamas, stored under her pillow, then grabs her phone. She's scrolling the screen as she disappears into the en suite. An Instagram addict, no doubt. She's the type.

Confidence is high.

I'll wait until she's asleep and leave then. I can endure this for hours. The army taught me that: stand here, march there, lie in that cold muddy ditch. Yes, sir. No, sir.

She's back.

The en suite light clicks off.

Her legs move to the end of the bed, then her arms appear as she grabs the dress. Her phone is still in her other hand as she turns towards the wardrobe, towards me.

It's happening too fast.

There's no time to react. She opens the door and stares straight at me. Her eyes blink as her mind tries to process what she's seeing. Recognition, fear, then panic. With a gasp, she drops the dress, turns, and runs for the door.

She's seen my face, spoiled everything. Stupid bitch. I explode out of the wardrobe, clothes flying off the hangers as they catch on my arms. Pelting through the bedroom door, I close in.

Eyes wide in terror, she risks a backward glance and her bare foot stamps on a discarded stiletto. Her ankle goes over on its side and sends her body into freefall over the top step.

I watch.

Brooke's scream is cut short as she lands heavily. Something inside her breaks and a loud crack echoes around the hall. As she tumbles, her arm slips between the wooden balusters and snaps against the momentum of her body's downward journey. The jolt spins her to a stop and leaves her lying upside down, head resting on the bottom stair.

I descend slowly, step by step, running the limited options through my mind before settling on the inevitable.

Whimpering in pain, she watches me approach, unable to move.

I pick up her phone and pause to look at it: the key to Millie. The key to my future.

'Please...help me,' she begs.

I flick the hall light back on and bob down on my haunches. When I hold the phone to her face, it recognises her features and unlocks. Standing back up, I find Millie's contact details and allow myself a hint of a smile. WhatsApp, Facebook, Instagram: they're all there. And she's there again in Brooke's sent messages, her photograph at the top hauntingly familiar.

Brooke's whimpering is starting to annoy me. Ignoring her, I tap on Millie's picture and a thrill surges through me.

I came here for her address and instead I've struck gold: Brooke and Millie are location-sharing.

Millie's photo sits on a B-road west of Epping centre, and when the cell-towers triangulate and lock on to her precise location, a green light pulses around her.

In sync, every part of my body pulses too.

After a few moments of savouring the green light's throb, I go into Settings and turn off the facial recognition and pin locks. Then I pocket the phone before turning my attention back to Brooke.

She's sobbing, pleading through the pain. Even now, she's still trying to manipulate me.

'What to do with you?' I bob down again and run my latex-gloved hand along her silky pyjamas. Cupping her breast, I squeeze hard before sliding my hand to her shoulder. 'Sssh, don't cry. It pisses me off when you cry. You *had* to open the wardrobe before I had a chance to sneak out, didn't you? You brought this on yourself. But it's okay, I forgive you. Here, let me help you.'

She shrieks in pain as I push her across the step until the side of her neck fits snugly against the newel post. Then I stand and look at her upside-down face. 'The problem is, you've seen me. You'll tell the police, and then she won't want to know me.'

'I...I won't tell anyone...please...' She sobs uncontrollably.

'You promise?'

She manages a nod through the tears and snot dribbling from her nose.

'Okay.' Bending down, I brush the hair out of her eyes and place both hands on the side of her face. 'Don't worry, I'll take care of you.' Without warning, I release an explosion of muscular power and jerk her head around the post. Her neck snaps and I watch her body quiver then go limp.

There's a rush.

A charge of electricity courses through my veins, then calmness returns.

I slide her away from the newel post and leave her head resting on the hall carpet at a right angle to her shoulder. Her eyes stare at me, glassy, lifeless.

Standing up, I flick off the hall and landing lights before walking back into the kitchen.

Mission accomplished. Not the way I planned it, but now that I know where Millie is – now I'll know where she is every moment of every day – Brooke's already forgotten. Pausing by the calendar, I pick up the spare set of house keys and exit through the back door, closing and locking it before walking away into the darkness.

[illegible] [illegible] [illegible] [illegible] [illegible]
[illegible] [illegible] [illegible] [illegible] [illegible]
[illegible] [illegible] [illegible] [illegible]

[illegible] [illegible] [illegible] [illegible] [illegible]
[illegible] [illegible] [illegible] [illegible] [illegible]
[illegible] [illegible] [illegible] [illegible] [illegible]
[illegible] [illegible] [illegible] [illegible] [illegible]
[illegible] [illegible] [illegible] [illegible] [illegible]
[illegible] [illegible] [illegible] [illegible] [illegible]

CHAPTER SIX

PAUL

As I look back over my shoulder at the door to the bedroom, a shiver of sweat runs down my spine. But then the TV switching on downstairs triggers a sigh of relief. I turn back to rummaging through Skye's chest of drawers.

Lifting out a stack of papers, I search underneath. When I find what I'm looking for, I stuff them in the front pocket of my jeans and grin with satisfaction when they rattle against the others. As I'm putting the papers back, three sheets fall out along with a photograph. As they float to the floor, I scrabble to pick them up while listening out for the sound of the television. He's still watching, still downstairs.

I study the photograph first. It's me and Skye. I remember that day at the fair, how happy we both were. Hand in hand, holding sticks of candyfloss, we're poking our pink-stained tongues at the camera, laughing.

So much love.

I slide the photograph into my back pocket and, as I'm returning the papers, the one on top catches my eye because it has my name on it. I study it first out of mild curiosity then in more detail before leafing through the others. The bottom sheet is a death certificate for my grandmother, Christine. I never knew her; she died shortly after I was born. I flick between that and the others.

Heart slamming in my chest, I walk out of the room and down the stairs, reading each page over and over as I struggle to make sense of them.

She lied to me.

Our whole relationship is a lie.

Stepping into the lounge, I look between the papers and the drunk piece of shit on the sofa, unable to decide what to do or say. A bottle of Balkan 176 vodka sits on the coffee table.

I reach for it.

My eyes snap open and the dream vaporises to reveal the cracked plaster of my bedroom ceiling. I'm back in my flat.

Twisting the key, I lock the memory up.

It's over an hour before the alarm's due to go off but I'm wide awake and restless. Rolling on to my side, I turn it off.

I work out for ninety minutes: weights, sit-ups, bag work.

Afterwards, in the bathroom, I check my reflection. Lithe and athletic, without an ounce of fat on my body, I'm unassuming when dressed; I keep my strength and power under wraps.

Twisting to flip on the shower lever, I catch sight of my back in the mirror. The scars stand out like deep tramlines. I ignore them.

That's over now, ended.

Showered and dressed, I check my computer before I leave. Brooke's phone has given me access to her socials.

Millie's Facebook and Instagram feeds are set to private except for friends and now I'm one of them. Pictures of her draw me in, look at me through the screen. She smiles and laughs. Calls out to me.

She has a Facebook business page, too. Millie's a personal trainer with a home gym for clients. There are pictures of her working out with men who leer at her arse and tits tightly covered in Lycra. I don't like that.

Taking a deep breath, I let the cloud clear, unclench my fist and turn on Brooke's phone. Once it boots up, I open Messages and tap Millie's picture.

She's still at home.

I want to drive to her house and wait outside, watch her, follow her. I need to find an opportunity to talk to her. But that will have to wait. I turn off the phone. It's too risky to have it turned on for more than a few minutes; not only can I see the location of Millie's phone, she can see Brooke's.

Anyway, I have to get going. I have to finish the job for Mrs Indecisive Clarke, then get over to Dexter's before he blows a gasket.

The day has gone badly.

I finished the grouting and all that was left to do was paint the walls. I should have known the annoying bitch would decide she'd picked the wrong paint colour at the last minute. I convinced her the walls would look better white; it was the only colour in my van. She was easily persuaded. Only now it's six o'clock and I've only just finished the final coat but at least she'll have paid the bill before she figures out the walls look shit in white.

. . .

I've got three missed calls and two angry answerphone messages from Dexter. I'm not in the mood to talk to him, so I just text. *On my way there now.*

Fuck, I'll have to work till midnight.

After stopping at Subway for something resembling a healthy meal, I head over to Dexter's house and park on the driveway. The grounds are empty, the house in darkness. Dex is either overseeing one of his many other projects or he's gone home to his multi-million-pound house opposite Theydon Bois golf club.

I finish the sub, placing the wrappers in a carrier bag I use as a bin to keep the van clean. Even less in the mood than when I left Mrs Clarke's, I give in to necessity and lug my tools inside.

After spending an hour or so fitting the radiators, I head outside for my brushes and rollers to paint the kitchen walls. The temptation to turn on Brooke's phone and check Millie's location is too great, so I hop into the van and grab it from the passenger seat.

I wait for the cell masts to triangulate Millie's position and for the *Locating* message to disappear. Her face emerges in the centre of town over a knife and fork icon. I tap it. The opening hours, address and website for Yakimono Robata appears – a Japanese restaurant on Epping High Street. I stare at it for a couple of minutes until the pulsing heartbeat of Millie's location tells me it's current.

She's inside.

I should turn the phone off and get on with the painting.

I should.

But I don't.

CHAPTER SEVEN

MILLIE

'It was insightful of you to know how much I'd get out of it.' James pops a sushi roll in his mouth and makes yummy noises at eating one of his favourite things while rhapsodising about another. 'I'm so glad you recommended it. I've been binge-watching it. It's not just the writing – obviously, that's brilliant – it's the colour and sound. Sheer magic. They aren't afraid of long silences; it doesn't need dialogue when the cinematography's so strong.'

I tip my head in agreement.

'That moment,' he says, 'where she looks at all the other handmaids through the window and then opens her hand to show them the detonator. Oh, my God...!'

I love his enthusiasm, and I can't help feeling pleased with myself that my recommendation is giving him so much joy.

He's completely carried away now: '...white hats falling, red cloaks flying and all against this backdrop of black glass as the building explodes...'

I hide my mouth behind my glass of wine, taking a sip and swallowing a giggle, but nothing slips by him.

'Sorry,' he says. 'I sound like a total twat, don't I?'

'No, of course not. I loved that scene too...for all those reasons. I just wouldn't have been able to articulate why. But yes, it is so much more than the screenplay and the acting. Honestly, you don't sound like a twat at all.'

'Not even a little bit?'

'Hmm...' I pinch my fingers together and James lets out a self-deprecating laugh. 'I'm kidding!' I say. 'Honestly, I love hearing you talk about filming like that. It's been a long time since I've heard a man talk about anything other than sex with that much passion. You notice things. Light. Shadow. I guess that's why you're a photographer. Whenever I take pictures, I cut people's heads off.'

'Everyone does that at first. I have dozens of unusable photos. I'd capture this great bokeh but have footless stumps in the ground. I used to be so self-conscious if people were standing around waiting for me to frame the shot. I'd rush and make mistakes. Eventually, I relaxed. I got better and could make light and framing decisions faster. Wildlife photography is good training for that; you have to frame a shot quickly.'

'You mean they don't pose...even if you ask nicely?'

He grins, pushes his empty plate aside and pours us a little more wine. Then he pauses. 'You really should come on this trip, you know? I could teach you photography, and you could help me get in shape. I bet the guys would even club together and pay for your tickets. It's a long trip, we spend hours sitting in one position and having someone like you around to take care of us physically would take the strain off. It's not like we can go for a run or anything. They'd be chuffed as nuts to have you there.' He looks right at me. 'I would, too.'

I take a deep breath then a gulp of wine. 'It sounds amazing, honestly. I just don't think I'm brave enough...breaking through the ice and all that. I'd be scared of something going wrong and freezing to death. Or the boat sinking and getting eaten by a whale. Or, even worse, having to eat my frozen shipmates to survive.'

'Don't knock it; we're all really tasty.'

I laugh. 'I want to, I really do. I just might take a bit more convincing. I mean, Chile...Antarctica? The most exciting place I've ever been is Crete. And that was a decade ago.'

Taking my hand, he says, 'Think about it, alright? We still have three weeks left and it'll be easy to add you to the crew. To be honest...' He clears his throat, and I wonder what he's going to be honest about. '...I think... I feel like we've reached this amazing place in our relationship...don't you? Made a connection, I mean. That's not just me, is it?'

I shake my head, slowly.

'Now I'm having to leave for six months, and I don't want to go without you. I don't want to jeopardise this. What if you forget all about me while I'm gone, fall in love with some other guy?'

'Some *other* guy? Who says I'm in love with you?'

'Him!' James points at the waiter on his way to our table. 'He told me you were in love with me, while you were in the bathroom.'

I laugh.

'Can I get you any desserts?' the waiter asks.

A few moments ago, a chocolate ganache was delivered to the table next to us. It looked so delicious, I was set on having it. Now the thought of eating frozen dead people has put me off.

James picks up the dessert card. 'Oh, sorry, we haven't looked.' He scans the options then looks up at me. 'Do you fancy one?'

I pause, unsure whether to say what I think I'm going to say. 'Actually...I was wondering...if you'd like to come back to my place?'

James thrusts the menu at the waiter.

'Just the bill, thanks.'

CHAPTER EIGHT

PAUL

As I pull into a loading bay opposite Yakimono Robata, the green pulse over Millie's photo tells me she's still there.

Brooke's phone is a risk. I've left it on too long, cell towers triangulating my journeys. But its digital history, logged in the service provider's databanks with millions of others, will remain hidden. Unless the authorities go looking. I turn it off and put it in the glovebox. I will destroy it, but for now its value is too great.

I get out of the van, grab my hoody off the back of the passenger seat, and slip it on over my overalls. I flick up the hood and tilt my head down, masking my features from view as I cross the road.

My heart's beating fast.

Hopefully Millie's with another girlfriend, a better one than that slut Brooke.

How can I turn this into a coincidental meeting?

I check the menu in the display cabinet beside the door.

They do takeaway. That's my excuse to enter. Before I do, still facing the menu, I take a half-step to the side. Through the window I scan the restaurant out of the corner of my eye, searching the tables for Millie.

I don't see her.

Anxiety washes over me until I realise she's sitting with her back to me. Her hair shakes as she picks up her wine glass and laughs. Her movements captivate me, make me smile. She laughs again, leaning to one side to reveal her companion.

A man.

Tanned, with smooth features and surfer-blond hair, he laughs with her. His eyes are locked on hers. Not in the way friends look at each other. No. Like lovers, flirty...sexual.

Unable to breathe, I back away stunned.

I fight the urge to stride into the restaurant and walk right up to them, grabbing his wine glass and smashing it on the table edge, grinding it into his fucking neck.

How dare you touch her!

I want to grab him by his pretty-boy hair and slam his face into the table over and over until it's a bloody mess, unrecognisable.

The darkness in my head is too much. I'm losing the control I work so hard to maintain. The mask I wear is slipping, the fury that burns inside on show for all to see. I have to get out of here.

As I run to the van, my hands shake so much I fumble with the keys. I pull the door shut and sit in the driver's seat, eyes wide, my vision disconnected from the real world, incoherent thoughts spinning around between tumbling, nightmarish apparitions.

I'm trapped in the dark.

The key turns and pulls out of the lock.

He's home early. He glances at the wardrobe door as if he knows I'm in here.

It's stuffy, pitch black. I can't breathe.

I have to get out.

Face hot, veins on my neck and temple pulsing, I grip the steering wheel and roar at her to let me out because if I stay in here a moment longer my head will explode from the screaming inside my mind.

Walking hand-in-hand past the van, a couple turns and stares, their pace increasing when a vision of insanity stares back at them. My roar fades, replaced by suffocation. Hyperventilating, about to black out, I take slow, measured breaths.

It's an eternity until my vision clears and the tremors fade. Finally, barely in control, I start the van and drive the fifteen-minute journey to my flat.

Before the van comes to a complete stop, I yank the hand-brake, lock the wheels and slide into the space at the far end of the car park.

Emotionally exhausted, I'm cranking the rear doors open to grab my tools when a familiar voice attacks me from behind.

'Paul! I've been calling all fucking day! I've just come from the house and you've only done the radiators. You haven't painted the walls and the fucking kitchen fitters will be there in the morning! What the fuck, man?'

I turn to find Dexter standing right behind me. This time there's no apologetic tone or stooping to make myself smaller. No longer the assured alpha male, his expression flips from uncertainty to shock, then intense fear.

Suddenly twice my size, my face close to his, unfamiliar in its contorted rage, I grab the front of his jacket with both hands. Pulling him clean off his feet, I dump him flat on his back in the rear of the van. Dex lashes out with wild punches as he tries to stop me. They're weak, pathetic. Nothing like my father's.

With gritted teeth, I power my head forward, head-butting him in the face. Cartilage and bone give way as his nose collapses and blood gushes into his mouth.

'She's with him! She can't be with him!'

Dex thrashes harder in a desperate attempt to get free but I clamp my hand around his throat and pin him to the floor of the van. With my free hand, I reach up to the racking and grab a litre tin of white gloss. It fits snugly in my grip. A look of utter terror crosses Dex's face as I raise it above his head. Drops of blood and spittle fly from his mouth as he pleads, but I can't hear him. He's not a man. He's just a target for this uncontrollable fury.

Releasing every ounce of explosive power I have, I smash the paint can into the side of his head, the tin denting as I hit him. But his shocked mind is too slow to register the blows.

I hit him again and again. 'She. Can't. Be. With. Him.'

By the time the lid blows off, splashing sticky gloss across the van's floor, Dex is barely conscious. Releasing his neck, I dig my fingers into his cheeks, forcing his mouth open before pouring what's left of the paint down his throat.

'Not. Anyone. But. Me.'

Dex gurgles and convulses, failing with what little stamina he has left to move his head out of the way. His body goes limp, the blood from his nose mixes with the gloss, and candy pink swirls run down his cheeks.

I step back from the van.

The rush of electricity is stronger than at Brooke's: amazing, powerful, indestructible. But it fades fast, the reality of my actions returning with my self-control.

Fuck!

I look from left to right. How could I be so stupid? What if somebody saw me?

There's no view into the van from the flats and it's dark, late. There are no kids playing football on the patch of grass behind me.

Reaching inside, I unwind a length of clean blue tissue from the roll. As I wipe the paint and blood off my hands, I scan the parking area for Dexter's car. His yellow Lexus LC500 coupé is easy to spot near the road. Throwing the tissue inside, I swing Dex's legs into the van then rifle through his pockets. After pulling out his house and car keys, I shake open a stack of dust sheets to cover the body. As I shut the doors, there's no panic, no remorse, just annoyance at my loss of control. A problem has presented itself: a problem that requires a solution.

After a few minutes, I calmly crank one of the rear doors open again, just enough to lean in. Reaching for the racking, I pull out a pair of latex gloves and two sets of plastic shoe covers, then shut the door. I ram the gloves and one set of shoe covers into my pocket before pulling on the second set.

Without leaving painted footprints in my wake, I run up to my flat and change into a brand-new pair of overalls, fresh from their plastic bag. Then I transfer the contents of my pockets across. Back down in the car park, I look around, then put on the gloves and a clean set of shoe covers before getting into Dexter's car.

At a housing estate two miles away, I leave the car parked in the shadows before jogging back. I need to get rid of the body and clean every trace of it from the van. I also need to burn the overalls, gloves, shoe covers and dust sheets, but that won't be easy.

Thinners!

There are thinners at Dexter's, at least half a dozen five-litre bottles, locked in the shipping container he's rented to use as a material store. Carl, the foreman, ordered them thinking they were 500ml bottles and Dexter tore him a new arsehole for making the mistake. But he's done me a favour. There's also the freshly dug trench for the extension footings. It's a metre deep and isn't overlooked thanks to the high hedges that circle the grounds.

By the time I back the van up the driveway of Dexter's new property, it's after ten. I unlock the door and go inside, turning on all the lights to flood the rear garden. Grabbing the keys for the container and mini-excavator, I head out back. The digger sits silently beside the trench that, tomorrow morning, will be filled with concrete.

Jumping into the seat, I start it up. Soon, deep in the footings, there's a two-metre-long ditch.

CHAPTER NINE

MILLIE

'Wow.' James scans my grandmother's hallway. As I lead him to the lounge, he peers left and right through the open doors. 'It's like going back in time.'

'I haven't changed much. Nanny decorated. It reminds me of her, but there are traces of Grandad too. I can't bear to part with any of it.'

The Persian runner, side table and sideboard, plus all the pictures on the walls, are all exactly where Nanny left them. My mum died when I was seven, then Grandad when I was thirteen. Dad was always away with work, so Nanny became my only parent. Her belongings – her presence – fill every room, corner to corner. And now in her absence this cottage has taken her place. It's my warmth, my comfort and my safety. I don't tell James this place is a mother to me – he'd think I'm crazy – but that's how it is.

When I'm alone, I talk to Nanny all the time and I know she can hear me. There's an old Ouija board in the loft which Shawn and I have played with many times. Nanny always shows up to say hello. She spells out things Shawn couldn't possibly know, so I don't doubt that she's there. I sense her behind me sometimes, feel her hand slipping into mine the way it used to. And, now and then, the lavender scent of her talcum powder fills the air. Of course, I don't tell James that either. I've just got him here; I don't want to scare him off.

I wonder if Nanny likes him – no doubt she's following us down the hallway, checking him out in the same way he's checking out her house – I think she'll approve. But then again, Nanny always said that men who seem too good to be true inevitably are. And James – so far – has definitely been that.

His too-good-to-be-trueness makes me cautious.

He's the perfect amount of handsome: groomed but natural, still untidy around the edges. Blond hair grazes his shoulders and he has olive skin. I've never asked if that's from shooting outdoors so often or from another heritage in his bloodline. And his dark eyes shine with so much exuberance, they're like the mirror glaze on that chocolate ganache I was craving earlier. But what really feels too good to be true is how nice he is to me, how thoughtful. He remembers everything I tell him about my upcoming week and then asks me about it on our next date.

I open the lounge door and step aside so he can go in first. 'Can I get you a drink? Wine? Beer?'

'Wine would be great.'

'Red?'

'Sure.'

'Go in, take a seat. I'll just be a minute.'

When I come back from the kitchen carrying two glasses, James is on the sofa staring into the inglenook. He glances up when I hand him his wine but a second later his eyes are back on the fireplace. It's the same with everyone who sees it for the first time. It's the heart of Nanny's home. The red-brick chimney breast has a half-metre-deep wooden mantelpiece that takes up the entire back wall of the lounge. Inside, there's enough room for two seats and two log stores on either side of the open grate. If I leave all the internal doors open it's big enough to heat the entire house, and everyone who comes here loves sitting around it, staring into it.

'That's incredible,' James says.

'I know.' I kick off my Skechers, take the seat next to him and pull my feet up close to his thigh. There's a nip in the air and my feet are cold. 'You don't see many inglenooks like that these days. This room used to be the cooks' kitchen in a larger house. But it was bombed in the war, and never rebuilt. This is all that survived.'

'Do you ever light it in the summer? Just for the hell of it?'

'Sure, if it's cold enough. Or if I want something to stare at. Occasionally I light it for no reason, if I'm in an outrageously naughty mood.'

I lean across him and place my wine glass on the coffee table before leaping to my feet. Grabbing Nanny's pewter matchstick-holder from the side table, I use its striker to light one of the extra-long matches. Slipping the flame between the gaps in the grate, I touch the newspaper firelighters one by one. I let James think I keep the fire made up all the time but in truth I did it for him. I thought it might be romantic.

Staring at the blue flames as they slowly take hold, I say, 'This *whole* house reminds me of Nanny, but that fireplace most of all. She used to keep her teapot warm over it and she'd even cook on it sometimes. She had this huge cast-iron cauldron that she made soups and stews in. It was copper-plated. I can still see it sparkling in the flames. I swear her food tasted better for being cooked over an open fire.' I laugh. 'She used to...' I stop. I'm boring him with memories of Nanny, becoming disconnected from the present.

'What?' James asks.

'Never mind. It's silly.'

'Tell me. I won't judge.'

'Whenever she was stirring something over the cauldron, she used to act out that scene from *Macbeth*; it made me laugh every time.'

His face is blank.

'You know...' I do an impression of Nanny stirring. '*Double, double toil and trouble, fire burn, and cauldron bubble.*' There's a hint of recognition in his eyes, so I clue him up with the next line. '*By the pricking of my thumbs, something wicked this way comes.*'

'Oh, you mean *Harry Potter*!'

I laugh. 'Yep, that's right, *Harry Potter*.'

'Aren't they bringing in some law about open fires, putting a stop to them?'

'It's not the fire itself.' I return to the sofa, pick up my glass again and pull my knees up to my chest while I wait for the room to warm. 'It's the fuel. There are rules about the types of wood suppliers can stock. But I have a whole supply in the garden. Nanny felled a giant eucalyptus years ago and its wood is still going. I thought about replacing the open grate with a woodburner once. They're far more efficient. But, when it came to it, the quote to get that removed was enough to change my mind.'

'I can imagine. It must weigh a ton.'

I laugh caustically. 'People say that about heavy things all the time, but in this case it's actually true. They said they'd need specialist equipment to move it.'

We stare into the fire for a while and then James puts his glass down on the coffee table. When he takes mine as well, I know what's coming. I slide my feet to the floor, so that my knees pressed to my chest aren't a barrier between us. It's not as though we haven't made out – of course we have, lots of times – but this time, when our lips meet, it's hard to breathe.

He pulls out of the kiss and says, 'I didn't bring anything. I thought you weren't ready, so I stopped putting them... I mean, I didn't know we'd reached the *come back to my place* stage. If I had I would have...but then it would have looked like I'd come prepared and was expecting... Not that I'm expecting it now, of course... I mean...just because you said—'

'James...' I look directly at him. 'When I said "come back to my place" I meant exactly what you thought I meant.'

He laughs, more out of relief than anything. I'm surprised he's as nervous as I am. Nanny will see that as a good sign. Not too cocky, too confident. I fall back into his arms and he kisses me again, his tongue brushing mine, his fingers in my hair. I push the coffee table aside and we slide off the sofa on to the rug. Then I wince as I sit on one of my Skechers, lying on its side with the thick sole up-ended. I laugh, imagining what Brooke would say about me trying to be romantic with a Skecher stuck between my bum cheeks.

When I unwedge it and toss it across the room, James laughs too. Then he pulls me towards him and lays me down before gently lowering himself on top. Straining against me, he's already there, but he takes his time. He kisses my lips, my neck, and my shoulders. But, with a dress all the way up to my neck, that's as far as he can go without kissing fabric.

Getting undressed in front of someone for the first time is always nerve-racking for me. Perhaps he senses that, because he gets to his feet and goes to one of the floor lamps by the fireside. 'Shall I turn this on?'

'Sure.'

Then he makes his way to the door and flips off the main ceiling lights. In the dim glow of the lamp, his eyes fix on my every move. I slip out of the long cardigan Brooke would have chastised me for wearing over my little black dress. Then I deliberately turn sideways as I lift that over my head, so he catches a glimpse of my lace cheekies. I don't take those off, though, or my bra; I'm not quite ready for that.

It's not that I'm ashamed of my body. I mean, there's nothing wrong with it: I don't have one boob ten inches lower than the other, or a nipple where my belly button should be. I just...I don't know, I'm old-school, I guess. Shy when I'm naked. Nanny brought me up to believe that the first and only man to see you naked should be your husband on your wedding night. And if he didn't find you sexy at that point then tough shit, he'd already married you!

These days, there's a sense of judgement. It's like we're all on that bizarre dating show where all the contestants are in the buff, and people decide whether or not to date you based entirely on your wibbly bits. Our bodies are so deeply personal, inextricable from ourselves and yet not at all who we are. It's wrong to be judged at such a superficial level, but that's what happens. It's like standing on the edge of a cliff wondering if he'll take one look at you in your birthday suit, and think *thanks, but no thanks!* then push you off.

I want this and yet at the same time I'm afraid of it. I dread that sickening feeling when he stops calling after the first time you've had sex. So you're left imagining not only the worst things about your body but the worst things about yourself as well. And each time it happens, a sliver of my faith in men gets chipped away. I have to retrain myself all over again to believe they aren't all devious three-year-olds who've just discovered their winkies are fun to play with.

On a more practical level, there's another advantage to keeping your undies on as long as possible: if you don't slow a man down with a bra clasp, it's all over in the sand of an egg timer.

The magic has scattered. My wandering thoughts have ruined it again. But then James unbuttons his shirt and I forget what I was thinking about. Eggs or something.

Although we've made out dozens of times, I've only ever seen James with his shirt on. It had crossed my mind that he might have tricked me with the sensitive guy act. Naked, he could turn out to be one of those rippling muscle "look at me" types. Someone who spends all his time in the gym because appearances are the only thing that really matter to him. But then he works the fabric off his shoulders and I realise he's a normal guy. Slim – but I knew that already – toned, but not rippling.

As he leans forward to pull down his jeans, a pendant swings from his chest and catches the firelight. On its silver snake chain, it sways back and forth before nestling in his chest hair when he stands.

I've never seen a pendent like it. Its steampunk design has a sturdy brass cylindrical base with an ornate silver hinged lid. A ball and loop clasp keeps it shut, suggesting something's hidden inside. Still in his boxers, he runs his hands around the back of his neck and unhooks the clasp, the action solemn. It's as if the chain might snap at any moment from a weight too heavy to bear.

He then turns his back to me slightly, forcing me to lean sideways on the hearth rug to see what he's doing. He places the pendant in his cupped palm, carefully piles the chain on top, and, before placing it on the mantelpiece, he kisses it. The action is quick, surreptitious, as though he's crossing himself in the presence of an atheist.

When he turns back to me, I point at it. 'That's unusual. I've never seen a necklace like that before.'

He just nods.

'What is it?'

'A cremation urn. My sister.'

'I'm sorry... You've never mentioned her.'

'I don't like to talk about it. Amanda lost her baby. Cot death. And then, four months later, she hanged herself. I always wonder if there was something I could have done, or said...something I didn't do that I should have.'

'James... I'm—'

'Don't. If you start me off I won't stop.' He glances at the pendant on the mantelpiece. 'I never take it off, but it feels weird, you know...doing this with...well...Amanda sort of in between us. Can we change the subject?'

'Of course.'

He resets himself, finds the moment again. My eyes widen – just a little – when he slides down his boxers. And when I blush, I tell myself it's the heat of the fire.

Clearly he's not as troubled as I am by getting his kit off. So when he sits back down on the rug I prepare myself for a runaway train. Only that doesn't happen. He pulls me to him, wraps my legs over his, and kisses me again.

We sit together like that for a long time. Him pressing his lips to mine, then to my neck, then down to my breasts just above the cup line. He doesn't rush to take off my underwear; he's tentative. With his arms wrapped around me, he caresses my back.

When he finally unclasps my bra and my naked chest presses against his, our tongues meet in a deep, sensual kiss and the spark sets off a fire that neither of us can control.

I pull out of his embrace, lie back on the rug and slide off my panties. Not needing any more of an invitation, he dives between my legs, kissing me gently before sliding his tongue inside me. But I'm already so worked up, I have to pull him back by his hair to stop things ending too quickly. After three months of flirtatious dating and doorstep kisses that eventually turned French, and after late-night fumblings in his car when he dropped me home, now I'm lying naked in front of him with my legs apart, James isn't the only one who's too impatient to wait any longer.

So, when he works his way up my body, kissing my stomach, my ribs, my breasts and finally sinking into me, I don't hold him back or tell him to go slow. I wrap my legs around him, put my tongue in his mouth, and take pleasure from the knowledge this won't last long for either of us.

When we're curled up under a blanket on the sofa, warm from the fire, my shyness returns. I don't know whether it's because I can't stop myself from worrying if he thought I was terrible, or because Amanda is back between us. James put his pendant back on the moment it was over, saying he didn't feel right without it.

I wonder if she would have liked me.

James senses my inhibition and instead of looking at me he stares at the fire, his cheeks glowing like the embers while he rubs the back of my thumb. I try to forget about Amanda and focus on what we just did, how sexy he is, how happy he makes me, and how much I want to make him happy too.

'I would have done that for you as well, you know?' I nod suggestively below his waistline. 'If we'd had more time.'

'Sorry.' He laughs. 'It was a bit too much all at once. I hadn't planned for tonight to happen. I'll do better next time.'

'Oh, no, you did great. I'm just saying...if you'd wanted...'

He lets go of my hand, runs his fingers through my hair and kisses me deeply. 'Oh, I wanted! Next time. And I'll be thinking about that all week now...'

Will he? I said that in the hope it *would* make him think about me all week, that there *would* be a next time. But with my track record, it's more likely that he'll turn out to be a three-year-old looking for his next toy to play with.

The early summer sun streams in through the bedroom window. It was late when we came to bed, dark. I didn't think to close them.

'James... James.'

He stirs and groans. 'What time is it?'

'Eight-fifty.'

'What?!' He half-opens his eyes and looks around as if he's forgotten where he was.

'We overslept.'

Brushing sleep on to his cheek, he finally focuses and his face falls. 'You're dressed. Why didn't you wake me?'

'I tried. You just groaned and rolled over. I have to go. I have a yoga class. Brooke'll be here any minute. But stay... sleep. I brought your clothes up.' I point to the end of the bed and he nods appreciatively at not having to wander back down to the lounge naked. 'Help yourself to anything you want – coffee, toast – and then let yourself out.'

I peck him quickly on the lips but as I pull away he drags me back for a longer kiss. 'I had a great night,' he says. 'When can I see you?'

'I don't know. Call me?'

'Sure...later today? And maybe tonight we can—'

'Tonight?!' I twist my face into an expression of shock and revulsion.

'Well... I mean...if next week is—'

I grin. 'I'm just teasing you! I'd love to see you tonight.'

He flops back on the pillow. 'Oh, my God! You totally got me! For a minute there I thought you'd used me for sex and I was getting dumped.'

I bend over and kiss him again. 'Not a chance. But now I really have to go. I'll see you tonight.'

'I'll call you.'

At the bedroom door, I turn back to look at him one last time before tearing myself away. Grrr...bloody yoga class! The only thing I'm in the mood for this morning is crawling back into that bed and doing some downward-facing dogs with him!

As I run down the stairs to the front door, my mind refuses to budge from this one solitary thought: I hope his little speech up there wasn't rehearsed, and he really will call. Because if James is everything he seems to be...

He might just be *The One*.

CHAPTER TEN

MILLIE

Standing on the pavement outside my house, I stare up the street at the empty road.

Brooke's late.

She knows she has to pick me up by nine at the latest because I need time to set up the studio. It's at times like this that I wish I could invent a good reason to not share a ride with her. I hate being late, it makes me flustered. And the last thing my students need is an instructor who arrives more stressed out than they are. It's hardly an advert for yoga when the teacher looks as though she's about to have an embolism.

I wish I were one of those people who goes with the flow, but I'm not. I need order. I need to know what's going to happen next, and I can't cope when things upset my equilibrium. That's why I studied yoga in the first place, so I could take back control of my life...or at least fool myself into thinking I had control over it. It's helped, but what I really need is a personality transplant.

I check my watch again. Brooke's rarely late. If anything, she's usually on the early side. She likes being the first to arrive so she can snag her spot in the second row and stare at Richard's arse for an hour. Richard's always the last to arrive and ends up in the front row where nobody likes to be.

I try her mobile. It rings and rings before going to voicemail. That worries me. Brooke never lets her phone go to voicemail. She has an acute case of FOMO. She even returns missed calls from unknown numbers to ask why they called her. I would never do that. If I don't recognise a number, I don't even answer it.

Brooke and I location-share so I don't have to wait outside if it's raining. I usually check she's en route while I'm getting ready but James distracted me this morning. I open the Find My app and wait for the *Locating...* message to clear. It takes longer than usual, and I don't know whether that's because everything slows down when you're running late or whether her phone's off.

The message vanishes and the green sphere throbs over her avatar.

I stare at it in confusion.

Brooke's on the other side of town. I'm about to zoom in on her exact spot when the *Locating...* message reappears. It must have been a blip or got stuck on her last mapped position. Knowing her, she was out on a date last night with some rich, hot guy who owns one of the big houses out there. Maybe she forgot to charge her phone. She's probably sobering up in his king-sized bed.

I can't wait any longer.

Cursing her under my breath, I slam the gate behind me and stomp back up the garden path. But, once inside, I can't find my car keys; they aren't in their usual spot in the hall drawer. I have to go back to the damn Find My app to locate the AirTag I have attached to them. I hit *Play Sound* but can't tell where the beeping is coming from. So I waste another two minutes using the *Find Nearby* arrow. It takes me to the gap between the sofa cushions that my keys fell through.

I am *not happy* with Brooke!

Fortunately the traffic into town is light, because by the time I found the keys and got Mini Monty out of the garage Brooke had cost me twenty minutes. I'll have no time to relax before class now and the whole session will be frantic.

It's not the first time Brooke hasn't shown up. The first time was when Shawn had his motorcycle accident and nearly died. Neither of us showed up to class that day; we both spent it by his bedside praying he would wake up. Since then, she's been sick a few times – code for hangover – but she always texts to let me know.

This is only the third time in five years that she hasn't shown up without texting. But on the previous two occasions I could see it coming. She'd been frosty on the way home from the previous class because I hadn't let her bully me over something or other. And I'd been able to pre-empt her absence with a text to say I had an errand to run afterwards and would take my own car.

I rack my brains for snippets of stored conversation from the journey home on Monday. I don't remember pissing her off. I don't remember her being frosty about anything. But I do remember her being crabby about me wearing my black dress on the date with James. She wanted me to borrow one of hers. Maybe she took my refusal as an insult. She gets pissy about the smallest things.

I make good time and arrive at the leisure centre with a few minutes to spare. I do some deep breathing while the students organise their mats, blocks and towels around the studio. But, once everyone's ready, I can't help staring at the empty space in the second row. Nobody fills it because Brooke has indelibly stamped her name on it. Once, a new student took that spot and Brooke forced her to move. Afterwards, the student hung back to speak to me, saying, 'I didn't realise the spaces were allocated.' I just smiled, winked at her and said, 'They aren't.' She took it in good humour and never tried to take Brooke's coveted spot again.

I warm up the class with a basic sequence: cats and cows, extended child's poses, and downward-facing dogs. Only my mind isn't in the room; it's still on the conversation with Brooke. I keep running over what I said and did. I'm training with Shawn this afternoon, so maybe he can tell me what she's in a strop about; she tells him everything. He'll explain it; I just have to be patient. But I'm not my usual centred self.

CHAPTER ELEVEN

PAUL

'Alright, Paul?' Carl, the site foreman, approaches my van. 'Jesus, it stinks in there, mate. You're gonna get fucking high driving that.'

'Yeah, I had to drive with the windows open. I was here late last night finishing that bloody kitchen ready for the fitters. I dropped a full tin of gloss as I was packing up. Fucking shit went everywhere. It took an hour to clean the van with thinners and I had to burn a load of dust sheets in the oil drum out back.'

'That's shit luck, mate.'

'I borrowed the thinners from the storage container but I'll square all five away with Dex. I've kept what's left in my van.'

'Okay – make sure you do, though. I can do without one of his bitch fits today. And don't let him catch you using the oil drum; you know how he gets the arse about burning waste on site.'

'What he doesn't know won't kill him,' I say with a smile.

'Well, I won't tell him if you don't.' Carl grins and walks off to check the back garden.

I call after him. 'You here all day, Carl?'

'Yeah.'

'Look, mate, I've only got to give the utility room a final coat, then I'm done. If I show the kitchen guys what's what, can you lock up when they're done?'

'Sure, no worries.'

The kitchen fitters turn up around nine, and, while I'm showing them where everything is, the cement lorry and pumping rig arrive. I watch from the kitchen window as the long boom arm appears over the house and pumps concrete into the footings at the back. The liquid flows all around the trench, covering the area of dirt above Dex's body in no time. The extension's foundations will soon be a metre of rapid-set concrete.

Leaving the site to Carl, I exit the house and hop in my van. I'm tired but relaxed, back in control. All bases are covered. Nothing from Brooke or Dex can lead back to me.

Well, almost nothing.

Flipping the glovebox open, I stare at Brooke's spare set of house keys and underwear then grab her phone.

Just one more time, then I'll get rid of them.

I go through the rigmarole of turning her phone on and waiting for it to boot up, then open the app to locate Millie.

I'm patient this morning. Maybe it's feeling secure in the knowledge that my tracks are covered. Maybe it's just lack of sleep.

Either way, I wait for Millie's location dot to pulse over her house.

She's home. I stare at it for a long time, eyes unblinking.

Eventually the dot moves along the road, heading into Epping. It shifts around the streets before stopping at the leisure centre.

Remembering *yoga with Millie* on Brooke's calendar, I suck in a breath and exit suspended animation.

I should be good for at least an hour.

Turning off the phone, I grab hand sanitiser from the door pocket and squirt a liberal dollop on the display. I work it over the surface with a paper towel until the alcohol evaporates, leaving it free of DNA and prints. Holding it by the paper towel, I shove it into a plastic bag and repeat the process with her keys.

Reaching back into the glovebox, I run my fingers over the black lace of Brooke's underwear. It triggers the memory of her slipping out of her clothes. I want to keep them, but I can't risk it. Shaking off the image before things stir, I soak them in the sanitiser and add them to the bag. I'll dump it in a rubbish bin somewhere in town.

The clock's ticking and I need to get to Millie's house.

I start the engine and check my watch. An hour is plenty of time for a quick look.

The countdown begins.

Her place is old, not what I expected. The bricks need re-pointing and the lead windows have paint peeling from their wooden frames. They're all closed and the drive's empty. No one's at home. As expected.

I park in front of the property, hiding in plain sight: just a workman on a visit. No one pays me any attention as I walk up the path to the front door. The thin latex gloves stretched over my hands are invisible from anywhere more than a couple of metres away.

The door has an old deadlocking nightlatch. Yale. Its brass disc is drilled into the heavy oak just above waist height. That makes it awkward to slide my picks in. Standing tall to hide what I'm doing from prying eyes, I feel my way. The six pins lift one by one.

Two minutes.

The lock clicks and draws back. Leaving it on the latch, I nudge the door open and step inside. When I push it closed, a breeze from outside moves it slightly in the frame.

Millie's lounge is a weird mixture of old and new. Outdated wallpaper and old furniture sit next to a large high-definition TV. An Apple laptop and iPad lie on an old leather sofa like an alien invasion.

The explanation for the old and new sits on the sideboard: old family photos in frames. Several were taken inside this house. A woman in her fifties or sixties with a little girl next to her. The same woman much older, with Millie standing beside her looking just as she does now. Next to the photographs there's a wooden plaque engraved with *Nanny. In Loving Memory.*

This was her grandmother's place.

I pick up the last picture on the sideboard and run a finger across her beautiful face. It's how she looked the last time I saw her. Staring out of that window. She wasn't supposed to be there. She was supposed to be at work, and she would have been if her bus had shown up. She was only twenty-six.

I fight the urge the break the glass. Set her free.

There's a creak from the hallway. Shit. I put the frame back down and move light-footed out of the lounge. Reaching the front door, I turn as a pair of legs appear at the top of the stairs. A man's legs. When he descends, I'm confronted by that bastard from the Japanese restaurant.

Flipping character, I fix on a warm smile and place a hand on the door as if I've just closed it. 'Hello! Anyone home?'

The long-haired fucker's surprised face meets mine. 'Can I help you?'

I clock his concern: he's wondering how I got in.

'Yeah, sorry, I was looking for Millie Holland. The door swung open when I knocked.' My face a picture of innocence, I sweep the door back and forth on its latch to demonstrate.

He stops on the stairs in his T-shirt and jeans.

No socks.

He fucked Millie last night, plied her with wine and smooth conversation. He tricked her into the sack with come-to-bed eyes.

My Millie.

I'll cut those fucking eyes out of his head while he begs for his life.

'Sorry, she's not here. Who are you?'

'Oh...er, okay. I saw her website and was hoping to book some sessions. Look, it's no problem...' I casually turn to leave. 'If she's not here, I can come back another time.'

I have one foot out the door when he descends the rest of the way to the hall.

'Millie's clients book online; they don't just show up unannounced. And the system doesn't give out her address until you've paid for the initial consultation. I know because I helped her set it up. So how did you get her address?'

I turn back to face him. 'She trains a friend of mine. He gave it to me.'

'Who's the friend?'

'Um, what?'

'The friend that Millie trains?'

'I told you. Just a friend. He gave me her address, alright.' Let it go, you stupid fuck.

This is not the time to deal with this prick, not now, not here. Brooke was a necessity, and Dex was a mistake. I lost control. That was stupid of me.

'Like I said, I just wanted to book some training sessions.' I turn again to leave. 'I'll come back another time.'

He comes towards me, more confident of himself. He's not going to let it go.

'So you thought you'd just turn up at her house? Your friend shouldn't be giving out Millie's address. Tell me his name so I can let her know.'

Time to go. I smile politely and pull the door open. 'I'll call back when she's in.'

His eyes move to my hand on the door and his body language changes from confident to fearful. I track his gaze to my latex glove and when I turn back to face him he's pulling his phone from his back pocket. 'Look,' he says, 'I'm warning you: leave now or I'm calling the police.'

You just had to push it, didn't you? And now you leave me no choice.

Closing the door, I click the latch.

'Get out, I'm warning you.' He moves along the hallway towards me. 'Don't make me fuck you up.'

His comment amuses me; no one's been able to fuck me up since my father.

And he regretted it.

When they took me into care, there was nothing left. Just an emotionless void that filled up with fury whenever anyone pushed me. I joined clubs: jujitsu, Thai boxing, mixed martial arts. Later, cage fighting. I moved on each time I was chucked out for losing control. As soon as I was old enough, I joined the army.

They taught me restraint.

The prick does that thing untrained men do when threatened: puffs himself up to look intimidating. Sliding his phone back into his pocket, he comes out swinging.

I duck under punches you can see coming from a mile away then bring my knee up into his stomach. The hard bone sinks into his soft flesh, compressing his organs before knocking him two feet back on to the floor.

He lies there like a deflated balloon, desperately sucking air into his lungs. Before he can get up, I jump in with a vicious kick to his balls. His body slides along the polished wooden floor. The battle already won, I loom over him as he curls up, coughing and wheezing.

Beside me, there's an old-fashioned coat stand. On it hang Millie's scarves and coats. Fear and pleading fill his eyes as I grab the thickest scarf and move closer. When I step over him he retches helplessly. Winding both ends around my knuckles, I drop to my knees and pull it tight around his neck.

It takes a surprising amount of time to strangle someone. Their arms scrabble and flail while their legs dance across the floor. After three minutes, their movements die down to the odd twitch and they lose consciousness. But they're not dead, not yet. You have to keep the pressure up for another three minutes until the brain is starved of oxygen.

I'm bored by this stage. I no longer feel the buzz. This shouldn't have happened, not here, not in her house.

Our house...soon.

There are too many problems: who is he to Millie? One date? A relationship? What will she do when he disappears into thin air? And how will I get him out of her house without being seen?

Unwinding the scarf from his neck, I hang it back on the coat stand in the same place it was before. Then, stepping over the body, I head up the stairs into Millie's bedroom. The clock's ticking and my desire to look around, find out more about her, is soured by fact that he's been here before me.

Had sex in our bed.

Bastard.

His wallet and keys are on Millie's nightstand and his socks and shoes are beside the bed. I pocket the wallet and keys and bring his socks and shoes downstairs. I drop them on the body along with his leather jacket which I find on the coat stand.

I open the front door just wide enough to look around.

No one left or right.

My van blocks the view from the houses opposite. I move swiftly down the path and pull the van's side door open. I grab new dust sheets and a roll of duct tape, and leave it open while I return to the house. Wasting no time, I wrap him and his clothes in the sheets, taping them tightly around his body.

This looks bad, but time is short. And a glimpse of something possibly body-shaped being carried to a van is still way better than an actual body.

Checking the coast is still clear, I leave the front door open and hoist him over my shoulder. It's hard lifting his dead weight, but I've squatted heavier. Moving as fast as I can, I dump the body inside and the van booms when he hits the metal floor.

I take a few deep breaths and slide the door shut.

Another quick check in either direction, and I head back into the house to take a last look around.

Everything appears normal.

He isn't a serious boyfriend: there's no toothbrush, no shaving kit, no clothes in the wardrobe.

There's no sign he's ever been here before today...before last night.

The hour's nearly up but I need something good to come from this cock-up. So I take a souvenir, something Millie won't notice is missing.

Leaving quickly, I drive out of the estate, keeping to the speed limit and indicating where necessary.

Just a white van leaving a job site.

CHAPTER TWELVE

MILLIE

Inevitably, Brooke's still on my mind while I prep the gym for Shawn. Hopefully he'll have spoken to her since yoga on Monday and can give me the lowdown on whatever awful thing I apparently did.

He'll be here soon.

While I'm waiting, I send a quick text to James to let him know I had a great time last night and see if he still wants to meet up later. I'm just adding kisses to the end of the message when the doorbell rings.

I don't say anything until Shawn moves on to floor work because I know how tough bench-presses are for him. Talking at the same time is too much to ask, so we're always quiet through the first part of his routine. But once I've adjusted his stance and he's comfortable squatting with chains I ask, 'Have you heard from Brooke lately?'

'Yeah, I saw her Monday night, we went out for Chinese. Why?'

'She didn't show up for yoga this morning. Did she say anything about being pissed off with me?'

'Not that I remember. But you know Brooke, she's always pissed off about something.' Shawn rises out of the tenth rep, the muscles in his legs tensing. He's getting stronger every day, definition returning to his thighs. He couldn't walk for three months after the accident and was in physio for another six. He lost all his strength and muscle mass.

He adds, 'Actually, now I come to think of it, she did seem a bit agitated.'

'Why?'

'She said something about you finally finding the one and not making an effort with him. But you knew that already. I told her not every guy was interested in a tight dress and high heels. I'll leave you to imagine her response to that.'

'That's so silly. Why does she care what I wear on a date? Is she really pissed off at something so pathetically small?'

'Well, when Brooke's having a hissy fit, it usually is something pathetically small. I love her to death but what is it they say about little things and little minds?' He puffs out a quick breath and instinctively I reach out to take the weight. But then he gets a second wind. 'That's not fair,' he says. 'I shouldn't say things like that about her. It's too easy to see Brooke as one-dimensional when she's not. You just have to peel back the top layer. Honestly, she thinks the world of you – well, you and the commission on her latest apartment sale.'

'And how many views her latest social media post got.'

'So true. But fussing about how you dress on a date is her way of showing she cares. I know it seems superficial to us, but these things are really important to Brooke. Let's face it, she's never going to be preoccupied with climate change or have the weight of the world on her shoulders...speaking of—' He winces and I rush forward to take the weight. 'I'm alright... I'm alright.'

'You're not, I can tell by your face. Let it go. I've got it.'

He lets go of the bar and the chains clink as I lower it slowly to the floor. He bends forward, panting, 'Lucky one of us has some muscle left.'

'I told you you weren't ready for another chain. I don't know why I let you bully me into these things.'

'Sorry.' Shawn winces again, grabbing his lower back. 'It's just taking so bloody long.'

'Well, it'll take a hell of a lot longer if you injure yourself. Why don't you listen to me? Come on, let's get you into the lounge; I'll get you a heat pack.'

When I come back into the lounge, Shawn's leaning forward on the sofa with one hand on the base of his spine. I sit down next to him and press the heat pack against his back. When he tries to take it from me, I say, 'Don't twist. I've got it.'

We sit in silence for a while, staring into the fireplace. Even when it's not lit, it still holds your attention.

'Is that helping?' I ask.

He nods. 'You know...I wouldn't want to wish the summer away, but I miss our winter sessions. Having a beer after a workout, curled up on your sofa, staring at the fire.'

'That's the *only* thing I miss about winter.' The moment those words leave my lips, I realise it sounds as if I miss curling up with him on the sofa. I quickly add, 'The fire, I mean.'

'Why don't we ever sit in here in summer after a workout?'

'Because the gym's only cold in winter. I worry about your temperature dropping too fast after a session. We wouldn't want you getting stiff.'

He looks right at me. 'No. We wouldn't want that at all.'

I shake my head, rest a hand on his shoulder, and lean around him. Then I move the heat pack its width distance further up his spine. 'Does it still hurt?'

Shawn doesn't answer. I sit up and our eyes meet again.

A second later, his lips are on mine.

The heat pack slips from my fingers and lands on the sofa. I quickly pull away. For a moment he looks shocked, hurt. But then he chuckles. 'Sorry. I was just messing with you.'

I don't know what to say so I don't say anything. Then my phone pings on the coffee table. Saved by the bell, I snatch it up. It's a Facebook notification: a post from James. I wouldn't usually read Facebook posts while I still have a client in my home but it's Shawn. And it's a welcome distraction. Any excuse not to look at him when my cheeks are burning.

James has posted a photograph of an elephant seal with a huge trunk-like nose. My heart skips a beat with the idea that I might go with him, that I might actually get to see one of these fascinating creatures in the flesh.

But then my face falls.

'What's wrong?' Shawn asks.

I hand him my phone and Shawn reads the Facebook post out loud.

> Decided to head out to Chile early and see if
> I can shoot some of these beautiful ladies…
> a hell of a lot more attractive than the
> women I've been dating lately! Wish me
> luck! See y'all in six months…

'What the fuck?'

I take the phone back from him. 'I told you, it's my gift: one shag and I turn princes into psychopaths.'

'You only slept with him last night!'

'Apparently that's all it takes.' I slump down in the sofa, determined not to cry in front of Shawn. He's my best friend, but when we're in gym gear he's a client. I need to remain professional. But then I burst into tears anyway.

'Oh, come here.' Shawn pulls me into his chest and wraps his arms around me.

'I can't catch a break,' I sob. 'All that shit about us having a connection and not wanting to break it. All that stuff about me going to Chile and Antarctica. It was all just a pile of bollocks to get me in the sack. And I fell for it hook, line and sinker! What a fucking idiot!'

'You're not an idiot. Good liars are bloody hard to spot. Especially when you're wired to think the best of people.'

'What the fuck is wrong with men? Is getting your dick wet really so fucking important that you'll do absolutely anything for it: lie, trick, cheat. Do *any* of you have *any* feelings at all? Any shame? I'm starting to think you're all just a completely different fucked-up species!'

'Hey,' he says softly. 'We're not *all* like that.'

I fight for breath between sobs and he pulls me tight. Forgetting our client-trainer relationship, I cling to my best friend's T-shirt and cry it out.

CHAPTER THIRTEEN

PAUL

I stop the van outside Starbucks and grab a coffee. The lack of sleep and having to deal with that fucker in the back have taken their toll.

The swig of a strong Americano kicks in as I rifle through James Buckley's wallet. Thanks to his bank cards and driving licence I now know his name, date of birth and address. Unfortunately his phone doesn't have fingerprint or face recognition, and I don't know the PIN. Not to worry. I drain the last drop of coffee. I know a guy who can unlock it.

At the phone repair and accessories shop on the high street, with my thirty quid in his hand, the guy shows his usual lack of interest about where it came from. He unlocks it. No questions asked.

Yawning, I leave the shop and drive to James's house. It's on a busy street with young mums pushing buggies. And fucking dog-walkers, more intent on watching what the neighbours are doing than picking up their mutts' colossal crap.

The path to his house is long and exposed; there's no way I can get the body up there without being seen. I have to give up my plan to get him inside and stage a robbery gone wrong.

Leaving him in the van to deal with another way, I casually walk up to his front door as if I'm supposed to be there. From a distance, the overshoe-covers look like blue trainers and hands in my pockets hide my latex gloves. I slide his key into the lock, turn it, and go inside.

The house is big, modern, designed to look cool. Dotted around the walls, blown-up photographs of endangered animals give off a save-the-fucking-planet vibe.

Well, he's past endangered now.

Sitting in James's office chair, I rifle through his desk drawers, trays of papers, and shelves of box files. I check his calendar, and flick through notes pinned to the corkboard above his computer. While scanning for anything of interest, I shuffle together fragments of James Buckley's life.

Spinning in slow circles, I scroll through his mobile, read his emails and look at photos of Colombia, Africa and Australia. In his phone's Wallet app he has tickets for an upcoming trip to Chile and Antarctica. But when I find a text from earlier this morning I stop turning and plant my feet on the floor.

> Had a great time last night. Do you still want to meet up later? Millie xx.

The message is for me. She wants to meet me.

A second later, real life drags me back. It's not for me. It's for him: the long-haired dead fucker in the back of my van. It pleases me that he's dead, and pleasure isn't an emotion I experience often.

I switch on his computer, which presents me with a password request. Knowing the number of people who write them down, I rummage through his desk again. Finding a black diary I tossed aside earlier, I flip to the back page. Sure enough, there's a list of passwords, all but one of them expired and crossed out.

One password.

For everything.

He's bookmarked his online banking and the browser autofills the user ID and passcode fields. James Buckley was a fucking idiot.

The second login stage is a verification code which the bank sends to James's mobile, held eagerly in my hand. Just six numbers and I'm into his accounts.

Freelance photography must pay well, because he has over forty-nine thousand in savings. Forty-nine thousand! Millie can wait. Just a little longer.

For various reasons – mostly illegal – I have an offshore bank account under another name, registered to an address in Stockholm. With the contents of James's account transferred into it, time is of the essence. I'll have to get rid of the body tonight and fly to Stockholm tomorrow. Once I've withdrawn the cash and closed the account, I can fly back on Friday.

Now to get this fuckwit out of her life. Permanently.

A poser like him is bound to be all over Facebook: *look at me next to this fucking huge walrus, aren't I cool?* And I'm right: his posts go on forever. Photo after photo with amusing comments and witty banter.

Not so funny now, are you, mate?

Scanning through his Pictures folder, I find a photo of a large seal thing with a trunk like an elephant and post it with the message:

Finishing up, I plug the phone into the charger on his desk and leave it on. If Millie calls or messages, it'll ring and ping, never to be answered, as if he's totally blanked her.

Now it's time to clean.

In his kitchen, I find antibacterial spray, cloths and bin bags. I start at the furthest away point and work my way to the hall. Despite my latex gloves, I clean everything I've touched. The spray, rags, James's wallet and keys all go into a bin bag I take with me. Then I shut the front door and walk casually to my van.

When I'm clear of his estate, I pull over and Google cleaning suppliers. I find one on an industrial estate in nearby Harlow. They stock twenty-five-kilo bags of sodium percarbonate – oxygen bleach – and large, heavy-duty bins. I saw a programme on forensic pathology where the victim's body had been washed with sodium percarbonate and it destroyed all trace of the killer's DNA. I locked that in my memory banks.

After collecting the supplies, I'll pop over to Dexter's house tonight after dark. There's an outside tap and hose for filling the cement-mixers. I can dissolve the bleach there before driving James deep into Epping Forest. I'll find a remote spot, strip him naked and soak his body in the bin before burying it.

CHAPTER FOURTEEN

PAUL

A plane rumbles overhead, the engine so loud I could be on it instead of in this house.

Skye calls from the bedroom. 'Pauley, come here.'

'I'm going to be late,' I yell back as I make for the stairs.

'Don't ignore me! Get your useless arse in here.'

I don't need to step through the doorway and breathe it in; I can tell from her voice that she's already high. The room stinks like burning plastic. A smoky haze floats in the air, swirling across rays of sunlight that cut through the narrow gap between the curtains.

'Come. Lie next to me.' Her tone is urgent as she drags me into the room and on to the bed. She puts her crack pipe down and looks at me with dilated pupils. Then she pulls my head down on to her chest. Inside her unbuttoned pyjama top, her left breast moves up and down as she breathes. We stay like that for an eternity.

I don't move or speak.

I know what's coming next, what always comes next when she's like this.

'Make me feel good, Pauley. Like I showed you.' There's no tenderness in her voice; that's gone. It's a command. Always a command.

'No. I don't want to. I'm going to be late.'

I try to move off the bed, but she grabs my arm and pulls me back. 'Don't you walk away from me!' Her face contorts with anger, and she punches me hard in the ribs. Never the face, never where it shows.

I suck up the punch. My eyes water, but I don't cry. That makes her angry.

'I'm sorry, Pauley, why did you make me do that?' Her face softens as though the outburst never happened.

I put a trembling hand on to her belly, sliding it down until it slips under the waistband of her pyjama bottoms.

'That's it, Pauley, keep going.'

My fingers weaved through her pubic hair, I stop. 'I don't want to. I have to go. I'm late.' Pulling my hand back and lifting my head off her chest, I try to get off the bed again. But Skye grabs the neckline of my jumper.

'You ungrateful shit!' She yanks me back so hard, I fall off the bed. Then she picks up one of her shoes and I curl into a ball on the floor while she beats me with it as hard as she can.

I don't make a sound. I just shrink inside myself.

Deeper and deeper.

Untouchable.

The shoe comes down again and again while Skye shouts, incomprehensibly, 'You need to put your seat up!'

· · ·

I jolt awake, flinch away from her.

'Sorry, sir,' the stewardess says, 'but you need to put your seat up. We're beginning our descent into Arlanda airport.'

I flick the seat vertical, close my eyes and shake off the memory.

Untouchable.

Despite my skin crawling from being trapped in this flying tin can for two and a half hours, I slept most of the flight. Exhausted after last night's trip into Epping Forest to bury the fuckwit, I'm sick of being surrounded by people. Flight attendants touch me, families breathe too close to me and I'm stuck in an aeroplane seat that's been polished by a thousand arses.

I didn't have time to get rid of the dust sheets or my clothes after burying the body. That bothers me. I've still got those leftover thinners in the van so I'll burn the rest as soon as I get back.

After clearing customs, I get on the Arlanda Express to Stockholm Central Station. The trains run every ten to fifteen minutes and the journey takes less than twenty, so I don't have to worry; the banks are open till three.

To work.

I like Stockholm, its clean streets and grand architecture. I like the anonymity; I'm an invisible stranger, a nobody, wandering the streets while the locals go about their lives.

On the way to the bank, I pop into a department store, buy a thick jumper and ask for a large carrier bag. Before going outside, I stow the carrier bag in the front pocket of my backpack then put the jumper on under my jacket. It's tight and it pads me out. To a CCTV camera, I'm now ten kilos heavier.

I go on my way. The bank's just up ahead.

I catch my reflection in a shop window. I'm him now.

Brown contact lenses conceal my distinctive grey-green eyes. I'm heavier-set, wearing a baseball cap and horn-rimmed glasses. His passport's in my pocket along with a wallet containing his driving licence, some cash, and a couple of photos of his wife and kids. They're not fakes – they're legitimate, acquired by months of work to steal his identity.

Why this man?

For no other reason than that he looks like me.

In the bank, I'm relaxed; I'm Simon Carlisle. Heading for the counter, I tilt my head. The tip of my baseball cap obscures my face from the domed security camera, top left.

A young woman, blonde, greets me in perfect but accented English. And when I ask to close my account – withdraw over six hundred thousand in five-hundred-krona notes – she doesn't blink an eye.

Swedish efficiency.

With a smile, I hand her Simon Carlisle's bank card and passport. She smiles back, her lips heavy with lipstick. Excusing herself to get the transaction authorised by her manager, she walks away. Her thighs and arse in a tight pencil skirt leave nothing to the imagination. With nylon-covered calves, defined and tense, she balances in high heels. Tights, or stockings? Tights: the skirt's too short to hide stocking tops. I haven't had sex for over a week. I'm horny as hell. I'd like to take hold of that long hair and fuck her lipsticked mouth.

The manager glances over at me and I look confidently back. He scans the passport and bank card, then me again. That's right, dumb fuck, it all checks out. Hand them back to the slut and go get my money. There's a good boy.

She returns to the counter and slides the bank card and passport back to me. 'Thank you, Mr Carlisle. Can I ask what the money is for?'

I'm prepared for this question. The bank is legally obliged to make sure I'm not being scammed or coerced. The money only being deposited yesterday is a red flag. It could trigger a currency transaction report. But I'll be long gone by then.

I open my phone on a screenshot of a red Alfa Romeo 4C Spider. I pulled it from a Swedish car sales website. The sticker price is six hundred thousand krona. Holding it up to her, I say, 'I sold my beamer yesterday; I'm picking this up tomorrow. What do you think?' The car's audacious design and the question, loaded with charm, derails her suspicion.

'Stunning.' A broad smile breaks through her efficiency. 'Maybe you could take me for a test drive.'

'I'd like that.' I wink at her. 'But I'm leaving tomorrow and not coming back any time soon. Hence closing the account.'

'That's a shame. Well, my manager is seeing to your request. I'm afraid we don't carry that much in the cashiers' drawers. But it won't be a minute.'

'No problem.'

Here he comes. In under two minutes, his counting machines have checked and double-checked the withdrawal and I close the account with my well-practised version of Simon's signature. I hate to shut it down; it's been useful over the years. I've stashed profits here from all manner of small business scams. But I can't risk any paper trails and for this amount of dosh it's worth it.

With the help of the blonde, the manager wraps the note bundles into bands and passes them under the counter. I feed each one into a smaller green rucksack hidden inside my large backpack.

Leaving the bank, I keep my head down to avoid facial recognition on traffic cameras. I cross the street and enter

Sturegallerian shopping centre. Having memorised a map of the centre, I move swiftly past the stores with intent. In the toilets at the furthest end of the building, I lock myself in a cubicle.

First I take off the jacket, turn it inside out and hang it on the back of the door. Reversible, it changes from black to brown. The contact lenses are carefully pinched out and flushed. Putting the baseball cap facing upwards on the toilet lid, I fill it with Simon Carlisle's passport, wallet and horn-rimmed glasses.

Setting the green rucksack of money aside, I empty the remaining contents of the black backpack on to the floor. Everything has to go.

The backpack and jumper go in the carrier bag that came with the purchase. A bottle of alcohol-based sanitiser gets drained into the upturned cap and worked over the contents to destroy any fingerprints or DNA.

Finally, I slip on the now-brown jacket, a pair of Ray-Ban sunglasses and the green rucksack. The baseball cap with its soggy contents gets dumped in the bin nearest the toilets, and the carrier bag in another just before exiting the way I came in.

Walking back past the bank, I'm a different man again. When the investigation into a missing James Buckley and his money gets this far, which I have to assume it might, there is no CCTV trail.

Declaring a large sum of cash at the airport is a no go; it raises questions about the money's origins but you can't smuggle it, either. Baggage X-ray machines detect it and body-scanners are sensitive. They pick up the metal embedded in each note. So, after a short walk, I enter a branch of Western Union, pay the fee and transfer three hundred and fifty thousand kronor into one of my UK accounts.

My flight back isn't till ten-thirty tomorrow. Under another different name, I've booked a room in a cheap chain hotel.

With the rest of the day to kill and business all done, my thoughts return to Millie, how to get close to her. What she likes. The type she likes.

The fuckwit. That was her type.

He was smooth, he had money, an extravagant lifestyle. He wore expensive clothes and took her to fancy restaurants.

I still have twenty thousand pounds' worth of kronor in my rucksack and I'll have to declare anything over ten. So I head for the upmarket shops in the Bibliotekstan district.

I have a plan forming of who I am...or who I will be: a property developer like Dexter, but with the boyfriend's style. First stop: Ralph Lauren. I purchase a suit and various other mix-and-match outfits. Browsing the other shops, I spot a leather jacket in a window that's similar to the fuckwit's, so I buy it.

Clothes shopping done, I check the time. My cheap watch stares back at me. Looking up and down the street, I see a Rolex sign protruding from a jewellery shop. I know watches, mostly stolen ones. If you buy a Rolex today with all the correct paperwork, in a year's time it'll be worth only slightly less than you paid for it. Sell it in ten years and it'll be worth several times more.

I enter the store, browse the pre-owned section and finally settle on an understated Datejust, for a hundred and fifteen thousand kronor – just over nine thousand pounds. A subtle statement of wealth without shoving it down her throat. Also, anything pre-owned won't draw the attention of passport control and raise questions about when or how it was purchased.

.   .   .

Next morning, after using the self-checkout and leaving the hotel, I buy a small carry-on suitcase. In the station toilets, I change into some of my new clothes and swap my cheap watch for the Rolex. I remove the tags from the remaining new clothes and pack them in the suitcase.

When I leave the toilets, I dump one carrier bag of tags and receipts in the nearest bin. A second carrier bag, containing my old clothes, watch and green rucksack, gets dropped next to a homeless guy. I also hand him a five-hundred-kronor note which he's too busy staring at while muttering his thanks to even look up at me. As I walk away, he puts down his bottle of cheap, stomach-burning spirits and checks out the contents of the bag with filthy fingers.

Just over twenty-four hours after I set off, I'm walking back through Heathrow. Paul Cooper again, but a different Paul Cooper. A better one, a more successful one. A property developer. A man of means.

The right man for Millie.

CHAPTER FIFTEEN

MILLIE

Biting back tears, I sit in Starbucks with my hands cupped around my latte. I don't know why I'm cold; it's eighteen degrees outside. I've chosen a seat at the back in the corner, well past the counter where nobody will notice me. Brooke and I never sat back here; she always wanted to be at the front or outside. For the first five minutes, I sat at our usual table, until the empty seat across from me gave me chills and I had to move.

I've cancelled my yoga class for tomorrow. I just couldn't stand the thought of staring at Brooke's vacant spot. There was no way I'd have kept my emotions in check. I'd have been screaming at the new girl, *For heaven's sake, take Brooke's spot!* because I wouldn't have been able to look at it.

My first instinct was to call James but there is no James. Not really. The kind, thoughtful man I thought I knew doesn't exist. And the real James has fucked off to Chile without me. The only person I really want to be with is

Shawn – and I'm sure he needs me as much as I need him – but he's dealing with the police.

I'm not sure who else to call.

'Millie, right?'

A deep voice snaps me from my thoughts, and I discreetly wipe away tears with my napkin. Pretending to pat my nose and mouth, I turn to look up at the person standing by my table.

It takes a few seconds.

The face is vaguely familiar but either his clothes or the coffee-shop setting throw me off-kilter. It's as if the barista had stripped out of his white shirt, tie and apron and turned up at one of my yoga classes head to toe in Lycra.

The penny drops.

'Paul...?' I almost add *the tyre guy* but stop myself just in time.

He nods. 'Are you alright?'

I shake off the confusion realising it's not the setting that threw me off, it's his clothes. 'Yes, sorry. It took me a moment to recognise you without the overalls. Nice suit. Special occasion?'

'Nah, business meeting.' He smiles, almost laughs uncomfortably, as if to evade the attention. 'I wear the suit for the investors; it makes them feel more comfortable when they part with their cash... Sorry, you probably thought I was a painter and decorator; I'm actually a property developer. Well, a jack-of-all-trades really. You never know when someone's gonna let you down at the last minute, so I try to keep my skills up. Plus I enjoy the graft. I get lost in mundane, repetitive tasks. It's almost spiritual, don't you think?'

I nod as enthusiastically as I can.

'May I?' He indicates the empty chair opposite.

'Oh...' I don't really want the company of a stranger right now, the effort of conversation. 'Um, sure.'

He peels off his jacket and I clock a Ralph Lauren logo on the internal pocket. The fine detailing of the silk lining screams extravagance. Nanny taught me to sew when I was little, and I've seen enough stitching in my time to know a well-tailored suit when I see one. When he hangs it carefully on the back of the chair, the blue face and silver bracelet of a statement watch slips out from beneath his shirt cuff. It looks expensive too, a Rolex maybe. Although I can't see the logo properly and don't want to be caught staring.

Not that I care – I don't think clothes or money make the man – I'm just taken aback. He's a different Paul from the one who changed our tyre: presentable, confident in his own skin. Not that he wasn't confident before but...I don't know... it's not just the clothes. *He's* different.

He must notice the attention I give to his watch, fitted shirt and tailored trousers, because he adds, 'It may seem superficial, but with the kind of money my company invests, you have to look the part. But, in truth, I'm more comfortable in my overalls...you know...doing an honest day's work.'

I force a smile.

'Are you sure you're alright? You seem upset.'

It's the worst thing anyone could say at a time like this, and, as hard as I try to stem their flow, the tears fall. Paul runs a hand across the table and takes mine, but he doesn't say anything; he waits for me to speak.

'My friend,' I manage between sobs. 'The one whose tyre you changed. She died.'

'Oh, my God, I'm so sorry. What happened?'

'She fell down the stairs. Broke her neck. Her brother found her early yesterday morning. She'd missed yoga twice, and I got worried and called him. He went to her house

Friday night, but she wasn't answering the door or her phone. He went back yesterday and she still didn't answer. So he smashed a window and found her at the bottom of the stairs.'

'Do they have any idea when...?'

'The coroner said that she'd been dead for days. Late Monday, they think.'

'Jesus. That's awful.'

He gently squeezes my fingers. I should feel weird holding a stranger's hand but for some reason I don't. I guess it's because, after he changed the tyre, I feel like I know him already. He's clearly a nice guy or he wouldn't have done that.

'I feel so guilty. When she didn't show up for yoga on Wednesday, I thought it was because she was pissed off with me. Instead, she was lying at the foot of her stairs. But I just went ahead with the class and left her there. I didn't even try to *phone* her until Friday afternoon. I should have gone round to check on her. Instead I assumed she was being petty and sulky. I left her to die.' I sob out the words that are so hard to say, but I have to say them. Admitting it is a form of penance. 'While I was thinking the worst of her, she was lying there...needing my help...and I could have—'

'You wouldn't have been able to do anything. If she broke her neck, the fall probably severed her spinal cord. It would have been quick. Anyway, unless you had a key to her place you would have thought she was out, just like her brother did.'

'I guess. I still feel terrible.'

'Because you didn't go round there, or because you never really liked her all that much to begin with?'

'What?' My sobs end abruptly, the tears on my cheeks evaporating in a sudden drought.

I glare at him in shock.

'Sorry. I tend to say it like it is. I have a talent for reading people. I could tell she got on your nerves that first day we met. That you weren't close friends. It was all over your body language.'

I wipe my face with the back of my hand, incredulous that he would say something like that when he doesn't know either of us. With no idea what to say in response, I just stare at him.

'It's okay,' he says. 'She got on my nerves too. Liking or not liking people doesn't make bad things happen to them, so you have no reason to feel guilty.'

He smiles, softly. And in spite of myself a tiny smile escapes my lips: an outpouring of relief more than anything. All that emotion trapped inside, suddenly released by someone saying something so completely inappropriate and close to the bone. Because he's probably right: that my true feelings for Brooke are the real source of my guilt.

'How's her brother? You said he found her?'

'Shawn? He's a mess. They were really close. I feel so sorry for him. He broke his back in a motorcycle accident last year and then his partner left him because she couldn't cope with his full-time care. Now this. He's really going through the mill.'

'Poor bloke... Do they know what happened? The fall, I mean...it was an accident, I assume?'

This takes me aback, makes me defensive. Because of course it was an accident. Why would anyone hurt Brooke? But he did say he *assumed* it was, and I suppose it's a normal question to ask. I'm overreacting, my emotions on a knife edge. If anything, Paul's questions are making things easier to deal with. I can focus on them instead of Brooke's last moments and whether he's right: whether it really was quick. Or if she died slowly.

It's nice of him to consider Shawn, too. I doubt many men would think to ask about him, or question what happened. I didn't think I wanted to talk to a stranger but it's oddly comforting and Paul is easy company. Most men would just grunt, without the first clue what to say.

Shawn had sounded broken on the phone yesterday; he could barely speak. I relay what he told me to Paul. 'He said Brooke was always leaving shit everywhere. Always tripping over things she'd left on the floor. Apparently the lights were off, and she tripped over a pair of shoes in the dark. She fell from the landing, all the way down the stairs.'

I picture her hallway, cloaked in darkness, and wonder what those last seconds were like, whether she was frightened. Then I think of Shawn again. How dreadful it must have been to find her. The kiss slips into my mind unbidden and I push it away. He didn't mean anything by it, and, even if he did, what would it matter now? We'll never be able to look at each other again without remembering Brooke. Our friendship will be forever tinged by grief.

Paul says something, but I'm buried so deep in thought that I don't hear him. 'Sorry?'

'Can I buy you another coffee?'

I check my fitness tracker. 'Thanks, but I don't have time. My buckets will be full in...' I do the maths '...twenty minutes.'

'I've been subjected to any number of brush-offs in my time, but *my buckets will be full in twenty minutes...* Can't say I've ever heard that one.'

'It's not a brush-off, honestly. Things always come in threes. My boyfriend dumped me, my best friend died, and my house is flooding.'

'I can't help you with the first two, but I might be able to help you with the last. What's causing the flood?'

'My plumber fitted a new radiator on Thursday and over the weekend two of the others started leaking. He can't get back again until Tuesday so until then I'm stuck changing buckets. Every two hours and forty-five minutes to be precise. I've timed it down to the minute.'

'What about at night?'

'Yep, night too.'

'Jeez, what a pain. Why don't you let me come and take a look?'

'Because he'll fix them for free. After all, they weren't leaking before he fitted the new one. He must have broken something.'

'I'll do it for free,' Paul says. 'As it happens, I've just dropped some supplies off to the lads on site, so I've got my van and tools. I can come now if you like. Then you'll get a full night's sleep without a bucket-change.'

'Umm...' I don't know this guy and I'm not sure I want a stranger in my house. But he did change the tyre that day and didn't expect anything in return. It's easy to get caught up with warnings of stranger danger, only to forget all the stories of the kindness of strangers. I don't want to turn my nose up at that; it would be rude.

I think about getting out of bed every few hours tonight.

'That *is* tempting. If you're sure you don't mind?'

CHAPTER SIXTEEN

MILLIE

'I really appreciate this,' I say as Paul takes off his jacket. He hangs it over the back of one of the chairs surrounding my small kitchen table.

'It's no problem, honestly.' He runs a finger over the part of the radiator that's leaking. Then he takes out a set of keys from his pocket and singles out a funny-shaped gold one. Slipping that over the radiator part, he turns it but the leak doesn't stop. 'The bleed vent's gone. I've got a couple of spares in my van.'

He goes outside, and I watch him through the kitchen window. His van looks odd from the driver's side. Half the company name and telephone number are cut off by a gleaming new side door. When he comes back in, carrying a small wrench, I point at his van outside and ask, 'Is that a side gig?'

'Huh?'

'Servicing the props that hold up chicken coops?'

He tilts his head to one side and narrows his eyes in confusion.

'Coop Prop Serv.'

He laughs without humour. 'Cooper Property Services. Some idiot pizza boy rode into the side of my van.'

'So it's Paul *Cooper*, then?'

He tips his wrench at me as if it's a hat, then turns back to the radiator. After closing the valve at one end and turning the thermostat off at the other, we stand side by side as if watching a movie together. The water still trickles steadily into the bucket.

'Was that supposed to fix it?'

'Patience, grasshopper.'

That makes me smile. It's a clichéd but cute expression that I don't expect from a no-nonsense man like him. Perhaps there's a softness and humour beneath his tough exterior. But the water still runs and I didn't bring him here for entertainment. I glare at him, confused. I'm starting to think he knows nothing about radiators and this is all just a trick. My heart beats a little faster.

Paul smiles at my impatience. 'Wait for it...'

The water tapers off, dribbles, then stops.

'And there it is.'

Okay, so clearly he does know what he's doing after all. He removes the bleed vent and puts in a new one.

While he's changing the vent on the second radiator he says, 'It's pretty common. When you drain down a system and refill it, that's usually when parts show their wear and tear. Did your guy put inhibitor in with the new rad?'

'Did my guy do in-hibby-what-now?'

Paul laughs. 'It prevents corrosion in the system.'

'I'm sure he did. He services my boiler every year. He's pretty good.'

'Who is he?'

There's a possessiveness to his tone. As if fixing my leaking radiators gives him a sense of ownership over my heating system. And now nobody is allowed to go near it in case they screw it up again. But I like a man who takes pride in his work.

'In-Heat.'

'In-Heat as in Arthur *Doggett*?'

I nod.

'I know the guy. His memory is as sound as his sense of humour. I'd better check it; I've got a test kit in the van. I'll be back in a minute.'

Paul returns with a tiny bottle into which he drops two tiny white tablets. Watching him do that triggers a sudden sense of vulnerability, as if he could just as easily have slipped those into my coffee. Then, as he opens the valve again with his key and tops up the bottle with system water, I realise I'm just being stupid.

'These'll take a few minutes to dissolve,' he says. 'Is it alright if I use your bathroom while we wait?'

'Sure.' I point at the door. 'Take a right, down the hall. It's under the stairs.'

Paul disappears through the kitchen door, and I watch him go.

When he comes back from the bathroom, he holds the tiny bottle up to the light. 'This shouldn't be clear,' he says. 'The liquid should be yellow. I think Arthur's cheating you. He's been charging you for inhibitor and the time it takes to add it, but then never putting any in.'

'Arthur?! He doesn't seem the type.'

Paul waves the bottle at me. 'The proof's right here. Honestly, this should be bright yellow. Without inhibitor, you'll have corrosion in your pipes, limescale build-up in your boiler, all sorts of problems. That means more work for Arthur and more bills for you. You can't trust that guy. Just call me any time you have a problem, or when the service is due, and I'll do it for you.'

'How much do you charge?' I throw him a cheeky grin.

'For you? Mates' rates. Just pay for the parts and buy me a beer after.'

'You're so sweet. So I need to go and buy some of this inhibitor stuff, then?'

'Nah, I've got some in the van. I'll put it in for you.'

Paul pushes a plastic adapter, with a clear tube attached, into the radiator vent. Then he opens the valve back up and screws the can of inhibitor to the adapter.

'These things can be a bit temperamental,' he says. 'Usually I like to top up from a towel rail but this'll—'

'I've got a towel—' Before I can finish my sentence, the adapter flies out of the radiator and inhibitor explodes from the can. It sprays all over the walls, Nanny's kitchen drapes, me and Paul.

'Whoa!' Paul grapples with the can as if it's an out-of-control fireman's hose. He finally manages to stem the tide by unscrewing the connector from the can. Given its size, it's under surprisingly high pressure.

When the excitement is over, we stare at each other for a few moments then burst out laughing. Our hair is drenched in inhibitor and my white yoga top looks like a wet T-shirt competition. Blushing, I quickly draw the attention away from myself and say, 'Oh, my God, your shirt! It'll be ruined.'

'Nah,' Paul says, 'it'll be fine, I'll just put it in the washing machine when I get home.'

I laugh.

'What's funny?'

'I'll bet you the cost of that shirt that it's at least fifty per cent silk.'

'So?'

'So, it'll be dry clean only. Take it off.'

'Excuse me?'

I pretend his boyish grin isn't increasing my heart rate and say, 'Fine, if you don't want to take it off you can buy yourself a new one. But I can probably rescue it. I'm pretty good with fabric and stains. I'm the product of a frugal grandmother.'

Paul concedes and, while slowly unbuttoning his shirt, he stares straight into my eyes. I can't tear mine away. His are grey-green. And his smile accentuates a dimple in his chin from that small scar beneath his bottom lip. I noticed it the first day I saw him. I wonder how he got it. This is a train wreck waiting to happen but, staring at his unusual cupid's bow, I can't bring myself to step on the brakes.

'Millie?'

'Hmm?' My eyes move down his bare chest and my mouth falls slightly open. Bizarrely, half-naked he appears taller than when he's dressed. He's at least six foot six, with a body I've rarely seen. And it's my job to create this kind of perfection. Clothed, you would never imagine this physique is hidden beneath. His arms are wire-taut, his skin toned. Beneath the surface, thick veins curve snake-like around tight sinew. His pecs protrude above a ripple of muscled ribs and his flat stomach descends in a sharp V. I track it into the waistband of his suit trousers.

'Millie?'

I fight to focus my attention on his eyes and finally find my voice. 'Sorry... Well...you certainly don't need a personal trainer.'

'That's alright.' He takes a step towards me. 'I'm not looking for a business relationship.'

In one movement, he tilts my chin up with his forefinger and presses his lips to mine. He's gentle at first, but then he wraps his arms around my middle, lifting me off my feet without effort. Then the kiss becomes urgent, questioning, searching for my body's response.

With my feet off the ground, I can't step back from him or put any distance between us. If this gets out of control I'm vulnerable in his grip. Momentarily I'm cautious and afraid. But then I remember all the nice things he's done: changing Brooke's tyre; listening to me talk about her and Shawn, then coming back here to repair my heating system. Paul's one of the good ones, and I didn't realise just how attracted I was to him until this very moment.

Perhaps all my previous relationships have been leading to this one, and he'll be the one to finally break the curse.

Brooke's voice echoes in my head. *Your problem is that you hold out for too long. And you place too much emphasis on sex. If you got it out of the way on the first date and they ran for the hills, you'd have only wasted one night with a loser, instead of months and months.'*

She's right. I should listen to Brooke. I should take her advice as if it were her dying wish for me. After all, my way hasn't worked in the past. Why not try something new? Give Brooke's method a run for its money.

Returning Paul's kiss with equal urgency, I run my palms over his shoulders and around his neck. Then I slide them down his back. I grip the swollen triangle of his trapezius muscle and press my wet T-shirt into his chest. Sinking deeper into the kiss, I lift my legs and wrap them around him. And when I slide my tongue between his lips and tease his,

Paul groans. He grabs my backside with both hands and forces our bodies hard against each other.

We both smell of inhibitor, so I pull out of the kiss and whisper in his ear, 'Shower?'

'Upstairs?'

I nod.

With me still wrapped around him, Paul walks out of the kitchen door. But, so like me in a moment such as this, the cost of his shirt presses on the back of my mind. I grab the architrave and pull him to a stop.

'Your shirt! Let me put it in to soak first.'

'Forget it, I'll buy a new one.'

He takes another step, but I cling tight to the doorframe. 'But you'll have to wear *something* when you leave here.'

'I'm never leaving here.' He kisses me again, even more deeply. Groping my backside, he presses himself against me. And this time when he walks out of the kitchen I don't protest. He climbs the stairs two at a time as if I'm not even in his arms, and I can't help but laugh.

He carries me to the bathroom without breaking a sweat or even catching his breath. Lowering me to the floor, he lifts my yoga top over my head before diving in for another long kiss. And while his lips are on mine and his tongue is in my mouth, he's unclasping my sports bra one-handed. In one smooth move, it slips off my arms as he drops to his knees and takes my breast in his mouth. He's caressing me with his tongue while sliding my leggings down to my ankles but I stop him again. 'Shower!' I command. He ignores me and tugs down the front of my panties, about to slide a tongue between my legs. I have to push him away.

He looks up at me, that adorable cupid's bow almost touching my skin. 'Spoilsport.'

'Eager beaver!'

Paul laughs and gets to his feet, while I reach into the shower and turn it on. The water takes a while to warm up, so I turn back to him and kiss him softly. I remove his ruined shirt, unzip his trousers and pull them down. Leaning back into the shower to check the temperature is just an excuse to marvel at his physique for a moment longer. I imagine the hours he must spend training, the dedication.

He's the antithesis of most of my male clients. They confuse size for power and concentrate entirely on muscle gain. Instead of easing off the weights and maintaining a fit body, they forget the initial goal they set for themselves and push well past it. If they had any sense, they'd realise that a bodybuilder's shape only appeals to a niche sector of women. It's men who find excess muscle appealing: a towel-snapping contest in the men's locker room.

That's not Paul.

Paul is controlled, contained. He knows exactly how far to push his body without straining it. And the power confined in those compact muscles is enough to steal your breath.

I run my wet palms over his pecs and down his ribs. With my forefingers, I trace the V-lines either side of his stomach all the way down inside the waistband of his boxers. Paul lifts his chin to the ceiling, closes his eyes and moans.

But I don't take it any further.

While his eyes are closed, I hop behind the cubicle's frosted glass, step out of my panties and wave them through the open shower door on the end of my finger: a white flag of surrender.

A moment later, having slid out of his boxers, Paul steps into the cubicle with me. That's when his size becomes really apparent. He tries to wrap his arms around me but clunks his funny bone on the shower valve. I try to lift myself on to tiptoes and kiss him but he's too tall. So he tries to bend down and kiss me only there's not enough space between us for his torso to be in anything but an upright position.

We both laugh.

'This isn't gonna work,' he says.

'Nope. I need a bigger shower.'

Paul takes the soap from the metal dish hanging from the riser. He quickly soaps himself down, including his thick hair, brushed-back and clogged with inhibitor. Then he pulls me close to him and runs the bar over my back, soaping up a lather. It runs over my backside and down my legs. 'I'll get out.' He hands me the bar and I finish showering.

When I step out, Paul is turned away from me, leaning over to pick up his trousers. I think he's fishing around in a back pocket and I'm about to ask him why when I'm distracted. Deep scars, dozens of them, crisscross his back in every direction. The sight of them makes me wince with the pain they must have caused. But when Paul turns around they're quickly forgotten. He's dried himself with a small hand towel and is holding up my bath towel. He throws it over my head and wraps it around my back; it's warm from the rail. He could have used it and left it wet for me; it's considerate of him. A good sign. Every one of these small gestures makes me like him more, trust him more.

Gripping my towel in his fists, he pulls me towards him, kissing me intensely as our naked bodies merge together with warm, wet skin. Then he tugs the towel harder, tongue in my mouth, pressing hard into my belly until I have to pull away to breathe.

Scooping me into his arms, he carries me to the bedroom, where he sits me down on the ottoman at the foot of my bed. Dropping to his knees, he pushes his body between my legs and kisses me on the lips. He lets the heat build between us while showing the restraint he's clearly a master of.

Pulling away, he bites my bottom lip so gently I shiver. Then he kisses his way down my breasts, ribs and stomach. I reach out to touch him, pleasure him in the same way, but he stops me. His powerful hands lock my wrists and pin them to the soft velvet of the ottoman. Diving between my legs, he kisses me as if he knows my body as well as I do. A moan escapes my lips, and I fall backwards on to the bed in submission. The world disappears with the touch of his tongue, and I forget where I am. There is nothing, no one. Only the shuddering intensity that travels all the way down my body to my toes, turning my legs weak, then all the way back up until it pulses in my ears.

I strain against his grip, reach out to touch him again but he won't allow it. He just pins my hands tighter. When he lets them go, he rolls on a condom so efficiently, I know it's something he's done many many times. I'm on the pill but this isn't about falling pregnant. I barely know this man and I suspect he's had a lot of partners. I didn't even notice it was in his hand when he carried me through from the bathroom and it's a pleasant surprise that he can do that without breaking the moment. By the time he gets up off his knees, sliding his arms beneath my ribs to lift me further up the bed, I'm desperate for him to be inside me.

I want to say that out loud, say something to let him know what he's doing to me. But his presence is breathtaking; his intimidating strength leaves me mute. I haven't been with many men, but I have never met one who knows this much about pleasuring a woman. His command over my body renders me powerless. It responds to his touch – back arching, legs falling open – as if it's under the control of *his* mind instead of my own. And when he pins my arms to the mattress and slides into me, slow inch by slow inch, I come before he's even fully inside me.

He knows it, too.

And yet, he has as much mastery over his own body as he has over mine. He still takes his time. Looking deep into my eyes, he whispers something about a beautiful sky, but I don't quite hear it.

When I come again and cry out, he stays deep inside me, climaxing at the same time but in complete silence. The only evidence is a tense jaw, the quiver of his heart beneath his skin, and the strained veins in his forearms that still pin me to the mattress.

Later, as we're relaxing in each other's arms, I ask a tentative question.

'Paul...?'

'Hmm?'

'How did you get those scars on your back.'

He tenses. 'An accident on a building site. A brick wall collapsed, and I was trapped underneath.'

They don't look like scars from falling bricks; they look like the marks of someone who was brutally whipped. From the glimpses I've caught, they're all different colours, some more faded than others, as if the beatings were a regular occurrence over a long period of years.

I have more sense than to press him into admitting they're the scars of abuse. If he wanted to talk about it, he would, and the last thing he needs is a relative stranger prying into a painful past. Whatever his history, it's none of my business. I quickly change the subject.

'What did you say to me...while we were making love earlier? Something about the sky?'

Paul's grip around me hasn't eased since I asked about his scars, and it doesn't now. But then he lets me go, shifts on to his side and looks right at me. 'Your eyes...I said they're as beautiful as the sky.'

'Aww, that's sweet.' I crawl back into his arms and yawn. 'I'm getting sleepy.'

'Me too.'

As I drift off, my mind turns over in a silent, repetitive conversation with itself. Not about his scars or how beautiful he thinks my eyes are but how he knows so much about a woman's body. I can't believe any man would know these things intuitively, or learn them on his own. It was as if he was inside my mind, responding to the electrical signals from my body as if it was his own.

Did someone teach him that?

A woman?

I think it must have been a woman. A very experienced woman, someone older than him. And not in one or two sessions of lovemaking, but over an extended period of time. Many, many years. A woman he knew deeply. A woman he loved.

Struck by that knowledge, I feel the emotional distance of what took place between us. As if Paul was touching my body but, in his mind, making love to someone else.

Suddenly, I feel very insignificant. Like a cardboard cutout of the woman Paul really cares for. Who is she? And why is he with me instead of her?

Is she dead?

I think she's dead.

CHAPTER SEVENTEEN

MILLIE

It takes a moment for me to sense the presence of another person in the room, to remember I'm not alone. Being alone has become such a fundamental part of who I am – the only state in which I feel safe – that a wave of fear runs through me. I quickly turn over.

As I scan the room, the peaceful dream I'd been immersed in slips through my fingers, replaced by memories. Yesterday floods back: the afternoon with Paul fixing the radiator, ending up in the shower, then in bed. Making love.

No. Not making love.

Having sex. Something I've never done before. I have always been in love first, or at least in the early stages of love, the forging of an emotional connection that I've been wrong about every single time. It's always been one-sided, the reciprocation of feelings always in my imagination.

I guess that's not really fair. I'm not prone to flights of fancy. The reciprocation of feelings was always a poker bluff to win the game. One I'm no good at playing.

Paul is sitting on the edge of my bed, leaning forward in his boxers and unbuttoned shirt. I couldn't sleep so I snuck out without waking him to hand-wash and hang it to dry. It's unironed, crumpled, and that rough-and-ready look is sexy as all hell.

There's a relaxed contentment to him that tells me he's been sitting there for some time, watching me sleep. The sun breaks through a gap in the curtains, catching the natural highlights in his light brown hair. It's brushed back from his face, mussed from sleep. His grey-green eyes pierce through me with an intensity I didn't notice yesterday. But his half-naked body I remember very well.

This is new.

The gorgeous new man in my life isn't scrambling into his trousers, making up an excuse about a football game he has to rush off to. He hasn't magically transformed into a scribbled note on the pillow that reads, *Thanks for the great night, I'll call you, babe* as if he's Cinderella's coach.

Yesterday it crossed my mind that Paul might be the one to break the curse. And here he is actually breaking it. He still wants to be here even after the chase is won...admittedly it wasn't much of a chase, but maybe Brooke was right all along.

The only problem now is that it's so unfamiliar, I'm not sure how to act. But I could get used to this...having Paul in my life.

'Hungry?' he asks. 'I was going to make you breakfast but you don't have much in. Shall we go to Harley's? My treat.'

I smile and pull the quilt up to my chin. I'm suddenly conscious of being naked while having a casual conversation about breakfast with a relative stranger. That's also a new one on me.

'I'll take that smile as a yes?'

I nod. 'Breakfast sounds great. But what about work? You don't have somewhere to be?'

'Not today. You?'

'I cancelled my yoga class. After Brooke...I needed some time.'

He pats my leg under the quilt, closes his eyes for a second and nods with sympathy. 'Sure... Is it alright if I take a shower?'

'Of course.' I'm grateful when he goes into the bathroom so I can get up and slip on a T-shirt and pyjama bottoms without him watching me. I don't know how to act when everything feels upside down: nudity and carnal knowledge ahead of getting even remotely acquainted. Throwing caution to the wind felt exciting yesterday, but, in the cold light of this morning, it feels like walking down the street naked while complete strangers watch, point and judge.

CHAPTER EIGHTEEN

MILLIE

When the waitress brought the bill for breakfast and Paul paid, I waited for him to make his excuses. He'd said he didn't have to work but I was still prepared for some other lame appointment in a fictitious calendar. It didn't come. Instead, he suggested we take in a matinee and drove us out to Enfield.

When we got to the cinema and looked at the listings, I squealed, '*Benediction!*' with a little too much enthusiasm. I'd been wanting to see it for so long, I got lost in the excitement. Realising that watching a film about a British war poet probably wasn't what Paul had in mind, I quickly added, 'Or the new *Jurassic* or *Spiderhead*. I've been wanting to see those, too.' I tried to put equal enthusiasm into those titles but it came across fake. I'm no poker player.

I thought he'd take control then, insist we see an action movie, but instead he said, 'No, *Benediction*. I've wanted to see that for ages as well.'

'Really? Do you even know what it's about?'

'Of course,' he said. 'I've seen the trailer, it looks great.' While he was buying the tickets, he glanced over and caught my grin of surprised amazement. 'What?'

'Nothing. I just didn't peg you for a poetry fan, that's all. I thought Pratt or Hemsworth would be more your style.'

Paul frowned as if he had no idea who they were.

'You know, exploding helicopters...bitchin' one-liners... dudes who are so badass that blowing a man's brains out is as normal as a conversation about burgers.'

He shook his head.

'You haven't seen *Pulp Fiction*?'

You'd think I'd asked him if he'd seen *Harold and Maude* instead of a box office smash that the whole world has heard of. But I think I hurt his feelings. He said, 'Just because I fix radiators, that doesn't make me a cliché.'

'No, I didn't mean—'

'I like films that challenge your perspective, give you something to think about.'

I looked at him for a moment. Was he just telling me what I wanted to hear and letting me choose the film because he was trying to impress? But his face was artless, sincere.

When he handed me my ticket, I said, '*Benediction* it is, then. But you can't hold it against me if it's awful. And I insist on buying the popcorn.'

'Okay, but if you're buying the popcorn, I'm buying dinner tonight.'

I took his arm, feigning indifference about the fact that he wanted to spend the whole day with me. In truth, my insides were performing *Cirque du Soleil*.

It was a perfect afternoon. We held hands in the empty cinema, flicking popcorn at each other and giggling whenever the movie turned serious. Which was pretty much the entire two hours. And now, at Courante's, I can't help being as surprised by his choice of restaurant as I am by his taste in films. I hang my jacket over the back of the chair and straighten the skirt of my favourite pink dress before taking a seat opposite Paul.

'I've been wanting to come here for ages.' I lay a napkin, embroidered with the restaurant's logo, in my lap. It feels like silk, too nice to use. 'Henrietta Courante was the winner of *Great British Menu* last year.'

'I know,' Paul says. 'That's why I booked it. Why haven't you?'

'Ever come here?' I half laugh, half snort. 'It's a little out of my price range.'

I've watched every series of *Great British Menu* and when Henrietta was crowned Champion of Champions and opened a restaurant ten minutes from my house I was so excited. A famous chef just down the road! But then I looked at the sample menu on her website and the prices changed my mind. At Harley's this morning, while tucking into my eggs Benedict and sourdough toast, I'd asked Paul if he'd ever seen *Great British Menu*.

'Of course,' he'd replied. 'I love that show.' And now I remember, he'd hidden a smile behind his coffee cup as if he was keeping a secret.

It was only after the cinema that Paul surprised me with where we were going next. He'd booked it this morning, while I was still sleeping. So when I brought it up at break-fast, he'd struggled to keep a straight face. He confessed that he'd been wanting to come here as well and it was such a coincidence that I would bring up the very restaurant he'd already booked us into a few hours earlier. Being here feels like kismet.

Paul's constantly taking me by surprise, and I love that about him. He's a contradiction, unpredictable. I never know what he's going to do next or what to expect from him. I didn't peg him for a foodie any more than I pegged him for a poetry-lover, let alone one with an interest in Siegfried Sassoon.

The second I think that, I feel like shit. I'm so judge-mental.

I've made assumptions about Paul based entirely on that first day I met him dressed in overalls and driving a white van. I created a person in my mind – a cardboard cutout of a labourer – who does that? I'm such a horrible person. I couldn't have been more wrong about him and, feeling completely on the back foot, I'm determined to make it up to him. Even though he has no idea I made those awful assumptions.

The truth is, we have so much in common. Far more than James and I ever had. Perhaps even more than me and Shawn.

This morning, on the way to breakfast, we dropped into Cole's to replace his shirt. I'd thought I'd got all the inhibitor out but when I ironed it for him, dried-in stains were hidden in the creases. When the guy at the checkout rang up £300 on the till, Paul didn't even bat an eyelid. It's a gorgeous midnight-blue shirt, so well made, the fabric top notch. I can't afford clothes like that, but I can live my love of dressmaking vicariously through him.

I don't care about money, I never have. But I'd be lying if I said there wasn't a flutter of excitement at being able to do things like this: eat at fancy restaurants, help him pick out clothes in swanky stores, and have things in common like books and movies. Maybe I could even join him on business trips like the one he just took to Stockholm.

A completely different person from the one I'd formed in my mind sits across the table from me, and I'm pleasantly surprised. After everything that's happened with James and Brooke, Paul Cooper has turned out to be my silver lining.

Paul orders a bottle of wine, and the sommelier tells him it's a good choice. I know nothing about wine so I can't help being impressed. I look around the restaurant, wanting to tell everyone that this devastatingly handsome, sharply dressed sophisticate is my date.

As I glance over the faces of the patrons, a man in a business suit, sitting in one of the velvet-lined booths, catches my eye. He winks at me then turns away and says something under his breath. He's surrounded by three colleagues, also in suits, and they all laugh as they look in my direction. I blush, knowing whatever he said must have been about me.

The sommelier returns with the bottle of wine, opens it at the table and offers me the tasting, but I insist Paul do it. What would I know?

While Paul's approving the wine, I feel the businessman's eyes boring into me and they're like a magnet for my own. I sneak a glance, and he doesn't look away. Brazenly, he holds my gaze, legs spread wide, jacket slung open, arm splayed along the back of the booth. He takes up all the space at the table and the air in the entire room.

When the waitress arrives at his table, he flaps his hand at her, shoos her away as if he's far too busy and important to answer questions from serving staff. Anyone would think he owned the restaurant. It's a performance, and, the whole time, his gaze intrudes on my date with Paul.

I take control of the situation and focus on my man.

'So...what kind of music do you like?' It's a lame first-date question but it's hard to relax and be sociable when any attempt to ignore the businessmen is met with raised voices and raucous laughter. The curved booth acts like a bass speaker we have to talk over.

'This and that.' Paul glances in their direction. 'What about you?'

'I love old music…the '30s and '40s were such classic eras. My grandmother got me into Louis Armstrong, Billie Holiday… Ella Fitzgerald. You probably have no idea who any of these singers are. And now I sound like an old fuddy-duddy.'

'Not at all. I completely agree. They don't make them like they used to. Nowadays it's all about selling what you see, not what you hear. And that's not what music should be about.'

'That's so true.'

'They're selling sex,' he adds. 'Bodies on stage, whatever it takes to make teenagers scream. These "artists"…' he uses air quotes '…don't even write their own songs or play their own instruments. They're all overproduced studio voices with no talent or true understanding of music. Ella Fitzgerald was a Renoir and now we're reduced to finger-paintings.'

Paul's appraisal is harsh, and now I don't know how to respond. That familiar need to spring to the defence of everyone under attack surfaces, the way it used to with Brooke. I'm not exactly a fan of boy bands but just because I don't like the style, that doesn't mean they aren't skilled musicians. There are a lot of talented pop artists, and, regardless, it takes guts to put yourself out there.

After an awkward silence, Paul chips in with, 'There are noticeable exceptions, of course. I'm just generalising.'

That makes me feel better and my defences drop. 'I can't say anything really; I don't listen to pop music. I just think the '30s and '40s were so romantic. Nanny and I used to watch all these old black and white musicals together. Nelson Eddy and Jeanette MacDonald in *Naughty Marietta.*

Deanna Durbin in *His Butler's Sister*. I miss that. I have nobody to watch them with any more.'

'I'll watch them with you. I love old musicals. Compared to modern films, the old Hollywood stars brought so much class.'

'Really?' He keeps surprising me. 'Any stars in particular?'

'Well, Deanna Durbin, of course. Who can argue with that? And Neilson Eddy, too. Great voice.'

'Nelson.'

'What?'

'It's Nelson Eddy.'

'That's what I said.' He looks around the room, his gaze faltering over the businessmen. 'It's so loud in here.'

The waitress removes our plates, and I glance over at the booth again. The man still hasn't taken his eyes off me. The others run through a scene-by-scene analysis of *Game of Thrones* – how much flesh is on show in each episode – while he undresses me with his stare.

'Anyway...' Paul reaches into the inside pocket of his jacket. 'I got something for you.'

He pulls out a blue velvet box and puts it on the table.

'What is it?' I don't know what else to say. It's our first date and he's bought me jewellery. 'And when?'

'When what?'

'When did you *get something* for me? We've been together all day.'

'When I was buying the shirt.' He pulls at the fabric, tight against his muscular chest.

I stare at the box.

'Open it.'

I look up, grimace and crank it open. Inside is a tennis bracelet that must hold fifty diamonds.

'Are those real?'

'Of course.' He gets up from his chair and takes the bracelet out of its box. In the booth, the conversation mutes as I look over and, no longer staring at me, the man watches Paul fumble as he unhooks the clasp.

I want to say no, I can't accept it, but he's holding open the bracelet, waiting for me to lift my hand which feels welded to the table. I can't humiliate him in front of those men. I can't make him sit back down with his rejected gift. So I offer my arm with a broad smile.

Paul fastens it around my wrist before sitting back down and we're quiet for far too many moments.

Finally, I break the silence. 'You really shouldn't have. It's too much. I mean, this is the kind of thing you get for a birthday or Christmas. And even then it's far too expensive.' I half-laugh. 'More like a tenth anniversary or something.'

I twist the bracelet around my arm. The diamonds catch the restaurant's lights. I have no idea when I would even wear such a thing. I spend most of my life in sweatpants, and even when I do go out I tend to dress casually.

Paul shifts in his chair, a little uncomfortable too, and when the silence drags out again he picks up the menu and says, 'Shall we order desserts?'

I hesitate. I'm not sure I want a dessert. Now things have become awkward, I don't want to prolong the meal. I say, 'I couldn't eat another thing.' Then a few moments later, add, 'It really is beautiful. Thank you.' But I'm out of sorts: the bracelet feels like a restraint, a shackle that chains me to Paul. Because if I decide he's not right for me after all, I'm going to have to give this back, and returning such a generous gift would be ungrateful after everything he's done for me. 'Shall we just get the cheque?' I get to my feet. 'Would you excuse me? I need to use the ladies' room.'

I don't really need to use the loo, I just needed to get out of there, so I sit on the closed seat in one of the stalls and take a few moments to collect myself.

When I get back to the restaurant, Paul is at the reception desk by the bar, paying for our meals. I guess he didn't want to wait for the waitress to come with the bill.

I need some air, so I float past the table, pick up my jacket from the back of the chair and make sure Paul sees me. I point at the door to let him know I'm heading outside.

Behind me, the restaurant door swings open, so I take a steadying breath and plaster on a smile before turning to greet him.

It's not Paul.

It's the businessman from the booth, the one who's been staring at me all night.

'Having a good time?'

I nod, glancing through the window where Paul is still at the bar. 'It's a nice place.'

'Special occasion? Wedding anniversary?'

I laugh caustically then realise he's looking at my wrist. I shake my head. 'No, we're not married.'

'Boyfriend?'

I shake my head again. 'Just a date.'

He nods at the bracelet. 'Some date!'

I lift my wrist, heavy with diamonds. 'Hmm, it was a bit extravagant.'

'It's a good trick,' he says.

I frown, confused.

'Buying a woman a drink in exchange for her company is one thing. What's the going rate for a band of diamonds?'

I shift from foot to foot and glance over his shoulder at the door, wishing it would open and Paul would come rushing out.

'Sorry,' he says. 'I wasn't trying to suggest... I'm just saying... Anyway, I'm glad he's just a date, because I haven't been able to take my eyes off you all evening.' He reaches into his suit pocket and pulls out a business card. 'Maybe one night I could take you out? I can't promise diamonds, but I can promise you a good time.'

I hold up a hand, a barrier to the card. 'Thank you, but no.'

'No? Why not? You said you were only dating. So date me. I'm quite a catch.'

'Because I'm dating Paul.'

'Well, that's the point of dating, isn't it? To try people on for size. Try me. I guarantee I'm a better fit than he is. For a start, I'm not the kind of guy who buys women with inappropriate gifts.' He laughs, but he's not joking.

'Thank you for the offer. But I'm not a serial dater.'

'Oh, but life's too short for one man at a time. Especially for a woman as beautiful as you. You could have your pick of every guy in that restaurant. In the world, probably.'

He takes a step closer, and I take a step back. 'Thank you, I'm flattered. But I'm afraid I only have the time and energy for one man at a time.'

He closes the gap again. 'You won't hear any complaints from me about that. Lose that guy and then you'll only have to make time for me.'

When I take another step back, my heel hits the low wall that encompasses the restaurant's patio. He leans in, while I peer over his shoulder through the window. I wish Paul would hurry up.

'Really...like I said, I'm flattered. But I'm dating Paul.'

'Come on—' He reaches out for my hand, but I snatch it away. His voice tightens. '*Paul* looks like a tosser to me. Why waste your time? You could cut him loose right now and come out with me. I know a great place for a nightcap.'

'I said no. Thank you.'

I can't back away any further. The man gets right up in my face, grabs my wrist and crushes the diamonds into my skin. 'What kind of man would I be if I took the first no for an answer?'

'Actually, it was more like—'

'Tomorrow night.' He slips the business card into my jacket pocket. 'I'll meet you here at seven-thirty.' It's not even a question. My heart thuds in my ears as I try to pull my arm away, but he's holding it too tightly. 'I'll show you what a real—'

Behind him, the restaurant door creaks open then jangles shut. His face falls and he lets go of my wrist while I breathe a sigh of relief at the sight of Paul.

CHAPTER NINETEEN

PAUL

Damn.

I was glad when Millie wandered outside while I paid the bill – my aim was to scare the living shit out of the piss-taker sitting in the booth with his mates – but now he's followed her out there. And the waitress is taking forever with the bill; she keeps getting distracted by other servers.

He thinks I didn't notice his looks and gestures behind my back all night. But I saw the fleeting flicks of Millie's eyes, her disguised annoyance. She looked at him again when I gave her the gift, her reaction a mix of awkwardness, embarrassment and displeasure. It was difficult to figure out which related to him and which to my misguided attempt to impress her.

Now, he's talking to her outside, inching closer, and she keeps glancing over his shoulder. She's looking my way for help as she politely tries to get rid of him.

This presents me with a problem.

I can't just take him out, even though I'm itching to pound his face until it's a bloody mess. Millie doesn't like violence and I'm already on shaky ground with the bracelet.

Finally, the waitress takes the cash and hands me my receipt.

I walk out of the restaurant, body language and expression set to friendly and confident. Then I stride across the patio and take my place beside Millie, standing purposely close to her.

'Hello. Is this a friend of yours?'

'No, we've never met before.' Millie's annoyance is barely concealed.

He's probably a manager of some sort, one who gets a kick out of leering at his female colleagues while barking orders at them; he has that oily, jumped-up-on-his-own-importance, office-type look about him.

I step forward with an extended hand. 'Paul Cooper.'

Expecting a dick-swinging contest, the oily fucker is confused by my approach but reacts the only way he knows how: to shake my hand and try to impress me with what a big man he is. The second his paper-shuffling fingers touch mine, I block Millie's view with my body and clamp down with a vice grip.

He glances at his crushed hand then back up as my expression alters. Fear flashes across his face as he stares into the eyes of an apex predator. The flick-knife in my free hand clicks open and he flinches as its razor-sharp point digs into one of his balls. The fabric of his trousers barely holds up to the pressure of the blade.

I lean in and whisper, 'Fuck off or you'll lose them, right here, right now.' My voice is controlled, as I hold him in place by his hand. But then I let go and turn back to Millie. 'Well, nice to meet you, anyway.' I'm warm and friendly. 'You have a good night.'

With the flick-knife already folded and slipped back into my pocket, I offer her my arm. We walk away leaving the oily fuckwit shaken and speechless.

CHAPTER TWENTY

MILLIE

'What's the time?'

Paul stirs and rolls over but doesn't answer.

Reaching over him, I grab my phone from the bedside table and turn it on. It's 8.05am. 'Shit!'

I never sleep this late, but we didn't exactly go to bed early last night. Well...we did go to bed early; we just didn't sleep.

Walking back from the restaurant, I was on cloud nine. That arrogant asshole from Courante's really shook me up. I thought Paul might punch his lights out or something, but instead he just shook the guy's hand and had a quiet word in his ear. I don't know what he said, but it was enough to get the idiot to drop his bravado. One word from Paul and he backed right off.

After that, strolling through the dark streets of Epping, with Paul on my arm, I felt safer than I ever have. It's a comfort to know you're with a man who doesn't need to resort to violence to resolve problems. There's something insanely attractive about powerful negotiation skills. A man with the kind of presence that keeps everyone calm in a crisis.

Suddenly the bracelet didn't seem so bad. That arsehole saying those awful things made me realise that it's only guys like him who think that way. Not men like Paul. Men like him think women owe him something; that's why they won't take no for an answer. If Paul had bought me a rose or some chocolates, I wouldn't have thought much of it. And to Paul – who clearly has more money than sense – it *wasn't* an expensive gift. I just needed to see it from his perspective.

In the haze of alcohol, the sex was even better the second time, and I didn't think that was possible. Now, I don't want to crawl out of this bed, I'd much rather slip under the covers for a repeat performance, but that's not an option. I toss my phone on to the bedside table and scrabble out from beneath the quilt.

Paul grabs my hand. 'Where are you going?'

'I have to get dressed. I have a client at eight-thirty.'

'What client?'

'Just a client.'

'A *male* client?'

I raise my eyes to the ceiling and shake my head at his grey-green-eyed question before getting to my feet and letting go of Paul's hand. 'I have to get showered.'

I head for the bathroom, but Paul grabs my wrist and pulls me back on to the mattress. Pushing me on to my back, he says, 'I think you're gonna have to quit that job.' Then he grasps the back of my neck and pulls me into a deep kiss. 'I can't have you spending your days with other men while you're dressed in hot yoga pants.'

I push him off me, playfully. 'Don't be stupid. I know the difference between a client and a boyfriend.'

I shuffle towards the edge of the bed, but Paul wraps his arms around my waist and pulls me back.

'So, I'm your boyfriend, then?'

I laugh. 'I'll tell you when I get out of the shower.' I peck him on the lips and try to get up but Paul's quick. He slides my body under his and turns the peck into something very French.

My mind wanders to Todd Markham. He comes for an early half-hour training session every Tuesday and Thursday and he's always on time. Then he leaves with as much punctuality as he arrives – as single-minded in his daily routine as he is in the intensity of his workouts – and he wouldn't appreciate my being as much as a minute late. Todd runs his own company, is a very serious businessman, and believes every second is money.

I pull out of the kiss.

'My client will be here any minute.'

'Cancel. Let's blow off work today, go somewhere nice.'

'I'd love to.' I kiss him on the end of the nose. 'But I can't. Not at such short notice. Besides, we both blew off work yesterday.'

As I shuffle out from beneath Paul, he pins me in place with his body and kisses my neck. His bare chest against mine ignites all the memories of the last two days and my body sparks. Sensing my response, he deepens the kiss while forcing my legs apart with his own. Then he slides between my hips with a slow grind.

An involuntary moan escapes my mouth as he presses against me while tracing his fingers down my ribs, hip and thigh. The straining fabric of his boxers is the last barrier between me and being late for my session with Todd. I wish I didn't have a client, I wish I *could* blow off this whole day and spend another one with Paul. But I can't.

When he pulls out of the kiss and moves down my body from my neck to my breast, I say, 'You're gonna make me late.' But 'late' comes out as a gasp when he takes my nipple between his teeth and bites just hard enough to make me shiver.

I squirm beneath him, desperate to keep my wits about me. 'Paul, I can't. I have to shower and change, or I'll be—'

He stops my mouth with another kiss. Then he moves down my body again until he's between my legs, his tongue knowing exactly how to break down the resistance I'm barely clinging to.

'Oh, God,' I groan. 'You have to stop.' I run my fingers through his hair and grab it by the roots. I pull hard in an attempt to lift his head from between my legs and end this. But if he feels any pain, it only intensifies his fervour.

When he slides a finger inside me, my body betrays my desire for him. And that betrayal is the only invitation Paul needs. He slips his hands under my backside, lifts me up from the mattress and plunges his tongue deep inside me.

'Paul!' His name comes out with a moan. I'm well aware of how unconvincing my protests are, but I'm running out of time. 'Please...don't...I have to—' He runs his tongue up my belly while driving his finger back inside me. And instead of saying, 'go', I groan with pleasure.

But a moment later he's sliding his boxers down and my senses return. Pushing myself up on to my elbows, I say, 'Tonight, okay? Let's save this for tonight?'

Paul doesn't hear me. He isn't listening. I turn my face aside when he moves in to kiss me. Pushing his shoulders back, I shuffle up the bed to get away from him, but he's already between my legs again, forcing them apart with his hips.

'Please...Paul...no! I don't have time.'

He takes both my wrists in his hands and pulls them apart at shoulder height before pinning them down against the bed.

'Paul!' I say his name louder this time. 'Sto—' But the word is stripped from my lips as he plunges into me, arching his back, eyes closed. When he pulls out, I catch my breath, struggle against his grip and shout, 'Paul! Please! Sto—'

Suddenly his hand is over my mouth. His thick fingers, tight against my nostrils, press my lips together and I can't breathe. When he thrusts into me again, a tear runs down the side of my face. I can't reconcile what's happening now with the considerate Paul I've spent the last two days with. But then he lets go and presses his lips to mine, his tongue teasing its way into my mouth as if he hadn't done what he just did.

As he moves in and out of me while kissing my neck, my body and mind disconnect. The fight leaves me, and I just wait for it to end. And yet, my detached and disloyal body responds to his skilled touch as spontaneously as it did last night.

While one word plays on a silent loop in my mind – *no... no...no* – I cry out an orgasm that's entirely devoid of emotion. The cry quickly turns to a sob; I'm sickened by my body performing this function. But for Paul it's a triumph, and while my thoughts whir in fear and confusion he comes deep inside me, shuddering against me before rolling on to his back.

The second I'm released from his body weight, I scramble off the bed, grab my T-shirt from the floor and use it to cover my body. Rushing to the bathroom, I say, 'Get dressed, you have to leave!'

Paul didn't put on a condom and with no time for a shower, I have no choice but to quickly put on period pants beneath my workout gear. I bite back tears as I get dressed.

By the time Todd knocks on the door, I'm sweating, red-faced, and ashamed. I'm ushering him in with a plastered-on but professional smile when movement at the top of the stairs catches my eye.

Paul saunters down with a self-satisfied grin.

'Oh...' Todd notices him then quickly checks his watch to make sure he isn't mistaken about the time. Then, as Paul makes his way along the hall, he holds out his hand. 'Todd Markham. Nice to meet you.'

Paul stops and looks him right in the eye as he wipes his middle finger across his mouth, wetting it on the inside of his bottom lip. Pausing momentarily to taste me, he grabs Todd's hand and presses a moist finger into his skin. Pulling out of the hard and aggressive handshake, Paul walks out and shuts the door behind him.

'Subtle,' Todd says.

I clear my throat and point in the direction of the gym. 'Shall we go through?'

As I see Todd out I say, 'Sorry about earlier.'

'New boyfriend?' he asks.

'Sort of.'

'What happened to the photographer? I thought that was getting serious.'

I open the door with a shrug. 'So did I.'

Todd raises his eyebrows and presses his lips into a tight line as if to say, Ah, well, *c'est la vie*. Then, as he turns and steps out on to the porch, 'What the fu—'

I follow his gaze to his car.

His passenger side tyre is completely flat, the weight of his BMW compressing it into the gravel of my driveway.

My heart thuds against my ribs.

I'm struck by *déjà vu*.

Brooke.

A motion-picture memory plays back. I tail her out of Starbucks and stare at the rear passenger-side tyre compressed into the tarmac by the weight of her 4x4.

CHAPTER TWENTY-ONE

PAUL

I don't know what happiness feels like for normal people, but if I had to guess I would think this is fairly close. Even Millie's prick client Todd turning up didn't upset me this morning. He's not a threat; he's weak, inferior.

Even so, like a dog pissing on his patch, I slashed his passenger-side tyre on my way out. Then I drove off in my van, a man in command of his universe.

In command of Millie.

After a few more dates, I'll make up some excuse about losing my flat. Ask to stay for a week that never ends. Then I'll put a stop to all this personal trainer shit. It's for her own good; she doesn't need the burden of all these lecherous fuckers. I know what they're like, leaning in to smell her floral perfume mixed with sweat as they work out together, imagining sliding her Lycra leggings down...

No, that won't do.

She can work out with me, look good for me.

Up ahead, the traffic light's still green as I approach the junction. But then the light turns amber and I pull to a stop.

Things will be different this time...

I'm in control now.

...not like before.

Skye throws open the wardrobe door and shoves me inside with such force that I stumble backwards and have to fight to free myself from her clothes. The door slams shut, and I'm trapped in the dark. Then the key turns and pulls out of the lock.

He's home early.

His stumble up the stairs is familiar, unmistakable. He pauses on the landing while his pickled brain weighs up his options: take a piss, fall asleep in front of the television and sleep it off, or head for this room.

I pray he'll sleep it off in front of the TV, then Skye will let me out.

The bedroom door creaks open.

His footsteps come closer, and I press my eye closer to the keyhole. He glances in the direction of the wardrobe, but the only thing visible from the bedroom is one grey-green eye lit by a tiny circle of amber from the streetlight outside.

It's pitch-black in here. Stuffy. Hard to breathe. But I don't make a sound.

Through my narrow field of vision, all I can see is Skye's leg on the bed, unmoving in the light that creeps through the gap in the curtains. After shutting me in, she sucked deep on her crack pipe and is already sinking into a dreamless sleep.

Her escape.

But there's none for me. I'll be trapped in here until she sobers up.

He steps into view, visible only from his fat gut down. He just stands there, a roll-up between his nicotine-stained fingers. I picture his face, leering at her, dribble seeping out of the corners of his mouth as he considers his next move.

And there it is.

He flicks the roll-up on to the carpet before his liver-spotted hands fumble with his belt. His jeans drop and he climbs on to the bed, dick half-soft from the booze.

Skye's waking up. Small, weak noises emanate from her chemically numbed mind. He's the reason she takes that stuff. And it keeps her under control, stops her from running away.

Stops *us* from running away.

I pull back into the darkness, slide my hands over my ears, and shrink inside myself.

A car horn shocks me back to the present, beads of sweat trickling down my temple. The light's green. I lock the memory back into the armour-plated box it escaped from and indicate to pull into the junction.

Back in check, back at my flat with time on my hands until I see Millie again, I change into work gear and head over to Dexter's house to keep up appearances.

I pull on to the property behind an unremarkable Ford Focus. Two men in cheap suits, straight-backed, arms folded, are talking to Carl, the site foreman, and some of the other lads. Jumped-up on their own self-importance, the suits are unmistakably plod. Low-ranking detectives at a guess.

I butt in on the plods' conversation. 'Alright, Carl. Is Dex about? I need paying for last week.'

'Excuse me, sir, you are?' Lead plod puts on his best authoritarian tone.

I jerk his chain. 'Who's asking?'

'Detective Inspector Morris.' He rams his ID card under my nose.

'Easy, mate. I'm just here to see the owner, get paid and bugger off if that's alright with you?'

'Can you tell me your name, sir? And the last time you saw Mr Tanning?'

'Paul Cooper. Dex... Um...I dunno. A week ago, I think. He was chewing my arse out about getting the kitchen painted in time for the fitters. Why?'

'And you haven't seen him since?'

'No. Why?'

'Mr Tanning's girlfriend has reported him missing.'

'Shit. I hope he hasn't done a runner, 'cause I need my money.'

'At this moment in time, we don't know what's happened to him. It's likely he'll turn up, but we have to follow up on these things.'

'Well, if he's not here and I'm not getting paid, I might as well go.'

'If you could give your contact details to my colleague first, Mr Cooper, then you're free to leave.'

I do as he asks before heading for my van. A smile forms as I climb in and drive off, knowing that, with every day that passes, another five hundred bricks will be laid on top of those foundations.

Stupid bastards.

It's still early. I have some errands to do, then I'll have a long workout. I need to look my best for when I head back to Millie's later.

CHAPTER TWENTY-TWO

MILLIE

I wave to Todd as he pulls off the driveway behind the roadside assistance van. They put a temporary fix on the tyre that will, apparently, hold long enough to get him to the garage.

His car disappearing from view reveals a horizon of dark clouds with a clear intention of steamrolling this summer afternoon. I glance at my fitness tracker. If I'm really quick, I'll just make it to the shops and back before my next client arrives. But the jog home will be a wet one.

Dashing into the house, I grab my shell jacket from the coat stand, but, when I move my scarf from one hook to another, something sparkles in the light from the front door. With a metallic clatter, it drops on the wooden floorboards by my feet.

Bending down, I inspect the fallen object without picking it up. It takes a moment for my mind to register what it is and, when it does, I'm afraid to touch it. It's sacred, haunted. When my fingertips finally connect with the cold brass and I pick it up, it's as if I've made a connection to the other side.

James's sister's ashes rest on my palm.

I stare at the tiny urn pendant, waiting for her to tell me how she got here.

She doesn't answer.

James never takes this pendant off. Except to shower – or make love – and, even then, he puts it right back on afterwards. Or was that just a show? A play on my emotions?

Given the way he treated me, and my luck with previous men, it's not unlikely that James is twisted enough to fabricate a dead sister. It would garner empathy from women and charm them into bed.

No...I don't buy it.

I may have been naïve in the past, been tricked into thinking men cared for me more than they did, but that's only because I see people through my eyes – doesn't everyone do that? You only see cruelty in other people if it's inside you – and perhaps I couldn't see it in James. But something doesn't sit right. With the previous shitheads I dated, the signs I'd missed – or, more accurately, chose to ignore – were obvious with hindsight. But with James, even looking back now, there were no signs. I spent enough time with him to feel the sensitivity in his soul. He had an almost spiritual lack of ego that came from spending so much of his life ih nature, around wild animals. And that night, beside the fire, he didn't put on a show of kissing this necklace after he took it off; he tried to hide what he was doing. If the pendant and the story of a dead sister was a ploy to get me in the sack, he wouldn't have turned his back; he would have made sure I saw him do it. Plus, if it was an emotional trick, what purpose did it serve at that point? He'd already charmed me out of my dress. I was half-naked on the rug. I was a sure thing.

Oh, what the hell difference does it make now anyway? He still strung me along with that phoney invite to Chile and Antarctica. He fooled me into believing that he didn't want to be parted from me for six months, then fucked me and left me the next day.

I storm into the kitchen and press my foot on the pedal bin. As the lid rises, I tilt my hand over it and the pendant slips down my palm. A split second before it drops into Saturday night's leftovers, I clamp my fist around the chain.

I can't do it.

James's sister hasn't done anything to me. And if he was telling the truth, she doesn't deserve this. Nobody deserves to have their ashes tossed into sticky sesame chicken from Wok This Way.

Back in the hall, I snap up my phone from the table, take three calming breaths to silence my petulant, battered ego and dial James's number.

It goes straight to voicemail; he must have it turned off. If he's moved on from Chile to Antarctica already, it's unlikely he'll have mobile signal for some time. But I thought he was staying there at least a week or two, and surely most places have wireless these days, even in Chile? I switch to the Facebook app and decide to leave him a message instead. I don't ever want to see him again after the way he treated me, but all I need is an address to send the pendant to. Then he'll be out of my life for good.

James hasn't updated Facebook since he posted the elephant seal picture. That surprises me; I expected him to be updating it with photos almost daily. Surely Chile is worthy of the odd Facebook post? I guess there's neither signal nor wifi wherever he's been staying.

Although it pains me to read that awful post again, curiosity gets the better of me. It's like a bloody wound that, no matter how much it stings, you still have to pull it apart to see how deep it is. I have to know if he's said anything else about me, made another snide comment. I grip his pendant in my fist, the urge to bin it resurfacing. There are twenty-two comments on the post: a lot, considering that Facebook only shows your posts to a small subset of your friends these days.

Curiosity mingles with dread as I run through the comments. I prepare myself for the inevitable wisecracks about me being less attractive than an elephant seal. But the first comment isn't at all what I'm expecting.

> Mate, I thought you said Chile, not Thailand! 😁

The comment is followed by a smiley face. If it's a joke, I don't get it. And what on earth does Thailand have to do with James's photography shoot? Did he lie to me about where he was going?

The next comment is just as confusing.

> Dude, when I hit on you in the uni bar, you said you liked girls. Now I'm hurt!

A series of droll comments follow.

> He's sexy and he nose it!

> That's what happens when you snort Viagra!

> I get it, man, that dude is 3 tons of raw sexual aggression!

> He's probably too much for you to handle, mate.

The wisecracks continue along the same lines, most of them teasing James about his sexual orientation. The seal must be male; his friends are unanimous about that. So I ask Siri if female elephant seals have trunks.

They don't.

I wasted so much time scanning through James's Facebook post and the rest of his profile that I ran out of time to go to the shops, then I had three clients back-to-back. Before hopping in the shower – and more of a reflex than a conscious decision – I texted Shawn.

It did cross my mind that the last thing he needs is me bending his ear right now, but he's the only person I want to talk to. I justified it to myself with the notion that listening to my problems will take his mind off his own.

Finally out of gym gear for the first time today, hair washed and make-up on, I pick out underwear that actually matches and my favourite pink dress that buttons all the way down the front.

As I come down the stairs, I pull at the fabric to straighten it, wondering if it's a bit too much just to pop over to Shawn's. And now I'm ready, I'm not sure why I've made so much effort. After grabbing my keys from the hall table drawer and dropping my mobile in the side pocket of my dress, I throw open the front door.

And come face-to-face with Paul.

CHAPTER TWENTY-THREE

PAUL

The door opens before my knuckles make contact with its weathered oak. Millie's standing in front of me. She's all made up, wearing the pink dress she wore on our date, a surprised look on her face.

I block her exit from the house and fix on a smile.

'Paul, you startled me. What are you doing here?'

I don't answer.

The seconds go by.

I still don't speak, just let the pressure of silence force her into offering up an explanation as to where she is going.

She doesn't.

Relenting, I say, 'I'm here to take you out. Our date. The one we planned this morning.'

Her eyes flick to the left as she searches her memory, rewinds back to earlier and rapidly replays our conversation.

We didn't plan it. But I've planted the seeds of doubt. Give it a few more seconds and she'll convince herself that we did. I don't offer up anything else, just remain blocking her exit until she does.

And there it is: confusion. She doesn't remember, but assumes we discussed it.

'I'm sorry, Paul, something's come up...my friend's having a meltdown, she needs a shoulder to cry on. I'm gonna have to cancel.'

The creative part of her brain has thrown her the distressed girlfriend line but her eyes dart to the right as she speaks. Her body language is off and she's clearly selected the dress and make-up to impress a man, not console a girlfriend.

She's lying.

I spin my reaction selector and go for a sadness with a touch of hurt, but, inside, the anger is building.

'Hey, it's no problem. How about tomorrow instead?'

'Maybe. Sorry, I've really got to go. I'll call you.'

You'll fucking call me, will you? She doesn't even try to make it sound genuine. The brush-off hits me hard. Face passive, I clench my fists tightly behind my back, nails digging into my palms. I'm a split second away from pushing her back inside and teaching her a lesson in obedience.

Then she looks into my eyes, straight into them. Into me.

They're Skye's eyes.

They knock me off balance and I'm falling again, wrestling with her clothes in the wardrobe as I fight to stay on my feet. The key turns and I'm powerless, alone in the dark with the only light a pale amber seeping through the keyhole. I crumple, physically shrink from the woman I've never dared challenge.

'Yeah...okay. You should go, see your friend.'

I move out of her way and as she squeezes through the gap I flinch involuntarily, fear resurfacing. She clocks my reaction and her expression changes from evasion to guilt. At the car, she turns back with a warm smile. 'I'm really sorry, Paul. I'll call you tomorrow, okay?'

She gets in, reverses off the drive, and the moment her car pulls away I'm punched back to the present.

Not okay. Not remotely fucking okay.

Fury, frustration and anger at my weakness send me running for my van. I start it and kick the accelerator down, lurching after Millie's ever-shrinking car in the distance. I have to know where she's going. I need to know what man is interfering in the perfect life that's just within my grasp, what to do to put it back on course.

Easing off the gas, I follow fifty metres behind. Millie indicates left and vanishes around a corner. Frightened of losing her, I drop a gear and punch the accelerator.

I take the corner too fast, paint pots and brushes falling off the racking in the back. I spin out of the bend and hit the brakes hard, stopping a few feet short of skip lorry skewed across the road. Its hazard lights are on as the driver man-oeuvres it slowly backwards on to a driveway, the skip fully loaded with shingle ready to be emptied.

I inch forward.

Noticing my impatience, the driver brakes. He pulls forward again in a pretence of straightening up to reverse at a better angle, when the lorry was already straight. He glances at me with a smirk on his weatherworn face.

He's a dead man.

One hand's cranking the door open while the other fishes around in the storage trough. My fingers curl around the flick-knife. I'm about to exit when, in the wing mirror, I catch sight of a police patrol car pulling to a halt behind me. Eyes flicking between them and the cocky fuck in the lorry, I slam my door shut.

I grip the knife handle, tense with the urge to get out and kill all three of them.

Normally this would be easy; the burning rage, the desire to end any prick who gets in my way would be buried before it had a chance to take hold. But after Millie's deception it's hard as hell. Reluctantly I drop the knife back in the trough and sit facing forward, knuckles white on the steering wheel. Slowly, the lorry backs on to the driveway and leaves the road clear to pass.

Finally, I can breathe.

I pull away with the police car close behind me but the road up ahead is empty. No traffic. No Millie. Taking the next right, I watch the police in the rear-view mirror as they continue straight on. Then I pull over to the side of the road and stare out of the windscreen.

I stay like that for a long time, not moving. Then I explode, punching the dash until my knuckles are numb and my vision grows dark.

Amber light bleeds through the keyhole and I punch the door again and again until it bursts open and slams into the wall.

Skye's at the window, staring down at the street below.

My eyes barely have time to adjust to the blazing orange flames before she turns and runs at me, screaming.

Flinching, I throw my hands up to protect myself.

My eyes snap open and breathing heavily, I sink into the driver's seat. A drop of sweat trickles down my temple.

This is all her fault.

Millie's.

My army training taught me to control my anger, to contain it until the time was right to release its power. The visions became short-lived, the memories fleeting.

But she's brought it all back.

She's broken the lock on the box with her lies and deceit.

Reaching into the trough again, I grab my flick-knife and leather pouch. Stuffing them in my pocket, I leave my van by the side of the road. I walk back to the junction and at the main road, the skip lorry trundles by. Dust and grit leave a trail behind it, the driver oblivious to how close he came to meeting the real me.

CHAPTER TWENTY-FOUR

MILLIE

Sitting on bar stools on either side of Shawn's kitchen island, we spent the first glass of wine talking about Brooke and how much we both missed her. But by the second glass, the conversation naturally turned to what I was doing there. I brought up James, the comments on the Facebook post, and Paul.

'What are you suggesting?' Shawn asks. 'That James didn't dump you? That he's actually missing, and Paul had something to do with it?'

I don't speak. I don't even nod, because when it came out of my mouth it sounded perfectly plausible, but when he says it it sounds ludicrous.

Perched on the stool, beneath the discomfort of his challenging gaze, I shift my bottom as if my half-cracked theories belong right there beneath it.

Shawn leans forward, rests his elbows on the counter and presses me further. 'And this supposition is based entirely on a necklace and a Facebook post of an elephant seal?'

And now we've gone from ludicrous to supercalifragilisticexpialidocious. In two sentences, Shawn has made me doubt everything I was so sure of when I left my house fortyfive minutes ago.

And I was *so* sure.

After finding Paul on my doorstep like that, I replayed our conversation over and over on the drive here. And although I think I remember suggesting we see each other tonight, we definitely didn't set it in stone. We didn't even agree a time. His expecting us to spend the evening together when we hadn't even made plans was – Brooke's word echoes in my mind – creepy.

I tried to come across genuinely sorry because, honestly, his being there freaked me out. It frightened me. But I was just appeasing him.

Shit! I wish I'd never slept with him.

I say, 'It's not just the necklace and the Facebook post, it's...' I have no idea what *it* is and struggle for a convincing explanation. 'It's...all these tiny things that on their own mean nothing at all. But put them all together—'

'Like a puzzle?'

'Exactly. You have to look at all the pieces together before you can see the whole picture.'

'I was being sarcastic. You sound like Miss Marple. What are the chances? Statistically, I mean. Something like ninety per cent of all murders are committed by someone the victim knows. And Paul and James never even met, did they?'

I try to remember. 'I don't think so. I don't recall them meeting.'

'So, he had no motive.'

'Okay...but if you met Paul it wouldn't sound as farfetched as it does. He put Brooke on edge the first day we met him, and I think you'd agree with her. You'd take one look at him and think it was entirely plausible that he would kill someone he doesn't know. I think he's capable of murder.'

'And yet, you fucked the guy.' Shawn says that with more than a hint of...what is that? Anger? Disappointment? I'm not sure, but it drips with sarcasm. '*You* obviously didn't take one look at him and think, hmm, he seems capable of murder, I think I'll fuck him. You obviously liked him. And you've only changed your mind about him now because you found James's pendant on your floor. A pendant that could have easily slipped from his neck when he was leaving your house.'

'It wasn't *on* the floor. It was caught on my scarf. How is that even possible?'

'Maybe he tried your scarf on before he left. Or maybe it was *already* on the floor, and you only noticed it when you kicked it or something.'

'No, it wasn't. It was a week ago. Roger vacuums every other day. If it had been on the floor, he would have picked it up.'

Roger is my iRobot. I also have Simon the Scooba who scrubs the floors and Brian the Braava who mops them. All of my cleaning robots are named after men; it's my token contribution to standing up to centuries of female subjugation. 'And I didn't kick it. I heard it drop when I picked up my scarf. Why is it that people only question your memory and your sanity when you tell them something fucked-up is going on? That might make sense if fucked-up things never happened in this world, if women were never stalked, raped or murdered, but it happens all the bloody time. I'm telling you, Shawn, it wasn't on the floor. And even if James was the kind of man who borrows his girlfriend's clothes, why would he need my woolly scarf in the middle of summer?'

'I don't know – maybe he tried it on for a joke. Maybe he was sniffing it or something.'

'*Sniffing* it?'

'You know, like your dirty underwear.'

'Ew, please! And what about the Facebook post? You think James doesn't know the difference between a male and a female elephant seal?'

'You didn't.'

I raise my eyes to the ceiling and throw up my hands. 'Well, I'm not a bloody wildlife photographer, am I?'

'Have you tried contacting his friends to see if he showed up for the trip?'

'No. He's friends with hundreds of people on Facebook. And if he did mention the names of the guys he's going with, I don't remember them. I'd have to message all his friends to find out if anyone's heard from him. And if I'm wrong...'

'You'll sound like a nut-job stalker.'

'Exactly.'

'Alright, let's say I humour you for a minute. You said it's not just the necklace and the Facebook post but dozens of other tiny puzzle pieces. So describe the pieces. Help me see the big picture.'

I have no idea where to start and I'm quiet for a moment while I lay out the corners and edge pieces. 'Well...there's the timing for one. Things between me and James had been fine for months. Paul steps into my life and suddenly James disappears.'

'Again – you did fuck the guy.'

'Paul?'

'No, James! You did fuck him, right?'

'Can you stop calling it that?'

'Okay. You went to bed with him, yes?'

I nod.

'So that could have been the reason he jumped ship: he got what he wanted.'

'You're right. But if all James wanted was a fuck – like you say – he could have got that from Tinder. Why put in three months of dates, paying for dinners and making conversation with a woman you have no interest in?'

'But that's exactly what happened with Rob. You kept him waiting for months, finally had sex with him and he fucked off. Why are you so convinced that James hasn't done the same thing?'

'This isn't the bloody nineties, Shawn. Women like sex as much as men and there are plenty out there who don't have my values. Rob was obnoxious, I have no idea what I saw in him. But James is a good-looking guy. He's smart and kind. He could have had any woman he wanted.'

He laughs caustically. 'You honestly think men have changed that much in thirty years? It's the *Cruel Intentions* thing, isn't it? Whoever wrote that script was bang on; he knew what men are like. Guys aren't interested in the Ceciles of this world – women who'll drop their knickers after one kiss – they want an Annette. They want the challenge.'

'*Cruel Intentions*? You're such a heathen.'

'I'm not a heathen! Obviously *I* don't think that way.'

'I didn't mean that, I meant *Cruel Intentions* is...oh, never mind.' It's as bad as James confusing *Harry Potter* with *Macbeth* and I'm not wasting time going down that road. I say, 'The thing is, no matter what I say, you'll find some way to debunk it. You refuse to consider, even for a second, that something bad might have happened to James. Or that Paul might have had something to do with it. But people are murdered all the time. Just because Paul and James didn't know each other, that doesn't make it impossible.'

We're both raising our voices now and I've never had an argument with Shawn before. Heat's rising from my chest, up my neck into my cheeks.

'I'm not saying it's impossible.' On the edge of his stool, he leans over the counter as if the marble between us is preventing him from getting his point across. 'I'm just saying it's implausible. How many people have you known who were murdered? How many people do you know who have even *known* someone who was murdered? None, right? Do you know what the odds are?'

'Alright, slim! But it's not *just* the timing, it's the *way* we met. Since I found that necklace, I've been replaying everything, paying attention to the details. I didn't think anything of it at the time but when Brooke pulled up outside Starbucks I remember her taking the space from someone. They were indicating to go in there and I was embarrassed because it was rude. But then I forgot all about it. Shawn...it was a white van. And, when we came out of Starbucks, Brooke's tyre was slashed. Guess who was right on hand to repair it?'

'Paul?'

'And guess what he drives.'

'A white van.'

'Exactly. I think it was *his* van. I think he slashed Brooke's tyre.'

'She probably hit the kerb; she was hopeless at parking.'

'Jesus Christ...can you stop inventing your own version of events and listen to mine for one minute? She *didn't* hit the kerb. I would have remembered that. And if she had, she would have checked the hub caps for damage. You know how much she loved that car.'

'I *am* listening,' he says. 'I'm just playing devil's advocate. It's not like you're asking me to believe he stole a Snickers bar from the petrol station. I'm just saying that before you go to the police and accuse a man you barely know of murdering your boyfriend, you need to be sure there's no other explanation – that these events aren't random and you're putting two and two together to make five.'

It is a lot for anyone to believe if they've never met Paul, never felt the hairs on the back of their neck go up when his personality alters. I pause for a moment, take a breath, and prepare myself for the hardest piece of the puzzle to talk about.

'There's something else... We had sex last night and he stayed over. When I tried to leave, get ready for my training session this morning, he wouldn't let me go. He made me have sex again and while—

'He *raped* you?'

'No.'

'You said he *made* you...forced you...that's rape.'

'Not *forced* exactly...' I swallow hard, remembering that moment. I feel as if we need a different word for what happened this morning. I was in bed with Paul. We'd already had sex, and when he wanted it again I wasn't exactly firm. I feel humiliated now by how playful I was with him. Why didn't I fight? Why didn't I punch him, kick him, do anything to make it stop? And what I can't even begin to reconcile is my body's response to him. While being absolutely certain that I didn't want sex, knowing I asked him to stop – more than once – my body still reacted to his touch. Can you call that rape? If it was rape, why did I come? Bile rises in my throat at the memory. I think I'm going to be sick. Since there's no word for whatever that was, I say, 'More... convinced. Coerced. But anyway, while we were having sex, he put his hand over my mouth.'

'What?! He tried to suffocate you?'

'Not exactly. It was only for a few seconds, but it was sort of...aggressive...domineering. It frightened me. *He* frightens me.'

'Jesus, Millie. Why do you have to fuck guys like that?'

'It's not *my* fault! It was your sister's bloody idea! She said I was *the girl next door* type, *the marriage and kids* type. She said blokes dump me after sex because I've already kept them waiting three months and any longer's a commitment with a girl like me. So they get what they want and run. I figured I'd take a leaf out of *her* book and get it over with on the first date. Stop being the girl next door.'

'You fucked him on the first date?'

I hesitate. 'Before that, actually.'

Shawn drops his head into his hands, elbows on the counter.

'Why are you angry with *me*? Brooke put the idea in my head. And if Paul had turned out to be a great guy it wouldn't have been a mistake, would it? How was I supposed to know what he was like?'

'Because you get a sense of these things. I don't know why you go around fucking all these guys anyway, not when—'

'I'm not *fucking all these guys*! Christ, Shawn! You make me sound like a slut! And you have no right to be angry about it. Who I have sex with is my business, and it's not like you're on the pussy-wagon, is it?'

He heaves in a shattered breath. 'I'm not angry. I'm just protective, that's all. Protective of my little sister's best friend.'

'I'm not your little sister's best friend! I'm *your* best friend! At least I thought I was!'

'I don't fucking well want to be friends!!'

'Fine by me!' I leap up from the bar stool and head for the kitchen door.

Shawn leaps up too, chases after me. Grabbing my hand, he pulls me back and spins me around to face him.

'I don't want to be friends. I've never wanted to be friends. And I don't want you fucking anyone but me.'

Then his lips are crushed against mine.

CHAPTER TWENTY-FIVE

MILLIE

With my key in the lock, I pause at the cottage door, lost in thought, unable to wipe the damn grin off my face.

That kiss.

I've never been kissed like that in my whole life. It wasn't lust... I daren't even think the other word, but those few moments of physical intimacy opened a door between us, an emotional connection I hadn't realised was there.

Perhaps it had been simmering beneath our friendship all along, I don't know. But it was so intense, so all-consuming, I forgot where I was, who I was. The world disappeared, and all that remained was that moment.

When I came to my senses, with his arms still wrapped around me and his mouth on mine, I expected him to take it further. He said he'd never wanted to be friends so I thought he'd rush to the next level, run his hand over my arse or grab a breast or something but he didn't. Perhaps it was because I told him what Paul had done and the last thing he wanted was to convince or coerce me into doing something I wasn't ready for. But the ache of wanting him to take it further during that prolonged and passionate kiss was more exhilarating than any fumble would have been.

When we finally broke away, our breaths fast and shallow, he said, 'Fuck me, I've wanted to do that since the first day I met you.'

'Why didn't you?'

'I did try...that day in your lounge.'

'I was with James. If I'd been single...'

He ran his fingers through my hair. 'You have to admit, our timing has been pretty awful. One of us has always either been dating or fresh out of a relationship. I didn't want us to start that way.'

'Our timing isn't exactly great now. I'm raw from the relationship with James and tangled up in a mess with Paul.'

'I know. But when you went to storm out of that door, I had to stop you. I didn't want you to leave. I still don't want you to. Why don't you stay? We could have another glass of wine, watch a movie or something. I'm not suggesting...you know...but stay.'

I've stayed over at Shawn's many times. Good friends enjoying each other's company, suggesting films we think the other person will like, eating popcorn in front of the TV. But everything's different now. It won't take much to get heated and the idea of sleeping with three men in one week...that's *way* too icky for me. If we're going to take our friendship to the next level, I want to start with a clean sheet...literally!

'I don't think so.' I glance at my fitness tracker. 'It's getting late. Besides, everything's changed, and if I stay...'

'I know. If you stay, we'll—'

'Don't get me wrong, I want to...you know...stay. It's just, I don't want to do it like this. I need to make it absolutely clear to Paul that it's over. I mean, it isn't exactly a relationship, but I get the feeling he's the kind of guy that assumes you're monogamous until you end it formally. If he saw us together, tomorrow or something, I'm not sure how he'd take it... I mean, you should have seen him with Todd—'

'Markham?'

'Yeah. He was my client this morning, when Paul... Anyway, you should have seen the way he behaved around Todd; you'd think I was running a brothel not a gym. When they passed each other in the hall, for a minute there I thought Paul might punch him.' I thought of something else then, something I forgot to tell Shawn. My brow furrowed.

'What? What's wrong.'

'Todd...when he left, after his session, his tyres were slashed. Just like Brooke's.'

'Are you serious? You think Paul—?'

'Oh, God, I don't know. You've spent the whole evening trying to convince me I'm paranoid, and after one kiss you're agreeing with me?'

Shawn heaved in a breath, then forced it out again. 'I don't know. But I'm thinking maybe you shouldn't go home.'

I laughed. 'You're just saying that because you want me to stay over!'

'I'm not. I mean...I am, I do – but I'm genuinely worried about you going home on your own. Maybe I should come with you?'

'You think we'd be any better at controlling ourselves at my grandmother's than we are here?'

He grinned like a naughty boy.

'Besides, if he shows up out of the blue tomorrow morning, the way he did tonight, and you're there... No, it'll be a mess. If we're going to do this, let's make it a fresh start. We've both been through a lot; maybe it's time to put everything behind us. I'll be alright, I promise. I'll make sure all the doors are locked.'

He kissed me again. 'Can I see you tomorrow?'

'Maybe,' I said, with a twinkle and a smile that meant, *yes, abso-bloody-lutely.* 'We'll just have to see.'

Finally, I turn the key and open the door to Nanny's cottage. The moment I step into the hall, that necklace is on my mind. Paul is on my mind. So I turn back to the open door, hold the frame for support and lean out into the dark night.

As I drove down the lane, I didn't see his van parked anywhere; in fact there were no unfamiliar cars. The road and pavements were empty, and they still are. Apart from a dog barking in the distance, everything is quiet and sleepy.

I secure the bolts top and bottom before heading for the kitchen to check the back door as well. Finally, I get out my phone and text Shawn to let him know I'm home safe.

I'm about to phone Paul but 10.31pm glows on the screen. It's too late to be making social calls, especially the kind where you tell the other person you never want to see them again. So I pocket it with the intention of calling him first thing; he's more likely to take it in good spirits on a fresh, sunny morning. And, anyway, he's hardly going to fall to pieces in despair; it was only one date.

I grab a wine glass from the cupboard and fill it with a pinot noir that's half-drunk in the fridge. I only meant to chill it for half an hour, take the edge off, but forgot all about it. Ice-cold red wine isn't exactly ideal but it's all I've got.

Too wound up to sleep, I take the glass through to the lounge. I'm in the mood for some mindless television while replaying that kiss with Shawn. I want to relive it over and over while the memory is still vivid, while I can still smell him on my clothes, taste him on my lips.

I lean under the shade of Nanny's standard lamp by the lounge door, switch on the light, and drop my wine glass.

On the other side of the room, Paul sits in her recliner.

CHAPTER TWENTY-SIX

MILLIE

'Paul!'

Shock strips everything but his name from my lips.

The stereotype of letting himself in then waiting for me in the dark removes all ambiguity from this situation. His message couldn't be more transparent. But I have no idea what the smart response is, so I just play along.

'What are you doing here? How did you get in?'

'How's your girlfriend?'

'What girl—' I stop myself. With my mind still jumbled by the evening with Shawn – that kiss – I struggle to remember my conversation with Paul at the door earlier. Before another lie can form on my lips, an instinct baser than fear – fight or flight – kicks in. It's as if Nanny's sitting in the recliner instead of Paul, looking out for me the way she always did when she was alive, speaking to me. *Watch your words, Millie, get your story straight.*

What the hell *did* I say earlier this evening? What excuse did I give him?

'The friend having a meltdown.' Leaning back in Nanny's recliner, Paul's face is soft, his smile warm, but his eyes are fixed on mine, unblinking. 'How is she?'

'She's fine. Now, anyway. She was grateful I came over. But you haven't answered my question. How did you get in?'

'Good, that's good. She's lucky to have you as a friend. You look like you've had a few drinks to cheer her up. And you've smudged your lipstick.'

Paul's tone is friendly, oddly calm. But his relaxed posture conveys a sense of title, as if I'm the one who's let herself into *his* house uninvited instead of the other way around. It puts me on the back foot. It's as if I've stayed out an hour past curfew and owe him an apology. Without thinking, I lift my fingers to my mouth and wipe away my lipstick.

He says, 'I came back to apologise for earlier. I must have got it wrong. I didn't mean to be pushy. The door was open when I got here; you left in such a hurry you can't have closed it properly.'

Is that true? Was I stupid enough to leave the door open?

He adds, 'I decided to wait for a little while, see if you came back. But then I fell asleep. It's a really comfortable chair. You woke me up when you came in and I wasn't sure what to do. Sorry.'

His apology throws me, flips the situation again and I'm reminded whose house this is. I stand up straight, about to demand that he leaves, when I'm struck by his posture. Although he's leaning back in the recliner, one leg resting on the other, hands draped over his knee, his stature is rigid. His biceps strain the seams of his shirt, and thick veins pulse beneath the skin of his forearms and neck.

Our eyes lock and the lounge empties of all Nanny's things. I'm on an isolated savannah, exposed. A lone gazelle staring into the hawk-eyed gaze of her predator.

I could run. But he'll run faster.

I glance down at the broken glass at my feet where spilled wine seeps across the floorboards. The white fringe of the rug is staining pink. I could say I need to clean it up, need to go out into the kitchen to get a dustpan and brush. Then I could bolt out of the back door. But Paul's not stupid. He'd offer to help, follow me out to the kitchen, insist on picking up the shattered glass himself. Then he'd use the activity as an excuse to linger.

And I need him to leave.

Right now.

The room throbs with the drumming of my heart, as if its rhythm is cut in vinyl, playing at full volume on Nanny's record player for Paul's enjoyment.

I say, 'I appreciate the apology, Paul. But it's late and I'm going to bed now. I'll call you tomorrow, okay?'

He springs upright.

I flinch and step back.

In his tight black shirt and close-fitting black trousers, he seems taller than before. His matching shoes and tan belt are city-slick. Cut-throat. Eerily calm, he strides towards me, and I'm convinced he intends to hurt me. But instead he steps past, saying, 'I'll clear that up and get something on that rug before it stains.' Then at the door, over his shoulder, he adds, 'We can't go to bed and leave it; your nan would turn in her grave.'

The words *turn in her grave* leave me cold. But *we can't go to bed* leaves me colder. The cupboard doors open and close in the kitchen as he searches for something to clean up the wine. I'm glued to the spot chastising myself for not being more forthright, for allowing him to make that assumption instead of being absolutely clear that *I'm* going to bed. Without him!

No. No. That's not right, Millie.

I have another quiet conversation with Nanny in my head. I *was* clear. I have nothing to chastise myself for. That's how Paul wants me to feel. And he shouldn't be assuming anything.

He shouldn't even *be* here.

Then I remember what he said about the door. Paul took me by surprise earlier this evening, being right there on the step when I set off for Shawn's. It's a reasonable explanation that in my distraction I forgot to close it. But Nanny's oak door is very heavy and over the years the frame has warped slightly, forced the hinges outward. Now it closes under its own steam, latches itself.

Paul lied.

He broke in. And, knowing that, I'm in no doubt that he broke in while James was here as well.

I bolt.

Halfway down the hall, there's a clatter behind me: the dustpan, brush, and cleaning spray, I think. But I daren't look back, daren't waste one second.

Hands trembling, I throw back the top bolt, then the bottom. Grabbing the latch, I heave the door open as Paul's hand shoots past my face. His palm strikes the oak surface and wrenches the latch from my fingers. It tears a nail from the bed as he slams the door shut. When the resounding crash stops pulsing down the hallway, his face touches mine as he speaks softly in my ear. 'Where are you going, Millie? Did you forget something at your girlfriend's?'

A traitorous tear rolls down my cheek.

'I know you're lying.' His lips graze my earlobe. 'His aftershave is all over you. But I forgive you; we all make mistakes. The friends we choose: Brooke. The lovers we pick:

James. It's forgiveness and understanding that makes the two of us so strong. Inseparable.'

James... Brooke.

He's heard Brooke's name more than once: when she introduced herself that day and when I told him about her death. But James... I try to recall if I ever mentioned him by name to Paul. I'm sure I didn't. I just called him my boyfriend. He'd have no reason to know his name unless...

Paul is calculating and controlled; I don't imagine he makes many mistakes. He knows as well as I do that he shouldn't know James's name. It's intentional. He's using it to induce fear.

Not wanting to give him the satisfaction, I stifle the sob that catches in my chest as his hand slips around my waist. He pulls me away from the door. Nausea crawls up my insides as his thick arm presses hard beneath my ribs. I fight to prise his fingers free as he drags me backwards down the hallway. But they only dig deeper, constrictors tightening around their prey with every struggle to free itself.

When we reach the lounge door, his breath grazes my ear. 'Let's clear that up, shall we?'

I squirm in his grip. 'Let me go, Paul. Let me go or I'll scream this house down.'

He throws me through the lounge door, and I stumble over the dustpan and brush, falling to my knees. Tilting his head back, he laughs, the pitch hard and loud enough to crack the ceiling plaster. Then he lowers his eyes and stares directly into mine. 'Nice old cottage. Thick walls. Almost soundproof. You could get up to all sorts in here and nobody would ever hear you.' To hammer his point home, he raises his arms like Christ the Redeemer, and roars at the top of his voice.

I don't waste a breath.

Stooping low, I grab the stem of the broken wine glass and thrust it deep into his calf muscle.

Paul's roar turns into a howl as he drops to one knee. 'You bitch! You fucking bitch!'

As he reaches out to grab me, I swipe the cleaning spray, direct it straight into his eyes and pull the trigger, hard. Clutching his face, he wails in pain as I bolt for the lounge door a second time.

Blinded, Paul shoots out a hand. His fingers only graze the bottom of my dress but then he reaches out again, snatches the fabric and twists it around his fist. He pulls me back with such ferocity that the buttons down the front of my dress rip off, all the way up to my waist, and my feet slip out from beneath me. Face-first, I slam into the floorboards and my jaw cracks, but a split second later I'm reaching out for anything I can grab on to.

My fingers find nothing but air.

As Paul seizes my ankle and hauls me back towards him, the rug's edge curls up beneath me, its rough backing burning my bare thighs and stomach. But then my right hand connects with Nanny's mahogany side table, and I grab the leg tight, dragging it with me. It catches on the rug, tilts towards me and drops the Tiffany lamp and Charlie – Nanny's solid brass bulldog – on to my spine. The glass lampshade shatters and showers me with fragments. With the wind knocked out of me, I don't even try to catch my breath before flipping over and kicking Paul hard in the face.

That's when I see him. *Really* see him. A different man.

A monster.

He's grown in size. Fury and adrenaline pump every muscle. The veins in his arms and neck jut through his skin and he snarls through rage-red eyes. When I kick out again he swipes my leg away, crawls on top of me and sits on my waist. His weight on the soft part of my stomach makes it impossible to breathe but then his hand shoots out and grabs my neck in a vice grip and my throat closes.

Scratching at his forearm with both hands, I dig my nails in. It achieves nothing. With my right hand, I try to prise his fist from my neck, scraping skin. With my left hand, I scrabble around for a weapon. My palm brushes the lamp, and I wrap my fingers around its base, but it's far too heavy to lift one-handed.

Unable to move my head, I flick my eyes left and right, scanning my peripheral vision. Then I track Paul's free hand as he slides it down his calf, the fabric of his trousers wet with blood. I freeze. A cold sweat soaks my armpits as he curls his fingers around the protruding stem of the wine glass. With gritted teeth, he yanks it free.

As he runs his forearm across his streaming eyes, wiping away tears and cleaning fluid, blood drips down the front of my dress and into my cleavage. His vision clearing, he leans over me, brandishing the shard of glass as he spits words in my face. 'I swore you'd never hurt me again.' Then he jabs the glass, stopping millimetres from my right eye.

His own are vacant.

He's going to do it.

I fight to turn my head, but his clenched hand holds me still. 'Please...Paul...please...don't.'

His face is frozen, locked in some internal conflict. He doesn't release the pressure on my neck, and, as my peripheral vision darkens, all I can see through the tunnel of light is the quivering needle of broken glass.

Muscles weak, my fingers stop clawing and darkness closes in. But with a sudden gasp, as if he's the one coming up for air, Paul eases his hold. With each deep breath, life returns to his eyes and a controlled calm washes over his body. Only now I'm not sure which man I'm more afraid of: the raging savage monster or this disturbingly cold psychopath.

Even though he still has his hand around my neck and the shard of glass at my eye, his anger is in check and he speaks softly. 'You have no fucking idea of the things I have done for you.'

Pinned beneath him, I lift my legs and try to pummel his back with my knees. Unfazed, he just slides back on to the tops of my thighs. It restricts my movements, but the shift is just enough for me to steal a breath from beneath his fingers. When he throws the glass stem away, the sigh of relief lasts only a second because I know, one way or another, he's going to make me pay.

'It's not your fault,' he says. 'It's the people you have around you: Brooke and James...and those other men you let into your house. They've all poisoned your mind. Including whoever you were with tonight. Whoever you felt you had to lie to me about.'

Finally Paul releases my neck. I claw at my throat as if that will help me gasp in each painful breath. But then he grabs my wrists and pulls them away. I wrestle against him but he's so strong, and when he forces them down by my sides it's as if I've put up no resistance at all. Then he kneels on my forearms.

Trapped, powerless to move, I lie stiff as Paul lowers his face to mine.

'You'll see,' he says. 'I'll set you free of them. It'll just be the two of us.'

The words barely register before he clamps my cheek between his fingers and presses his lips to mine. I grit my teeth and swallow bile as his tongue works its way into my mouth. Tasting his spit, I gag. But I gulp down the retch, terrified it will make him angry. Sliding his legs down, he presses his body against mine, the growing bulge in his trousers grinding against my pelvis. I'm about to plead for him to stop when he pulls out of the kiss and sits on top of me again.

Reaching into his pocket, he pulls out a silver object, then presses a button on its side. A blade flicks out with a sickening click and its metal reflects the rainbow glass of Nanny's broken lampshade.

He lowers the knife until cold steel touches my bare thigh at my panty line. When he slips the razor-sharp blade beneath the sheer fabric it offers no resistance. With a smile that turns my stomach, his bloodshot eyes trace the knife's progress to the thin waistband.

I'm exposed from the belly down, but it's not enough for Paul. He cinches my dress fabric tight at my midriff, hooks the knife under the first of the remaining buttons and slices it off before moving up to the next. And the next. When the final button rolls on to the floor, my dress falls open and he flicks the blade back into its case. Then he drinks in my bare flesh and lacy bra.

After tucking the knife back in his pocket, Paul casually undoes his shirt, one button at a time, while saying, 'Let's not fight. Let's pretend it's our first night together.' Then he lifts himself slightly to crank his belt and transfers his full body weight to his knees. They crush my forearms into the carpet and I let out a cry.

Instinct, the absolute necessity to end the pain, floods my body with adrenaline. Charged with courage I didn't know I had, I wait for the smallest movement from Paul. When he leans slightly to the left to unzip his fly, blood surges into my right arm at the negligible release of pressure. Fighting the pins and needles that race to my hand, I power my arm out from beneath his knee with such force, it smacks into Nanny's brass bulldog. Scrabbling desperately around the rug near my thigh, my fingers curl around Charlie. And the second I have a tight grasp around his body I jerk my arm up.

Paul's eyes flick from his fly to my arm as I swipe the dog hard against his temple. The blow knocks him to the floor, and, the second I'm free, I scramble to my knees and lift Charlie high above my head to strike again.

Then I stop.

Paul isn't moving.

CHAPTER TWENTY-SEVEN

MILLIE

Clutching my dress closed at the waist, I bolt down the hallway, pull back the latch and yank the front door open. When the cool night air hits my damp skin still steaming from the fight, Nanny's voice whispers on the breeze.

What are you going to do, Millie? Run? Where to? Next door? Get Doreen to call the police? How long will it take them to get here? Twenty minutes? More? And how long will it take Paul to come around? Five minutes? Less? He'll wake up, casually walk out of the door and be long gone before the police even pull on to the street. What do you think he'll do after that? You think he'll just let this go? Say, oh, well, and chalk it up as a missed opportunity?

Whether it's really Nanny's voice or the one in my head, it's right.

I shut the door.

What the fuck am I going to do?

I need time to think, and, to do that, I have to get myself out of immediate danger. An idea forms quickly, and I run to the garage and then my gym. I don't know if it'll work or if I have enough time – Paul could wake up at any second – but I have to try.

Eyes flitting between him and the fireplace, my hands shake so badly that I keep dropping things. I have to stop for a moment to take a few calming breaths. Finally composed, I work efficiently rather than quickly.

Coiling a weightlifting chain tightly around each of Paul's wrists, I connect them with quick links that I tighten with Grandad's wrench.

Paul is powerful, athletic, and there aren't many things in this room I could chain him to that he wouldn't be able to move. Given his profession, I'm not chaining him to the radiator; he'd probably know its weak spots and how to break the pipework. But the one thing he'll never break, not even be able to move an inch, is Nanny's fireplace. He's close enough to the hearth not to have to move his body and I'm grateful: I'm not sure I'd have the strength to drag him more than a few feet.

The brass finials on either side of the grate have a similar circumference to my barbell so the attachment collars for each chain fit snugly. Once I've locked the bolts in place by twisting the T-bar rods, I use the hole in the wrench handle to lever them even tighter.

Standing over Paul, I assess my handiwork for any potential weaknesses. Even unconscious, his muscles still bulge through the fabric of his shirt sleeves. All it takes is the recollection of his grip around my neck to realise he's strong enough to unscrew those collars even without a wrench. The

T-bar rods will give him all the leverage he'll need to unscrew the bolts. They have to go.

I dart from the room.

Two minutes later, back from the garage with Grandad's Dremel, I plug it into the nearest socket. I pray it still works while trying to figure out how to turn it on. The cutting disc turns slowly at first and I quickly figure out how to increase the speed.

The ends of each T-bar are hammered flat to stop them sliding through the bolt holes, and, when I start cutting, a Catherine wheel of flaming-orange steel dust skips from the Dremel. I half-close my eyes while hearing Grandad's voice in my head – *you really should be wearing goggles, young lady* – but I'm more afraid the sparks will set my hair on fire.

The stopper on the first T-bar drops on to the stone hearth, and I slide it out of the bolt before setting to work on the second. But then Paul's right leg twitches and I flinch, the cutting blade slipping out of the groove. The Dremel shakes as I struggle to locate the small indent I've made.

Focus, Millie! Work smart, not fast.

Paul groans and kicks out his leg, but I don't take my eyes off the steel.

'Come on! Come on!'

Sparks flying, adrenaline coursing, I grip the Dremel. Finally, the stopper falls off the second T-bar, but when I slide it out of the clamping bolt it slips from my fingers. Tools tucked under one arm, I claw around in the hearth until I find the severed metal rods. I snatch them up just as Paul's eyes fix on me.

I'm out of time.

Throwing the tools across the room, I scrabble away on my hands and knees as he jerks upright. But before I can open even a metre between us a hand grabs my left ankle and

Paul's fingers dig so hard into my flesh, I'm convinced he'll snap the bone.

As he drags me back towards the fireplace I know this is my only chance to escape: either I break free now or die. On nothing but instinct, I flip on to my back, bend my right knee close to my chest and kick out hard, striking him square in the face.

Paul roars and lets go of my ankle. As I shuffle away on my backside, he springs to his feet and launches himself at me. With his arms spread wide and his fists clenched like weapons, his open black shirt whips around his bare torso.

With no idea whether I've secured the chains tightly enough, whether the clamping bolts will slip from the finials, or if Paul's adrenaline-filled rage is strong enough to move that fireplace after all, I cower at his approach.

But then the chains stop him dead. They wrench back his wrists with such force that his shoulder joints crack and swell under the strain.

Breathing heavily, we stare at each other in raw silence.

CHAPTER TWENTY-EIGHT

PAUL

It takes me a few seconds to realise what she's done, realise I can't get to her. I'm shackled by each wrist, straining with everything I have. But there's no give, so I let the chains go slack and reverse into the shadows of the fireplace.

Back in check, emotionless once more, I stare at Millie, only at her. I won't give her the satisfaction of checking my restraints, figuring out what she's done. Not while she's right there, looking back at me.

She pulls her phone from the pocket of her dress, and, shaking with fear, stabs at the screen.

Who's she going to call? The police?

The police could work; I'll play the victim. We only went on one date and, when I told her I didn't want to see her again, she lost it. She knocked me unconscious, and when I woke up I found myself chained to her fireplace. The bitch is completely crazy!

With any luck they'll be male officers and I'll turn on the man banter. They'll buy the psycho girlfriend, *hell hath no fury like a woman scorned* bullshit. A few hours of police interviews and I'll be out on the street. Millie can say all she likes about Brooke and James, but there's no evidence, no motive, no link.

She glances in my direction, flicking her gaze away as mine unnerves her.

I smile.

I'm still in control. I'm always in control. And once I'm out of this mess, I'll come back for her.

Only, then, having the police involved could be a problem. Although they'd get me out of my present situation, if she manages to call them a second time, more questions will be asked. Reasons and motives will come into play; connections could be made between me, Brooke and James. And the officers investigating Dexter's disappearance have my contact details.

I need to stop her.

I laugh, but Millie refuses to look at me. So I force the sound out, harsh, loud and impossible to ignore. When she lifts her eyes from the screen, I lean forward just far enough for the lamplight to hit my face as my mouth curls.

'Who are you calling, Millie? The police? Fine...call them. One lover disappeared off the face of the earth, the next one chained to your fireplace. My, my, Millie, you have been busy. Call them. I'll be free, and you'll be in custody for false imprisonment.' I let the words sink in before I float back into the shadows a millimetre at a time. 'But I'll wait for you. I'm good at waiting. However long it takes. And when they eventually let you out, I'll be ready for you.'

The seeds of doubt planted, I stand still in the dark, barely breathing. I know she won't dial that number. I know it before she even knows it herself.

I might be in chains, but I still have the power.

CHAPTER TWENTY-NINE

MILLIE

My fingers are trembling so badly, I dialled four nines instead of three then deleted two of them by mistake and had to punch in another. Finally with three nines on the screen, my thumb hovers over the call button as Paul's words register.

His threat sinks in.

I glance up at him again, a monster in the shadows. But I can't hold his gaze, that proprietorial stare. It's as if I'm a meal he's ordered. Only the dish arrived late, served cold, and now I'm his to eat or send back.

Paul looks at me as if he intends to finish me.

I can't connect the man I thought he was – kind and thoughtful – with this animal chained to my fireplace. The fact that I slept with him willingly makes me sick to my stomach. I could say that he fooled me, made a fool *of* me, but, in truth, his lies and persona were utterly compelling. He didn't once dither or pause. How does a person lie so convincingly?

Surely, to do that, you have to *believe* your own lies?

I *know* I'm my own person – that I don't belong to anybody – and yet the look on Paul's face is convincing enough to believe otherwise. In his mind, I am absolutely and completely his. It's not normal to think anyone belongs to you, that you have the right to break into their house and take what you want from them, of them. Not after any length of time but especially not after one date.

But for whatever reason, this monster has made a connection with me that I'll never be able to understand, and if I can't understand it, I can't break it. How would I even begin to negotiate my freedom from a man whose conviction in his ownership runs right through the marrow of his bones?

Paul is not a man you contradict.

And he's certainly not one you bargain with.

He may be wrong about the police believing him over me; that could go either way.

But then again, I do have him chained to my fireplace.

I know in my heart that Paul killed Brooke and James but, without evidence, the police won't be able to hold him for long, let alone charge him. And they won't listen to a hunch – especially from a woman who chains men to her fireplace – which means, the only crimes they will consider are the ones that took place tonight, the ones that are taking place right now.

I play the interview with the police over in my head:

Yes, officer, I did have sex with him last night and the night before. Yes, it was consensual. And yes, I had sex with him again this morning – although consensual is the wrong word for that – but tonight, he definitely tried to rape me.

So you chained him to your fireplace?

Yes, officer.

Paul's right. The evidence of *my* crime is clear: false imprisonment. How long will it be before the evidence of his becomes clear? How long before the bruises start to show? And does it even matter? Paul didn't actually rape me tonight. Best case scenario, he'd get a few years for attempted rape. Worst case scenario, he'll go free, and I'll be arrested.

Plus, I've seen Paul's 'nice guy' act. He had me convinced.

I may have succumbed to his lies, but there is one thing he said that I believe with absolute certainty: regardless of which one of us is arrested, he *will* wait for me.

He *will* come back for me.

I throw my phone on to the sofa so hard, it bounces off the back cushion and lands on the floor.

CHAPTER THIRTY

PAUL

My eyes follow her phone. They're the only part of my body that moves as I track its progress on to the sofa, the floor, and then across the rug.

Having discounted the police as an option, Millie is now lost. Uncertainty is written all over her face. She's gripped by fear: fear of calling the police and fear of letting me go.

Inside the emotionless void, I'm surprised by something other than rage firing along the neurotransmitters: a brief surge of happiness. But it quickly passes.

All my focus is again targeted on Millie.

It's time to play, make her doubt what she thinks she knows. There's no time to waste. The mind is more susceptible when it's in a state of flux.

I run through the catalogue of faces in my repertoire.

My father got off on fear. As a child I learned to overplay it to gratify and placate him. Skye, too. I channel that now, slip on a mask of innocence, then move slowly into the light. The vulnerable boy who could stop one of Skye's cocaine-fuelled rages appears before Millie. My eyes lock briefly on hers before flicking away.

'Millie, this is crazy. It's got way out of hand. I didn't mean the things I said, what I tried to do. But you stabbed me in the leg. It really fucking hurt and I lost it. I'm so sorry. What can I do to make it up to you?' I resist the urge to blink until my eyes water. 'You're really scaring me now. You've got me chained to your fireplace, for Christ's sake. Look, I'm really sorry. You've made your point. Let me go and you'll never see me again, I promise.'

I bow my head, close my eyes and let the tears fall.

'Please forgive me, Millie. I truly am sorry.'

CHAPTER THIRTY-ONE

MILLIE

Too exhausted to stand any longer, I collapse on to the sofa. But I'm a bundle of nerves and can't relax. So I perch on its edge and watch Paul. His head is bowed, tears roll down his cheeks, and he's shaking. I can't bear to look at him any more, so I rest my head in my hands. Running my fingers through my hair, I close my eyes and pretend I'm alone in the dark.

I want to go to bed. It's so late and I'm so tired, I just want to sleep. I want to forget any of this ever happened, wake up and realise it was all a dream. Because this can't be real, can it? This can't actually be happening.

Paul is dead right: this has gone way too far. It's spun so far out of my control, I have no idea how to make it stop. I can't call the police, and I can't keep him here. So what the fuck am I supposed to do with him? I really didn't think this through.

Perhaps he's telling the truth. Perhaps he did just lose it. After all, I did stab him in the leg, knock him out with

Nanny's brass bulldog and then chain him up. I'm hardly innocent in all this. In fact, the way things stand right now, he's *my* victim, not the other way around.

I look at him again, cowering in the shadows of my fireplace, trembling.

It's not another act, is it?

Right there in front of my eyes stands a frightened child visible just beneath his skin.

This isn't me. This isn't how I behave, how I treat people.

I spring to my feet and snatch up the T-bars I threw across the floor. But the moment Paul looks up at me, realises I'm about to free him, the guileless child evaporates. That's how quickly he can switch. I see him then, wearing a different mask. His face twists into a hideous memory: that snarl, those glowering eyes, rage-red, as he held my throat closed. I pause, gripping the metal rods so tight, my fingers are numb.

He's a liar.

Paul didn't just lose it. That's not how it went. This wasn't some disagreement that spun out of control; it was premeditated. He broke into my house, waited in the dark for me to get home. And he came armed with a knife. A knife that's still in his pocket. A knife I'm somehow going to have to take from him.

I step back.

'You must take me for a fool,' I say. 'That's a cute little trick: playing scared, crying on cue. This didn't out of hand; it just didn't go the way you'd planned. And you didn't lose it because I stabbed you; I stabbed you because you'd already lost it. You broke into my house! And not just tonight. You broke in when James was here as well, didn't you? Brooke's house too. I know you killed them. And if I hadn't stopped you tonight you would have raped and killed me as well.'

I laugh without humour and impersonate him. '*Let me go and you'll never see me again, I promise.* I almost bought it. If I let you go, I'll be right back where I was earlier this evening: your prisoner. Well, now you're mine. And you aren't going anywhere.'

CHAPTER THIRTY-TWO

PAUL

I lock fear and confusion on my face while I spin the situation's status quo quickly through my mind. She's convinced herself that I killed them; it's a conclusion born out of fear, desperation and panic. It's true, but to a rational person it's still an absurd accusation. How could I do something like that? How *would* I do it? And why?

Time to turn this back on her. Make her doubt all she thinks she knows.

Make *her* the monster.

'*My* prisoner? You're fucking crazy! Broke in? How? I'm not some master fucking criminal; you're the one who left the bloody door ajar.' I switch to annoyance, but keep my voice calm and assertive to protest my innocence. 'Millie, listen to yourself, listen to what you're saying. Your friend Brooke, I met her once, just once. All I did was change a tyre for her, and I only did that because I fancied you. Kill her? That's insane – why the hell would I do that? I didn't even know her. As for James, I have no idea what he even looks like; I've never met the bloody man. You've seriously lost it!'

Her brow furrows as doubt creeps into her mind. The things she was so certain about a minute ago are now spinning around in her head as my words destroy her logic.

I'm winning.

'Look, I meant what I said. I really am sorry about earlier. But when you seduced me that first time, when you kissed me and took me upstairs to have sex, I thought you liked it a little rough. Maybe I crossed the line and I'm sorry about that, but kill you? Kill your friend? Kill some bloke I never met? Where's all this coming from? *This...*' I rattle the chains to enforce the madness of her actions '...*this* is insane. Look, I really liked you but you're scaring the crap out of me. You've had your fun. All I want is to get out of here and never come back.'

Shrinking away, I fold in on myself. Small and vulnerable, I look into her eyes, then flick mine away as if I don't have the nerve to make eye contact with a madwoman. And there it is, the questioning in her eyes: what if she's got it wrong, what if she's chained up an innocent man?

I know her.

Millie's sweet, naïve. She's never done anything like this in her life. This situation has to be killing her; all she'll want is for it to be over as soon as possible. She can't call the police, so what options are left open to her? Kill me? Yeah, right, like that's going to happen. Set me free? It's just a matter of time.

I can't lose.

I move further back, allowing enough slack in the chains to lift my hands, palms up, cuffs exposed to the light. I'm giving her the power to do what she already wants to do.

Now for the finishing touch.

'Please, Millie, just let me go. You'll never see me again.'

Let's see how certain she is now.

CHAPTER THIRTY-THREE

MILLIE

'Stop it! That's enough! I can't listen to any more of your begging and pleading. One minute you're sorry because it got out of hand and the next I'm fucking crazy? If you don't stop talking, I'll stab you in the other leg!'

I don't know what the statistics are, but I know that it's a lot more than half: over fifty per cent of women murdered in this country are killed by their partners or ex-partners.

And I bet, in the overwhelming majority of those cases, they never imagined the men whose charms they fell for were capable of killing. It's too easy to think that something that terrifying only happens on the news, to other women, not to you.

Paul is underestimating me. Belittling my instincts.

It's what all men do: they strip us of our intuition by laughing at it. They tell us we're crazy, make out that our sixth sense is just hogwash or snake oil, a figment of our silly imaginations.

But it's *very* real.

The ability to interpret another person's emotional state from one look in the eye, to read warning signs at a glance, is in our genes. We've been using it to protect our young from predators and invaders since we lived in caves.

Men denigrate intuition because they don't have it. They can't understand it. And because men denigrate it, women too often brush it aside. That's why they end up dead. Because they didn't trust their instincts. They ignored the red flags.

I'm not making that mistake.

Intuition is our power. It's our gift.

And it keeps us alive.

With the T-bars still in my hand, I step back. Paul tracks my every move as I restore the fallen table to its rightful place and put the metal rods next to Charlie where he can't get to them. Negotiation with Paul is out of the question but this message is loud and clear: escape is out of his reach.

The T-bars roll across the table, coming to a stop at its lip. They're so small, so seemingly insignificant, and yet they're all that stands between Paul and me. Between my life and my death.

Gathering up the wrench and the Dremel from where I threw them across the floor, I grip them tightly in one hand while reaching into the pocket of my dress with the other.

I have another point to make.

I pull out James's pendant.

'Do you know what this is?' I hold it up in front of Paul. 'It belonged to James. He never goes anywhere without it. Never. Yet somehow it got caught on my scarf in the hall. And that's not the only mistake you've made. You don't know much about wildlife, do you, Paul?'

I watch his face closely for the narrowest crack in his facade.

'Only male elephant seals have trunks.'

And there it is: the tiniest flicker of a response.

After putting the tools back in the garage, I head to the kitchen and rummage around in the medicine drawer for a first-aid kit. It's probably been in there for a decade, but it'll have to do. I couldn't care less whether Paul's in pain, but I can't have him dying on me from blood poisoning.

As I'm closing the drawer, a bottle of Nanny's pills rolls forward and I read the label as if it's a sign from her. Believing she's trying to help me, I take them out and put them on the worktop, sensing I'll need them later.

On my way through the hall, I drop the first-aid kit on the sideboard before taking the stairs. After stripping off my torn dress and changing into comfy pants and a T-shirt, I go back on to the landing, where I pull down the loft hatch and climb the unfolded ladders. The bulb's gone but there's enough light from below for me to find what I'm looking for.

Back in the lounge, I throw the first-aid kit at Paul. 'You'd better clean yourself up. That wound could get infected.'

Then I put Nanny's copper bedpan down on the rug. When I stored it in the loft, I was well aware of what an odd memento it was to keep. But, like everything else of hers in this cottage, I couldn't bear to part with anything she had touched. Nanny was bedridden for her final weeks and changing her bedpan several times a day was something I got used to. I'm grateful it has a lid, because changing it for Nanny was one thing; changing it for Paul is something else entirely.

I shove it with my foot, and it slides across the rug within Paul's reach. 'You'll need that, too.'

CHAPTER THIRTY-FOUR

PAUL

Millie's strength takes me by surprise. Stab me in the other leg?

She wouldn't do that.

She loves me.

She's just angry, that's all.

I stare down at the bedpan. Unable to maintain this submissive stoop, I grow to my full size and show my defiance and disgust. But Millie ignores me. She flicks off the lights.

I retreat into the shadows as the last flash of the bulb's extinguished glow shrinks to the size of a keyhole.

I'm locked up again.

Panicking, I blink quickly until my eyes adjust. The glow from the streetlights outside cuts its way through a small gap in the curtain.

Only, this time, I won't go back in the wardrobe.

I concentrate on Millie's outline as she lies on the sofa. Her eyes are open, staring at me, visible only as glassy reflections in the amber light.

I'm glad it's dark; she can't see the beads of sweat on my forehead and the fear in my eyes. I've managed to push the past away, but the weight around my wrists threatens to break the lock on the box where bad memories live.

I escaped once before. I can do it again.

In suspended animation, the only thing that moves is my eyelids. Every ten seconds they wipe away the sting of my drying eyes.

I've been standing here for over an hour but that's nothing compared to a military inspection. My breathing's as slow as a metronome tick. My heartbeat is no more than a stone that skims the water's surface, a ripple forming every time it pumps another seventy millilitres of blood around my body.

Millie's still lying on the sofa, still watching me.

Cortisol and adrenaline only carry you so far before the body burns them up and the mind blocks out the fear. Physically and emotionally exhausted, she stifles yawns and fights to keep her eyes open.

I need her to sleep.

I have work to do.

Ignoring the increasing need to pee, I crouch down on to my haunches. Millie's eyes snap open and her head whips up at my sudden movement, but I don't react. I just sit down and lean back against the fire grate.

Hands in my lap and head bowed, I shut my eyes and pretend to sleep.

So starts the internal clock in my head.

She'll watch me. She might not buy that I'm sleeping but in her present state, in the dark with no stimulus, a minute will feel like an eternity. She'll be asleep within half an hour, but I'll give it forty-five minutes.

Tapping my index finger rhythmically on my leg, I cross off minute after minute and, while I count, listen to her breathing. It starts with short, frequent breaths while she's awake, scared, and distressed. But as the minutes tick by, it slows, deep inhalations followed by long exhalations. Then she yawns.

She's struggling now.

Twenty-five minutes in and her breathing is shallow and rhythmic. At dead on thirty minutes, the desperate need to pee forces me to risk cutting the count short. My eyes snap open. Her dark shape is quiet and still on the sofa. Her face is in shadow, but I can't see the whites of her eyes.

She's asleep.

Raising my arms, I slowly lift the heavy chains off the stone hearth and pick up the bedpan. It shakes in my hands from the pain in my bladder and I glance up at Millie. The slightest sound could wake her and the last thing I want is for her to see me kneeling here with my dick out, her eyes ridiculing me as I take a piss.

It's tricky but I lower my arms until the chains silently kiss the floor and set the pan down on the hearth by my side. When the copper taps the stone, my eyes flick up and cut through the dark to the sofa. She doesn't move.

Rolling my legs around, I pop up on to my knees so I can undo the zipper on my trousers. Then I lift up the hinged lid and squat as low as I can before relieving myself. In my head the quiet trickle is as loud as a waterfall. Millie still doesn't stir.

Sliding it a millimetre at a time, I push the bedpan out of the way before zipping myself back up. Then I listen to her steady breathing for another full minute to reassure myself that she's still asleep.

Now the work begins.

To escape any situation you must first fully understand what you're getting yourself out of. But it's too dark in here to see, so everything has to be done by touch.

I stand and raise my arms, quietly lifting the chains completely off the floor to assess their strength. They're thick, heavy, around twelve kilos apiece. Although unbreakable, their size and weight have an advantage: as long as I move slowly, they barely chink or rattle.

I grab one chain halfway along and follow its links to the cast-iron fireplace. A metal collar attaches it to one of the grate's pillars and it's tightened down with a bolt that has a hole through its centre. I try to unscrew it, but my fingers slide around the smooth steel.

Millie dropped two metal rods on the side table, the action conspicuous. Now I realise she was sending me a message: without those bars to slip through the bolt holes, I have no leverage.

I'll never get these collars off.

Moving cautiously back upright, I lower my arms and rest the chains on the floor again. My shoulders and biceps burn from the stress of holding up twenty-plus kilos of steel. Reaching slowly into my pocket, I pull out my leather pouch of lock-picks and remove the thickest one. It's thin, but if she hasn't done the bolts up too tightly it might give me the leverage I need to loosen them.

I trace the chain back down to the collar, and slide the pick through the bolt hole. Curling my fingers around it on both sides, I twist. The bolt doesn't move. Aware the pick is flexing dangerously under the pressure, I carefully apply a little more, pushing its limits. There's a snap followed by pain as each half of the pick embeds itself into the palm of my hand.

Millie stirs.

I freeze.

Palm by my side with two halves of a lock-pick sticking out of it, I keep my breath shallow. Her shape moves, changes, as she gets comfortable in her sleep. Even though I'm chained up here, her outline still stirs feelings down below.

Patience. I can still make everything right. Once I get out of this, I'll make her see how things need to be. She'll understand, stop this silliness. We will be together.

Feeling my way in the dark, I pull the remnants of the lock-pick out of my palm and drop them in the fire pit behind me. I contemplate having a go with another pick, but the first one did nothing to loosen the bolt and the others in the pouch are even thinner. Putting that idea out of my mind, I turn my attention to my chained wrists. I run a finger around each link in turn. They're all smooth except one that has a machined-in crisscross grip on a threaded sleeve.

It's a locking link.

Gripping it tightly between my fingers, I twist the sleeve as hard as I can, but no amount of force will unwind it. Then I remember the wrench in Millie's hand. She must have used it to tighten the links. Pursuing this avenue of escape is also pointless.

If I can't undo the collar bolts or the locking links, my options are wearing thin, but I might be able to pull my hands out. Focusing on Millie helps shut out the pain as I hook my fingers into the chain links and drag them down my wrist. They only slide halfway before the knuckle of my thumb stops their progress. Still, I carry on, gritting my teeth as the metal tears my flesh.

It's no good. I have to concede. I'd need to dislocate my thumb to get free and I could end up breaking it.

Reaching out in the dark, I feel my away along the grate and grab one of the metal pillars where the chain is collared. Cast iron can last several lifetimes but it's also brittle, especially if it's ever been subjected to rust. With both hands wrapped around the top of the finial – its weakest point – I pull it forward, listening for an iron crack that never comes.

Finally out of options and in desperation, I drop my arse to the stone floor, plant my left foot on the grate and my right on the collared pillar. Then, with my entire body weight directed through my right leg, I force my foot forward with all the strength I have. But not only does the finial show no sign of snapping, the fireplace doesn't move a millimetre. It must weigh a ton or more.

Millie's not stupid. She cut the T-bars off the bolts to remove my leverage. She wrenched the locking links past finger-tight. And, of all the things in this room she could have chained me to, she picked the one thing I'll never be able to move or break.

The whirlwind builds in my head. Anger spirals beyond containment and I kick the finial over and over, yelling at the top of my voice, 'You fucking bitch!'

Leaping to my feet, I throw myself at Millie. The chains snap taut, but I'm so determined to get up in her face that the fireplace moves a millimetre across the stone with a roar that matches mine.

Startled, Millie sits bolt upright on the sofa.

Now I can see the whites of her eyes.

She presses her back into the cushions to get as far away from me as possible.

There we stay, shadows in the dark, neither of us moving.

Eventually, aided by the lactic acid build up in my screaming muscles, the weight of the chains wins, and I relent. Easing back into the shadows, I sit down on the stone floor and lean against the grate. I bow my head and close my eyes, slowing my breathing to its metronome tick, my heartbeat to a stone that skims the water.

CHAPTER THIRTY-FIVE

MILLIE

It's still dark. It takes a moment for me to realise where I am. Instead of waking up in my comfortable bed, I'm in my lounge with a killer just a few feet away.

After being wrenched out of an exhausted sleep by Paul's outburst a couple of hours ago, I finally dropped off again to the sound of his measured breathing. But what little rest I got was fitful and fleeting, plagued by nightmares.

What the fuck am I going to do?

I have no idea.

The one thing I definitely need to do is make sure nobody finds Paul here. I made the decision not to call the police and – for now at least – it feels like it was the right one. The last thing I need is someone removing that choice before I've figured out for myself what the best course of action is.

By the dim glow of the streetlight seeping through the gap in the curtains, I scan the room for my phone. Then I remember throwing it on the sofa last night and it bouncing off on to the floor. So I get down on my hands and knees and feel around the sofa in the dark, then beneath each of the armchairs. I find nothing but dust bunnies under the first chair, but, under the second, my fingers make contact with the smooth glass of my iPhone.

When I lift it up, the lock screen glares with life. Only it's not my phone. It's Paul's. It must have dropped out of his pocket last night when he was...

Not wanting to wake him, I place his phone quietly on the coffee table and feel underneath it, where I find my own. It still has charge, so I compose a text message to my client group telling them I've come down with flu and have to cancel all training sessions until further notice. Fortunately, none of my personal clients attend my yoga classes, so I can still take those. Most months I live hand-to-mouth; I have a little in my savings account for a rainy day, but I can't afford to lose all my income.

Once the text has been sent, I glance over at Paul to make sure he's still sleeping. He is, so I lie back down on the sofa, close my eyes and curl my legs up to my stomach for comfort. I wish Nanny were here. She'd know what to do.

I'm woken by the rumble of a car engine outside. Eyes closed, I listen, praying the noise will fritter away as it drives down the road. Only, instead, the engine cuts out.

My eyes dart to Paul. It's woken him, too.

He's straight up on his feet, chains snapping tight as he throws himself forward trying to get a look out of the window. We exchange glances, then I spring to my feet too, and peer between the closed curtains.

Fuck!

It's Shawn. As he gets out of his car and makes his way to the garden gate, I run through my options.

One: I could let Shawn in on it.

No. I'll probably end up in jail over this; I'm not dragging him down with me. And anyway, he'd probably call the police and Paul will be back on the street in no time. I'll spend the rest of my no doubt very short life wondering when I'll come home and find Paul sitting here in the dark waiting to pay me back for what I've done to him.

Two: I kindly ask Paul if he wouldn't mind awfully keeping quiet while I get rid of the very person who'd most likely help him out of his chains. Not likely.

Which leaves option three: knock Paul unconscious.

Nanny's brass bulldog, Charlie, did an excellent job of that last time. And this time I know where to aim: either the jaw or the temple, depending on whether he faces up to me or turns away to protect himself.

I stride towards Paul, snatch Charlie up from the table and lift him high above my head as I close the gap between us.

Paul glares at me, his expression defiant and challenging. But when he realises I have every intention of going through with this, it turns to shock. Lifting an arm to protect his exposed jaw, he ducks beneath the mantel. I stop. I expected to have a fight on my hands but instead we stare at each other, refusing to break eye contact.

A few tense seconds pass but then Paul sits down, pulls up his knees and rests his wrists on them like a well-behaved schoolboy.

Still holding Charlie aloft, I take another step forward.

'If you so much as *breathe* too loudly, you and the bulldog will get reacquainted. Do you understand me?'

Still staring, Paul gives a single nod.

I put Charlie on the side table and close the door behind me as I leave the room. As I make my way down the hall, I silently thank Nanny's old cottage for having such thick walls. Opening the front door, I catch Shawn unawares just as he rings the bell.

'Hey!' He gathers himself.

'Hi – didn't you get my text? I'm not feeling well.'

'Yeah. I was just passing on my way to work, thought I'd drop in and make sure you're still alive.' He takes a step closer, points past me through the open door. 'You should be in bed. Shall I make you some tea and toast?'

It's been a long time since Shawn needed or waited for an invite to come inside. Usually, the moment the door is open I'm heading back down the hall nattering away with him in tow.

This time, I take a step to the side and body-block the doorway. 'Thanks for the thought, but I'm fine. Although I'm probably contagious.'

'I don't mind. To be honest I'm looking for any excuse to get out of work.' He holds his fist up to his mouth and fakes a cough. 'I think I'm coming down with it too. I'd better call in. We could be sick buddies.' He raises one eyebrow. 'You know...curl up in bed together for a whole week.'

I attempt a casual laugh, but it comes out fake. 'That sounds great...' and even though that would be true at any other time, curling up in bed with Shawn loses its appeal when there's a madman chained to my fireplace '...but I'm feeling completely horrible. I'm really not in the mood for company.' It sounds like a lie because it is. I'm a hopeless liar; give me a paper bag and I couldn't act my way out of it.

'That's alright, neither am I.' He takes another step closer, his proximity insistent. 'We'll shut ourselves away from the world and won't answer the door to anyone.'

'No, Shawn, really. Thanks for checking in on me but I'm really not up to socialising.'

'It's me,' he says. 'You don't have to be sociable with me. I'll call in sick and be your beck-and-call boy. You won't even have to talk to me. You can just ring a bell whenever you need anything.'

'I said no.' The moment the sharp words come out, I feel awful. His soft-spoken, gentle Millie is gone, replaced by this grindstone of a woman who's just stripped his skin.

His mouth falls open slightly and I'm lost for words. I regret it instantly, but I'm scared that if I appease him he'll opt for the *let's go inside and talk about this* approach. I really didn't mean to snap at him, but even now I can't think of a believable excuse for why I don't want to see him. That snap was born of fear not anger. Fear for him.

He stares at me for a long moment. I'm about to confess the whole thing, admit that I want nothing more than for him to come inside, hold me, comfort me, tell me what fuck I'm supposed to do with the murderer chained to my andirons. But then he speaks.

'Honestly, Millie, I'm...not sure what to say. I thought last night meant something. But it didn't, did it? All I get from you is the same text you sent to all your other clients. Not a word about last night. All that bullshit about men who fuck you then dump you, but you're no better than they are.'

'Shawn, I—'

'I really thought more of you than this. If last night was a mistake, you could have just said so, told me you weren't interested. I would have understood. I wouldn't have pushed you for more. We could have stayed friends. But this... I never expected this from you.'

I open my mouth, about to tell him that last night meant everything to me, that it opened a door between our friendship and a place far deeper than I could have possibly imagined. I'm about to tell him I think I'm in love with him. But then my mouth closes. If I tell him all that, I have no idea how he'll respond, or how impossible it will become to get him to leave.

I sift through my brain, searching for that elusive excuse, anything that will make him simultaneously understand how much he means to me and yet still leave right this second.

Nothing.

My mouth opens and then closes again as if I'm a vacant guppy.

When I don't speak, he adds, 'What an idiot... Thinking you were...' His voice trails off and I'm desperate to hear the end of his sentence, to know what he thought I was. The love of his life? His best friend and sweetheart all rolled into one? The person who feels about him the way I pray he feels about me.

Only, I can't ask.

Knowing in my heart and soul what Paul did to Brooke and James, I won't put him at risk. If Paul lays one eye on Shawn, gets wind of how much he means to me, he'll end him. I witnessed that murderous jealousy over Todd and there was absolutely nothing going on between us. I can only imagine what Paul would do to Shawn if he had any idea how deep my feelings run. The power this decade-long relationship has over me, this intimate friendship that we sealed with a kiss just last night.

'I think...I'd better find another trainer.' Shawn turns on his heel, storms down the garden path, and a small cry lodges in my throat.

I slam the door on Shawn's retreating figure, tear down the hallway and storm back into the lounge, screaming, 'Fuck you! You fucking bastard.' Snatching Charlie back up from the side table, I hold it aloft and charge at Paul.

CHAPTER THIRTY-SIX

MILLIE

I breathe heavily, my chest rising and falling with the effort of stopping myself from slamming Charlie down on Paul's head, over and over, until he's a bloody mess in the grate.

Do it, Millie! He'll be out of your life forever.

He looks up at me with those cold eyes that strip all the warmth from my body. I search for a crack in the ice, a glimmer of humanity. It has to be in there somewhere, surely.

But all I see is a monster, hiding in plain sight, dressed in the shell of a man.

I slam Charlie down on the side table and storm out of the lounge, taking the stairs two at a time to my bedroom. There I lean over my dressing table, gripping its counter for support until my breathing returns to normal.

Running through all my options again, I play out the events like chess moves, trying to anticipate my opponent's based on his skill and previous gameplay. But every strategy ends in checkmate. I always lose.

I spin around, rest the backs of my thighs against the dressing table and try to think of a way out of this, a strategy I haven't yet considered, but nothing comes.

I have to keep my wits about me. Be smart.

But, right now, I have to get to yoga class. At least there I'll find some semblance of normality, even if it's just for an hour.

On my way back from the leisure centre, I pull to a stop and stare at the traffic light's glowing circle. I will it to stay red for all eternity. I've always looked forward to going home after a class; every time I walk up the path to my front door, I picture Nanny standing on the doormat, arms wide. After she died, the cottage still embraced me the way she used to. It's probably a figment of my imagination but I swear the scent of her lavender talcum powder and fruit scones baking in the Aga are infused into the wood of her furniture, her rugs and curtains.

Being away from the cottage is like being away from someone you love. But, right now, the relationship has turned toxic. And going home is the absolute last thing I want to do.

I *hate* Paul for that.

Tapping the steering wheel, waiting for these traffic lights to turn green, is an action I've performed so many times, it's as mechanical as my heart pumping blood. I know every building, every crack in the pavement and every road marking as well as I know my own face in the mirror. Which is probably why the fluorescent yellow plastic sign, attached to the traffic light pole with cable ties, catches my attention. The black text is small, but I can just make out the heading: *Antiques Shop Grand Opening: Everything 20% Off* and a finger emoji pointing to the left.

Antiques.

I would have taken Nanny there if she were still alive. Scouring antiques shops was one of her favourite things to do.

I should get home. Make sure Paul is still restrained. Make sure I'm still safe. And anyway, I'm in the wrong lane for the turning.

The amber light illuminates beneath the red. I stare down the left turn into the industrial estate as if it's an escape route. In my peripheral vision, the red and amber circles snap to black before the green light glows its sick threat.

Home.

I glance at the sign, then back at the light, then at the approaching car that swells in my rear-view mirror. At the last moment, I swing hard into the left lane to the sound of a blaring horn.

The sign on the traffic light pole is a Trades Descriptions Act violation: it's not a shop; it's a warehouse. Walking through the floor-to-ceiling glass doors with an imaginary Nanny by my side is like stepping into a bygone wonderland.

It could be 1962, all the furniture new, Nanny and me the same age, holding hands as we float around the aisles like old friends picking out furniture together. I try to guess which pieces would appeal to her. So many of them would.

Then, as I walk down an aisle of sideboards, it's as if time fast-forwards: the pieces wear with the years, the old-wood smell leaches into the grain, and dust greys the joints. Every sight and smell reminds me of her, of home. Only there's no Paul here. I could happily stay until closing time, until they throw me out on to the street kicking and screaming, forcing me back to reality.

Back to my nightmare.

I shake my head, pretend the monster doesn't exist, and force myself to concentrate on the sideboards. There are two or three that look just like Nanny's, and I run my hands over their surfaces, querying my fingertips for her approval. At the end of the aisle there's a row of Welsh dressers against the back wall; two are a similar colour to the one in my kitchen, and I don't need to run my fingers over their oiled wooden shelves to know she would have loved those.

Instead of the stark and unappealing walls you'd expect to find in a warehouse, these are draped with Persian rugs, crowded with old mirrors and paintings. Antique chandeliers drip from the ceiling and glint in the recessed lighting like some 1940s swing dance.

I move down an aisle of dining-room furniture, then up another of wardrobes and dressing tables, into a large side room of brass bedsteads and canopy four-posters.

The place is a shrine to artisans whose talents died with them decades ago. Thankfully, the care and precision they used to construct these artworks is reflected in the love and care with which they've been preserved.

Nanny always used to say that these days machines have replaced craftspeople, and the dump has replaced love and care.

'Can I help you with something?'

I leap out of my skin. A man in his late sixties has appeared out of nowhere on the other side of a king-sized carved wooden bed.

'Sorry,' he says. 'I didn't mean to sneak up on you.'

'No...I was off in another world.' I look around the room filled to the corners. 'This place is incredible. I've never seen so many beautiful pieces in one store.'

'Yes, it's quite the collection, isn't it?'

'Are you the owner?'

He laughs.

'I wish! No, I'm just the curator. I find and sell the pieces. Someone else holds the purse strings. Were you looking for something in particular?'

'An oil lamp, actually. Mine... Well, let's just say it met a rather violent end.'

'Follow me...' He walks me out of the room back into the main warehouse. Halfway down the nearest aisle, we go through another side door which opens into a huge room, almost as big as the one we just came from. 'Lighting, ornaments, clocks and décor are all in here. Most of the table lamps are in the far corner,' he points, 'over there, but if you can't find what you're looking for, let me know. I have a few dotted around the store. I'll leave you to browse. Call out if you need anything.'

'Thanks.' I make my way through a section of tables covered with ornaments. A matching set of two antique cauldrons catches my eye. I picture Nanny cooking soup over the fire and pick one up as if holding it will make the memory real. It's cast iron, heavy and copper-plated, just like Nanny's. Putting it back down, I check the price tag and my heart sinks. I can't justify buying them. Making my way to the corner, I discover a treasure trove of coloured glass and art deco metal.

Despite the overwhelming choice, it isn't long before a lamp gets my attention. It looks like a Tiffany, almost the same as Nanny's. The mosaic glass shade and base have a multicoloured peacock-feather design. Nanny converted hers to electric years ago and this one's oil. Perhaps I could convert it too – Nanny was a dab hand at anything practical and I was lucky to inherit that gene – but there's something romantic about oil so perhaps I won't. Plus, with the cost of electricity constantly on the rise, it must be a lot cheaper to run.

I flip over the little white tag tied with a piece of string to the burner assembly. It's half the price I had Nanny's valued at for the insurance; I had to have most of Nanny's things valued because every piece is unique and irreplaceable. Clearly the owner of this warehouse is more interested in a quick turnaround than holding out for the best price. I know a good deal when I see one and I'd be a fool not to snap this up.

I try to lift it but it's so heavy, it feels stuck to the shelf. And before I have the opportunity to really put my back into it, the curator calls out from across the room.

'Hang on.' He points to a sign on the wall above my head that I hadn't noticed, too captivated by all the beautiful pieces. *Lovely to see, nice to hold, but if you break it, consider it sold.* 'It's better if you let me take it to the till. If I drop it, I don't have to pay for it.'

'Thanks – it's a lot heavier than I was expecting.'

I follow him out of the room, gazing at all the clocks and ornaments I wish I could afford to buy. Clutching the lamp to his chest, he says, 'It's still filled with fuel, that's why it's so heavy. It only came in yesterday. I was planning on servicing it but someone's stripped the grub screw on the burner assembly. It won't come off. You'll have to get that repaired.'

'That's fine. It's a good price and I'm quite handy; I should be able to replace the screw myself.' I follow him back down the aisle of sideboards towards the front of the store. 'In fact, it's such a good price, I thought it might be a reproduction.'

'No, it's a Tiffany.' He puts the lamp down next to the till and cuts the price tag off, setting it to one side. 'But along with the replacement screw it'll need a professional service. I wouldn't try that yourself, there's a small chance of damaging the font when taking the burner off. The glass is fragile.'

'Hence the price.'

'Hence the price,' he repeats.

I stare at his hands while he separates the shade from the base and wraps each in tissue paper and bubble wrap. Then he dives beneath the counter and pops up with a flat-pack box that he deftly assembles. As he's filling the box with polystyrene chips, he pops one in his mouth, chews and swallows it.

My eyes widen and I turn to look at the door as if I might need an escape route.

He laughs. 'Sorry. I can never resist playing that trick on a pretty girl.' He squeezes another chip. 'Corn starch. You can compost them.' He laughs again, sealing the box with tape. 'You will get it serviced, won't you?' His voice is tinged with concern. 'I have no idea what's in there. It could be petrol or it could be olive oil for all I know. People try to burn the strangest things. I had one come in full of chip fat once.'

'Seriously?'

He nods.

'Well, I rarely eat chips, so I won't be trying that. Don't worry, I'll get it serviced.' I tell him that, but then he rings a week of my earnings up on the till and I know I won't. Not until I've had a go at it myself.

As I drive out of the industrial estate, I glance at the box on the passenger seat, wishing I'd wrapped the seatbelt around it to keep it from sliding off. Eyes back on the road, I slam on the brakes and have to throw my arm out to catch the lamp before it flies into the footwell.

Bumper to bumper, I stare at the back of a van.

My head spins and my heart thuds until a horn toots behind me. In my rear-view mirror, the driver of a black BMW wearing Maverick-style mirrored sunglasses nudges his car forward while honking his horn again.

He's almost on my bumper as I indicate and drive around the parked van. As I float past, my thudding heart stops dead as I take in the striking white side door next to the familiar signwriting: Coop Prop Serv.

Paul! He's escaped, followed me here!

As I inch past the driver's side window, I'm fully expecting him to be sitting right there, a vile grin on his face that tells me I underestimated him, that I was a fool to think I could pretend life was normal for an hour and jolly off to buy a new lamp.

As if my life can ever be normal again.

When I realise the van is empty, the cortisol and adrenaline slowly drain from my system. He must have left it here before breaking into my house. Obviously, his van parked on my driveway, or anywhere on my road, would have alerted me to his presence last night. And if I'd seen it, I wouldn't have risked going inside. I would have gone back to Shawn's.

Fuck...I wish I'd gone back to Shawn's.

CHAPTER THIRTY-SEVEN

MILLIE

I've been hiding up here in my bedroom since I got back from the antiques shop. I'm avoiding the lounge. Avoiding Paul.

The sight of his van on that industrial estate still haunts me. It's a stark reminder of the day Brooke cut him off to steal that parking space. The day this all started. If she hadn't done that, he wouldn't have slashed her tyre. Would he have noticed us at all?

I keep replaying my three options over and over: let him go, call the police, kill him.

Could I kill him? Do I have it in me to take a person's life, even a monster like him? I don't know, but I don't think so. And even if I did have it in me, what are the chances I would get away with it? No matter how or where I tried to hide his body, it would be found. Bodies are always found. We've had sex, we've fought, I've chained him up. My DNA must be all over him. And it won't matter what he's done to me, what the mitigating circumstances are; I'll end up in jail for murder.

I'd rather be dead.

Call the police, then? Would they believe me? Even if they did, the police don't care about facts they can't prove with evidence. And if there's no evidence linking Paul to Brooke or James they'd let him go. They'd have no choice. Then he'd come back for me.

Let him go? There's nothing else left. But he said it himself: he'll come back for me. And, when he does, he'll kill me for this.

No matter which choice I make, I can't win.

My life is over.

My stomach rumbles. I haven't eaten since...when? Yesterday lunchtime? I guess neither has Paul. I may not be able to win this war, but I can fight one battle at a time and hope that a chance opens up: a lucky strike.

Right now, I can make food. *That* I can do.

Heading down to the kitchen and diving into the fridge, I pull out the things I'll need to make a breakfast smoothie: strawberries, blueberries, spinach and Greek yoghurt. Then I grab a banana from the fruit bowl on the counter.

As I whizz all the ingredients together, I eye the bottle of pills I took out of the drawer yesterday when I found the first-aid kit for Paul.

They won't win the war. Nothing will. But they could be a lucky strike.

I think about it. Paul drove his van here and left it near the antiques shop so he could walk the rest of the way. Which means he must have the keys in his pocket. Perhaps there's evidence in his van that could tie him to Brooke or James. And, if I had that, I could call the police. At the very least I need to take that knife from him, along with anything else he might have in his pockets that could aid his escape. And not having to worry about him escaping for a while will buy me some time to think. If I could feel safe in my own home, even if it's just for a few hours, I might be able to clear my head enough to figure a way out of this.

I crush the pills into a fine powder and drop it into the bottom of his glass. Then I take a second glass for myself, leaving the smoothie in the blender cup with a long-handled spoon. In the lounge, I put the glasses down on the side table and pour Paul's first, quickly stirring it before he has the opportunity to clock the white powder mixing into the green liquid. Pouring us both a glass from the same blender cup is a show of trust. I just pray he'll fall for it.

When I place the glass on the fireside rug, an arm's length away from him, Paul stares at it as if I've blended up dog shit.

'What?' I ask. 'It's a breakfast smoothie. And while you're under this roof you'll eat what I eat or nothing at all.'

He peers over the rim at the tiny bubbles making their way to the surface, bursting slowly under the tension of the thick smoothie.

'For heaven's sake.' I lift my own glass and gulp down a few sips. 'It's not poisoned.'

Finally, reluctantly, Paul takes his from the rug and glugs it down. But I don't breathe out until he reaches the bottom. Without taking my eyes off him, I sit down on the sofa and drink my own smoothie slowly while counting silently in my head as the seconds tick by.

Scared to touch Paul, terrified he'll wake up at any second, I find it hard to pluck up the courage to even approach him.

His pulse is slow, but normal for sleep. I haven't killed him. I'm not sure whether that's a good thing or not. I had to estimate his weight and how many sleeping pills it would take to knock him out for a few hours, but I'm not sure whether I've over- or underestimated.

Not thinking straight, I almost dive into his pockets, only to realise that my fingerprints all over Paul's knife are the last thing I need. If I *can* gather enough evidence to link him to Brooke and James, I can tell the police he tried to kill me too. With proof, they'll have to believe that – despite being my prisoner – he's the real perpetrator here. But they're more likely to believe that if his prints are the only ones on his knife. I dash out to the kitchen to get my Marigolds from under the sink.

Clad in bright yellow gloves, I feel like Harvey Keitel as The Cleaner. He's the character in *Point of No Return* who dissolves dead bodies in acid. Maybe I could try that: drag Paul to the bathroom, drop him in the tub and melt him in the caustic soda I use to clean the oven. If only I had the stomach for something like that; it would be so much easier.

My fingers tremble as I force my hand into each of his back pockets then the front left. The front right proves more difficult because he's fallen asleep on his side. But that's better than on his back; rolling him over on the stone hearth wouldn't be easy with the added weight of those chains.

I lay out the contents of all four pockets on the coffee table and finish the dregs of my smoothie while I inspect them. There's a pouch of instruments that look like something a dentist would use. Lock-picks, I think. They're how he got in here. The first slot for the largest pick is empty. Either it was already lost, or – far more likely knowing Paul – he used it to try to undo the bolts holding the chain collars to the andirons.

Thank God it didn't work.

The other picks are thinner, less sturdy. Even though he probably broke the first trying to get free, I still don't want him trying again with whatever's left of it. Getting to my feet, I feel around Paul's body, searching the hearth and then beneath the grate. I can't find it. I don't have time to waste so I have no choice but to abandon the search.

Sitting back down behind the coffee table, I put the knife and lock-picks to one side and inspect the ring of keys. There are three silver ones; presumably a house key is among them. There's also a large black key for his van. Maybe Nanny really is here, helping me. Maybe she directed me to the antiques store because she wanted me to find Paul's van.

The only other thing from his pockets is his wallet. There's a lot of cash inside, a few hundred at a guess, and in the pocket behind the cash there's a photograph, old and worn.

I pull it out and stare at it for a long time, unable to make sense of it. It's a picture of me taken maybe ten years ago. I'm holding hands with a boy and we're both laughing, poking out our tongues, which are pink from the sticks of candyfloss we're holding.

I have no memory of this. And I hate candyfloss, always have.

I look more closely at the boy and see a dark scab over a deep cut on his chin. It's right beneath his cupid's bow. That's exactly where Paul has a scar. His grey-green eyes pierce right through me; it's definitely him.

But there's no way that's me.

Whoever this woman is, she looks so much like me we could be twin sisters. I remember the day Paul and I first met, the way he looked at me, the same way he's looked at me ever since. As if we know each other. As if we already belong to each other.

Not wanting to look at this bizarre reflection of myself for a moment longer, I shove the photograph back in his wallet and search the other compartments. There's a driving licence registered to an address in Loughton.

That's two lucky strikes. If there's no evidence in his van, there might be something at his home, something to put him in jail for double murder. Then I'll be safe. I won't have to look over my shoulder for the rest of my life or be terrified I'll come home one night and find him waiting for me in the dark.

I glance at Paul.

He's still out cold.

Snatching up his keys and wallet, I head for the door.

Driving in a pair of bright yellow Marigolds would have looked suspicious so I dropped Paul's keys and wallet on the passenger seat before taking them off. Now, pulled up behind his van, I put them back on.

I don't have long; it's nearly lunchtime and cars will soon be pouring out of this sinking ship of an industrial estate for the nearest café.

Attempting to look relaxed and natural, I pop the lock and climb into the driver's seat. I act as if this is my van and I have every right to be here. Then I close the door before scanning the street to make sure nobody's watching me.

The van smells strongly of paint or turpentine or something. I want to open the windows but that'll only waste time. Quickly, I run gloved hands through the door pockets, under the seats and through the centre console. The van is surprisingly clean, empty. Apart from a carrier bag of food wrappers, there's no other trash: no discarded coffee cups or empty crisp packets, the kind of debris you'd expect to find in a builder's van. I guess I haven't known that many builders and it could be a stereotype, but this van is cleaner than my car.

The last thing I check is the glovebox. Even that's tidy, but at least it's not empty. I pull out what's inside: a leather-bound manual for the van, an ice-scraper, a pack of blue medical face masks left over from the pandemic and a few sheets of pink paper. I shuffle through the sheets, scanning them one by one. They're carbon copies of invoices for work Paul has completed. All but one are for a man named Dexter Tanning. He's been using Paul's services for at least six months. With the exception of one invoice outstanding, all the others are stamped 'paid'.

I put the invoices back in the glovebox, crawl across the centre console and get out on the passenger side where there's less chance of anyone seeing me. The van's sign-writing is intact on this side: Cooper Property Services. Vomit rises as I think back to the day he fixed my radiators, and I joked about Coop Prop Serv. I thought I was so funny and flirtatious.

Pathetic.

I make sure the road is empty before making my way to the rear doors. There must be dozens of white vans on this estate, but I don't want to take any chances. His van is distinctive; someone here could know Paul, recognise it. They'd wonder what this strange woman was doing rummaging around in the back wearing a pair of Marigolds.

When I throw open the doors, I'm hit by acrid chemical vapours. They strip the insides of my nose and throat, and I have to turn aside to catch my breath. It's the same smell that was bleeding into the cab. Eventually, fresh air mingles with the fumes, trapped in the van for days, and I'm able to move in closer and still breathe.

On a shelf to the right, I discover the source of the fumes: paint thinners. The whole van must have been wiped down with it to create such a powerful stench. Which means, if

James or his dead body ever saw the inside of this van, all evidence has been wiped clean.

I take my time pulling open every drawer in the customised frames that line each wall. I rummage through every toolbox and bag.

Nothing.

Pulling up outside Paul's block of flats is far more daunting than checking his van. But it's not breaking and entering if I have his front door key. And, if anyone asks, I'll tell them I'm his girlfriend and he's asked me to pick up a few things for him.

As I make my way up to the third floor, I pass a dishevelled man sauntering down the stairs. It's only midday and he can barely stand up, so I doubt he'd remember me if anyone questioned him about a woman on the stairway.

Outside the door to Paul's flat, I check the corridor left and right before slipping my Marigolds back on. When I open the door, a small piece of cardboard flutters on to the mat by my feet. I look up, but there's no explanation as to where it came from.

Paul presents a sane and rational persona to the world but I'm beginning to recognise the man beneath that façade. Knowing his intensity and paranoia, he's the kind of man who thinks the worst of people, mistrusts everyone, thinks they're out to get him. And someone like that is always on guard. He's the type who would defend his quarters as if they're a bunker near enemy lines. I think that strip of cardboard lets him know if his foxhole has been breached. He must slip it between the door and the frame. I pick it up and slide it into the back pocket of my jeans, making a mental note to replace it on the way out.

I close the door by pushing my back against it. Then I lean there for a few moments while I gather my wits and wait for my hands to stop trembling. I reassure myself I'm safe here. Even if Paul has slept off the smoothie, he's still chained to my fireplace. Nobody is coming.

The carpet is spotless, there's not a mark on it, so I kick off my trainers at the door and move into his lounge in socked feet. It's immaculate. Sterile. There are no ornaments or picture frames on the counters, no paintings on the walls or rugs on the floor. There's just a sofa against the back wall and a punching bag in one corner that hangs from a sturdy hook buried in the ceiling.

There's not even a television. My heart skips out of its normal rhythm when I remember all those things he said on our date. He said he loved watching old musicals and *Great British Menu*. Paul doesn't love old films, and he doesn't watch television. He was just mimicking everything I liked, making me feel as if we were meant for each other. And I fell for it.

More determined than ever to find something on him, I open every drawer in his sideboard but most of them are empty. The others contain nothing of interest except a spare set of keys for this flat and his van. There are a few packs of batteries, random cables, and an iPhone. But that's dead, and it doesn't belong to either Brooke or James.

I search the bedroom, kitchen and bathroom but every room is as sparse as the lounge. It's like a show home, as if nobody lives here and everything inside is a prop. No plants. No life. Not that any amount of staging would convince a buyer that this is the perfect place to put down roots. It's devoid of comfort and love.

The only thing of any interest is a computer on a desk in the corner. But when I press the space bar to bring it to life it's password-protected, and a few attempts at the obvious get me nowhere.

This is a waste of time. I know Paul killed Brooke and James but he's not stupid enough to have brought either of them here, or to leave a hair of evidence in his van to connect them to him.

So I'm back where I started.

With nothing linking Paul to their deaths, the police will let him back on the street in forty-eight hours and he'll be coming for me.

CHAPTER THIRTY-EIGHT

PAUL

My eyes snap open but I can't move. Dazed, I'm trapped somewhere between sleep and waking up. The smell of the extinct fire behind me fills my nostrils, triggering flashbacks: his clothes stinking of smoke and cheap spirits.

Blinking, I try to prop myself up but the fog doesn't clear. I look down at my hands and will them to move but my arms are heavy, weighed down. My heart thuds in my ears as the chain on my left wrist morphs into pale, slender hands. The chain on my right into callused fingers.

I'm on the landing.

Skye pulls me one way as my father pulls me the other.

'Let him go!' she screams in his face.

'I caught the little bastard stealing from my wallet again. I'm going to teach him a lesson.'

With his free hand, he loosens his leather belt, the one with the big buckle.

'Don't you touch him, you bastard! I told him to take it.'

'You dare tell him to steal my money and talk to me like that?'

The yelling increases in volume as they pull harder, my arms coming out of their sockets.

'I got my fucking period, okay?! I needed the sanitary towels you never buy. What do you want me to do, bleed all over the fucking floor?'

I swing my head to her, eyes pleading not to push him further, but it's hopeless. This has all happened before and it'll happen again.

Unchangeable.

My father's face flicks from anger to confusion as his booze-soaked brain grinds through the events of the previous days. 'You told me you were on your period last week, you lying little cunt!' He lets go of my wrist and plants a fist into Skye's face. Her cheekbone cracks and she drops to the floor, dazed.

I tell myself to run, get out. But instead I fall to my knees and try to help her, shake her awake. She opens her eyes as the belt buckle bites into my back, the crack and sting of the leather hitting milliseconds behind it. I fall forward, winded, her soft breasts a strange comfort against the intense pain that's repeated time and time again.

Swaying, breathing heavily from exertion, my father walks away and his footsteps thud down the stairs as he goes. Our eyes meet through the banister spindles as I lie on top of Skye. He's the first to look away as a wave of shame hits him.

I push myself off Skye and help her sit up. Tears run down her face as she clutches her cheek.

'Mum, are you okay?'

I move in to hug her, only to get a backhand slap to the face.

'I told you, never call me that! It makes me sound old. Now get the fuck off me, you little creep.' She shoves me away, but I don't move. Then she pulls me back and squeezes me tight, her arms pressing into the fresh welts on my back.

I close my eyes and block out the pain because it's worth it.

Opening my eyes, I remember where I am. Both my father's and Skye's hands have morphed back into the chains around my wrists. Still light-headed, I remember the smoothie.

Millie drugged me; she made me remember.

She keeps opening the box.

And, when I'm free, I will punish her for it.

CHAPTER THIRTY-NINE

MILLIE

As I drive home from my Friday morning yoga class, I replay what just happened. I wonder if I could have stopped the brawl before it started. And I worry what the staff members will think once word travels around the leisure centre that a fight broke out in one of my classes. I mean, it's not exactly an advert for inner peace, is it? Maybe I should start a new trend: combat yoga.

With Paul pressing in on every area of my life, it's hard to keep perspective over smaller events like this one. But there's no escaping the fact that incidents like this can damage my reputation, my business, my income. And I'm not exactly flush with cash right now.

I run through each event in the lead-up to the quarrel and assess what I would do differently were something like that ever to happen again.

There was a new attendee. He'd never been to one of my classes before, but I'd seen him around. He was always in the weights room working up a sweat or on the treadmill running too fast on an incline as if he had something to prove. And a hardcore bodybuilder standing on a yoga mat in my studio wasn't something I was expecting to find first thing in the morning. I struggled to conceal my surprise.

Obviously I welcome new students – they're the life blood of my business – but I'd be lying if I didn't admit that I wasn't really in the mood for one this morning. Especially this particular student. I've never liked the way he leers at me whenever I walk past the glass-fronted weights room. I suspected he wasn't there for the yoga.

But it wasn't only that. My regular students are really experienced now, which means I can feather into the routine more advanced poses such as wheels and crows, and that makes it more interesting for everyone, including me. With a newbie, I have to tailor the class around their inexperience, provide beginner's alternatives, and that takes time away from my regulars. I have to monitor poor stances and correct mistakes.

Unfortunately, we didn't even get as far as the advanced section of the routine. We barely made it through the warm-up. We'd done the usual downward-facing dogs, high planks, and sun salutations and had just moved into the main section. I always start by opening up the hips and we made it through the seated forward folds without incident. It was when we moved on to the knee-to-chest – which admittedly is also called the wind-relieving pose – that Pam transitioned into happy baby and let out a corker of a fart.

That's nothing unusual; farts are just one of the chords in the regular symphony of a yoga class. But being a touch on the older side, Pam has a reputation for being able to carry a tune. They always get a giggle – something Pam usually starts herself – but everyone soon forgets about it and moves on.

Only, today, the not-so-incredible Hulk took it upon himself to whisper under his breath, 'Filthy bitch.'

In the space of a few seconds, Pam's giggles dissolved into quiet sobs. And before I could launch into my explanation that it's a perfectly natural part of yoga, Richard was on his feet demanding an apology on Pam's behalf. Richard's such a sweetheart, so kind and calm, that I've always seen him as a bit...weak, I suppose. So it was one hell of a shock to witness him standing up to the Hulk – who's twice his size – in the name of Pam's dignity.

Of course a Neanderthal like that was never going to fess up to his rudeness and apologise, and before I knew it Richard had taken a cuff to the chin. I was expecting him to crawl up next to Pam on her yoga mat and have a little blub himself, but he didn't do that. He danced back and forth like a butterfly, and, a few seconds later, stung like a bee with a right hook to the Hulk's chin.

Fortunately the Hulk was stunned into paralysis long enough for me to dive into the middle of the fight. With a palm on each of their chests keeping them at arm's length and with as much authority as I could muster, I demanded they stop immediately or they'd both be thrown out of my class. The Hulk stormed off, Richard apologised, and Pam's tears turned into hugs and smiles of admiration...or adoration, I'm not sure which. Probably a mix of both.

It took everyone so long to calm down – me especially – that the class never really got going again.

'What's eating your butt?' Paul asks as I storm into the lounge and in one co-ordinated movement throw my gym bag against the wall, flop down on the sofa and grab the remote control with one hand while clinging to a bowl of popcorn with the other.

'Don't!' I point at him as if he's a toddler, my voice hard and sharp. I need him to be silent. I need to pretend he's not here. I need just one hour of this godforsaken nightmare to feel normal. I want my house back, my privacy back, my life back. But in the absence of that, in the absence of any private clients or anything to do for the rest of the day, I just want to watch television in peace and quiet.

Paul doesn't speak again. He just watches as I flip between the channels to Amazon Prime and turn on the show I'd nearly finished when this whole fucked-up ordeal started.

We sit in silence while the drama plays out and I pretend I can't see him out of the corner of my eye.

Forty-five minutes in, the series finale reaches its pinnacle. Reese Witherspoon – in the best performance I've ever seen – says to her daughter, Izzy, 'I never wanted you in the first place.'

Emotions are running so high on the screen that real life seeps back in and the character's venomous words echo against my bones.

A tear rolls down my cheek and I glance over at Paul.

I never wanted *you* in the first place.

My eyes flick back to the television, and I try to focus on the storyline, immerse myself in the fantasy to keep reality at bay. But, in my peripheral vision, Paul is a stain on my attention. One I couldn't scrub clean if I tried.

I never wanted Paul. Not really. He was a distraction. A mistake. One I probably wouldn't have made if it weren't for Brooke and all those things she said right before she died.

I wanted James. At least I thought I did until that night at Shawn's. Now everything's different.

Brooke's death and James's disappearance cut through the veneer of my life, through the surface of my relationship with Shawn. And within that deep laceration I've witnessed the connection we've built over the years: a chasm teeming with microcosmic moments. The lightest brush of an arm, an inside joke, the static that prickles the air between us.

What happened at the door – him believing I'd rejected him – churns my stomach and I glance over at Paul again, this time with so much hatred, I wish him dead. Only Paul isn't watching my every move the way he usually does. He's staring at the screen with a frozen expression I've never witnessed on his face before, and would never have expected to see.

Fear.

And, this time, I don't think it's an act for me. He's afraid of the television, like a child seeing a monster behind the glass for the very first time and believing it's real. My eyes dart back to the show, questioning what event has created this reaction. It's not as though it's a horror; it's just a family drama.

One of Reese Witherspoon's sons has grabbed a fuel can and is standing in his sister's bedroom, about to douse it in petrol.

Paul speaks then but the words get caught in his throat. I think he said, 'Turn it off.'

'What?' I glance at him then back at the show. Reece's other son tosses a match on to the bedroom carpet and the room goes up in flames.

Paul clears his throat. 'I said, turn it off.'

It's my show and it's nearly finished; he doesn't get to tell me to turn it off, so I ignore him. One of Reese's sons is now at her bedside, shaking her, trying to wake her up. But she's too drunk to realise the house is on fire.

'Turn it off!' Paul screams so loudly that it rattles my insides.

I pause the show.

With his eyes squeezed shut, he's cowering in the hearth.

'It's off,' I say quietly.

And in the silence that follows, all the air is sucked out of the room, as if a small fire has started and if anyone opens the door it will explode in a backdraught.

CHAPTER FORTY

MILLIE

Paul hasn't said another word. Neither of us has spoken for almost an hour.

Having given up on the Reese Witherspoon show, I switched from Amazon Prime to BBC One, deciding that steering clear of fiction was a sensible decision. This show isn't something I'd usually watch but let's face it, how frightened can anyone get watching *Bargain Hunt*?

I can't focus on the host's patter because all I can think about is the terror in Paul's eyes. Since he attacked me, I've only thought of him as a monster, a psychopath with no empathy or emotion. But something on that screen triggered him.

Every now and then, I peek over at the fireplace wondering where that scared little boy has gone. But since I switched channels he's retreated into the hearth and his stony expression has returned.

I remember the deep scars on his back.

Something happened to Paul, something traumatic, probably when he was a child. Maybe whatever it was made him the man he is.

Does that mean he isn't to blame for what he's done to me?

Of course he is.

I'm being naïve as usual, desperate to believe there's a human being in there after all. Everyone is a product of their childhood, and not everyone who's had a traumatic childhood turns out to be a murdering rapist.

But there must be more to him than that. If he can feel that deeply, respond to trauma that viscerally, then he can't be a psychopath. Psychopaths don't feel anything – at least, I don't think they do. There's a feeling man buried in there somewhere.

I've been waiting for my lucky strike, a sign that there's a way out of this mess, and, if there is another Paul lurking beneath the monster, maybe I can delve inside and coax him out. And if I can reach *that* man, maybe, just maybe, he has a better, kinder nature I can appeal to.

Either way, I have to try. One way or another I need this man – or monster, whatever he is – out of my house. I need my life back, a life that isn't lived in constant fear.

I break the silence.

'Why did you make me turn off the show? Did it remind you of something? Did something happen to you when you were a kid?'

'It's none of your fucking business.'

'I'll turn it back on, then, shall I?'

Paul looks down at his feet. 'No.'

I'm no therapist, and, even if he was willing to talk about whatever trauma he suffered as a child, I wouldn't know how to handle that conversation. If there is a way to connect with that frightened kid – without Paul shutting down at having to relive the details – I don't know what it is.

But I can't let go of the notion that that scared little boy might be my way out of this.

CHAPTER FORTY-ONE

MILLIE

Something snapped between us on Friday. I guess it was inevitable. Like a balloon filling with the air of our mutual rage and hatred, it had to burst eventually. The fracture happened for both of us; unable to sustain that degree of suspense any longer, we were both craving some semblance of normality.

Perhaps it has something to do with the weekend. We both needed a day of rest so desperately and now it's Sunday, convention orders us to do just that. We've settled into a strange sort of routine, without realising it was always there in the background of our dysfunctional domesticity. We both have to eat, go to the toilet, sleep. But without the rage and hatred right there on the surface, this way of living has become our new normal. I'm still on edge but my hands no longer shake all the time, and my heart has found its rhythm.

But the fracture wasn't smooth; even yesterday, its jagged edges were still razor-sharp. When I handed him his lunchtime smoothie, he just stared at it and refused to take it from me. That made me angry. After everything he's done I should leave him to rot, but instead I'm keeping him fed, watered and clean.

'What the fuck is wrong with you?' I snapped.

'Is it poisoned?'

'Poisoned?'

'I know you drugged me and took my keys. Have you been to my flat?'

'Yes.'

Taken aback by my brazen admission, Paul was hesitant when he replied. 'You had no right.'

'No *right*? You want to lecture me about rights? You had no *right* breaking in here. You think everyone should behave according to your rules but not you – you don't have to abide by them. Why? You think you're special in some way, above everyone else?'

Silence.

I broke it. 'You lied to me on our date. You don't watch *Great British Menu*. You don't like old movies. You don't watch anything. You haven't even got a TV. I know what you were doing, I looked it up. It's called mirroring. You wait for me to tell you something I like, and you mirror it, say you like it too, so I think we have a lot in common. It's a game.'

'It got you into bed, didn't it?'

'Does that make you feel good? Knowing you have to trick women into sleeping with you? Because they wouldn't, would they? Not if they knew the real you.'

'I do okay.'

'With tricks. Lying, mirroring, creating a fake personality. You have no consideration for other people. It doesn't occur to you that the rights you assert for yourself impinge on the rights of the people you're taking them from. Because you have no empathy. That's how psychopaths think. I mean, that *is* what you are, isn't it?'

He shrugged.

'I know I don't feel what normal people feel. If that makes me a psychopath...'

I had no answer. I wanted so badly to reach him, have my words sink in, but they beaded on Paul's surface like rain on an oilskin.

'I don't have to lie,' he said. 'It's just that with you...I didn't want to...fuck it up.'

I stared at his chains, and he lifted them up by his wrists. Then we both laughed without humour. 'I'd say you made a pretty epic mess.'

'Just because I don't know how to act around people, that doesn't mean I don't want all the things normal people want. Happiness...love...'

'Well, you have a fucked-up way of showing it. And if you don't get what you want, you take it, right?'

He shrugged again. 'I wouldn't know what else to do.'

'Accept the things you can't have. Let them go.'

'I've been able to do that before...but...'

'But not with me.'

'No. Not with you.'

We drank our smoothies in silence, watching *Homes Under the Hammer*, him regaining some trust that I hadn't drugged his smoothie and me feeling some relief that the tension had finally snapped.

Only a day later, with the rage and hatred having ebbed even further, guilt has inevitably swept in to fill its void. I've been treating Paul worse than a prisoner; at least in jail, offenders get a mattress and proper food.

While Paul watches the men's final of the Queen's Club Championships, I cook a Sunday roast. It's not something I ever do for myself; it's too much food and effort for one person and it takes a lot longer than I'd planned. By the time it's ready, the tennis match is over and they're interviewing the players.

I put Paul's plate down on the rug before nudging it towards him with my foot. Then I throw him a cushion from the armchair, which he catches with a surprised expression that breaks with a hint of a smile.

'Thanks.' He slides it between his backside and the cold stone hearth.

Guilt rises again and I throw him another cushion from the armchair. 'For your back,' I say.

He stares at it for a moment, then places it behind him before reaching for his plate, the first proper meal he's had in five days, his expression warm with gratitude.

I take my usual spot on the sofa, put my feet up and settle my plate on my lap. I'm not a big fan of tennis so I ask, 'Are you enjoying this?'

'Couldn't care less.'

'Good. Let's watch something else.' I grab the remote and switch to Amazon Prime. While I was cooking I came up with a movie I thought he might like, one that doesn't contain any traumatic scenes that might trigger him, and purchased it on my phone.

Piling in mouthfuls of food as if he hasn't eaten in a month, he chews throughout the opening credits before questioning my choice. '*Chariots of Fire?*'

'I assume you haven't seen it?'

He shakes his head.

'It's a classic. I think you'll like it. It's about two athletes who run track in the Olympics.' With Paul's fanaticism for fitness – his only interest as far as I can tell – it seemed a good choice.

When we're about halfway through the film, I pause it and reach for my empty plate, abandoned on the coffee table.

'That was good.' He lifts his own plate off the rug. 'Best gravy I've ever had.'

'Thanks.'

'Was it Bisto?'

'I'm a personal trainer; you think I make anything from a packet?'

He looks impressed, surprised that I made the gravy from scratch. 'You're a good cook.'

'Thanks. Nanny taught me.'

'Not your mother?'

'She died of cancer when I was twelve. But I don't want to talk about that.'

'I'm sorry.'

'It is what it is. I was lucky: I had Nanny.'

I take Paul's plate, and it's only when I'm piling our cutlery together and sliding it beneath mine that I glance down at my feet and realise how close I'm standing to him.

Heart suddenly in my mouth, I snap my head up and Paul is eyeing my feet too, realising at exactly the same moment that all he has to do is reach out and grab my ankle.

He looks up at me and our eyes lock.

A few brief seconds of silence drag out.

My fear resurfaces with his anger, and they mingle together until their energy shudders with potency. Then he retreats into the fireplace, his movement small, barely discernible, but its significance is so deafening, it's as if he's screaming.

I step back, casually, as if I'm not aware of how close I just came to losing the power in this situation. 'Do you want some ice cream?'

'Are you having some?'

I nod.

'Alright, then.'

In the utility room at the back of the kitchen, I lean into Nanny's chest freezer and try to collect myself while fishing out two tubs of ice cream from the bottom. The freezer is so big, nearly two metres long and almost a metre high, that I have to dive into it to reach anything at the base, but I could do with cooling off; I have no idea how I could have been so stupid.

When I come back into the lounge carrying two bowls, I put Paul's on the rug at arm's length, vowing never to make the same mistake again. I don't know why he didn't react when the opportunity presented itself. Perhaps my words didn't bead on him after all, perhaps they did reach him and have some effect.

Or maybe he's just figured out that – particularly in the comfort of one's own home – nobody can sustain their guard for very long.

All he has to do is bide his time for the perfect moment.

By the time the movie ends, the tension is no longer fizzing from our close encounter. Throughout the film the relief that normality has finally crept into our lives was so overwhelming that I found myself tearing up, even before the emotionally charged finale.

When I look over at Paul, for once his face isn't expressionless. He's blinking and swallowing, as if to contain the emotion that's welled up inside both of us.

'Did you like it?' I ask.

He nods and clears his throat.

It's not his fault that so little stirs his sentiments; he's wired that way. Moments like this – that people with a full emotional range take for granted – must be few and far between for Paul. In that respect I feel sorry for him. But choking up over a film must mean that there is a feeling man somewhere beneath the veneer. Perhaps, if he isn't buried *too* deep, there's still a chance for us to negotiate a way out of this nightmare.

Anxious to preserve our delicate equilibrium, I switch back to the TV and flick through the channels looking for something innocuous yet as emotionally inspiring as the film.

I'm relieved when I switch to the BBC and find that a re-run of *Seven Worlds, One Planet* is on; you'd have to be a cardboard cutout not to be moved by David Attenborough's compassion for animals. After it finishes, the BBC switches to the news and I take the opportunity to clear the empty ice cream bowls.

When Paul lifts his up to me, he holds it out at full arm's length, which can't be easy given the weight of the chain around his wrist, and I can't help being touched by the gesture.

'Thank you,' he says. 'For the cushions, too.'

'You're welcome,' I say. And there's warmth in our connection that goes beyond anything I felt when I first met him. For the first time, it feels genuine.

. . .

After washing up the plates and bowls and making us both a cup of tea, I come back into the lounge as the programme switches from the *BBC Weekend News* to our local headlines.

'*Good evening from BBC London, I'm Victoria Hollins.*'

Again Paul stretches out his arm so he can take his cup without me having to get close to him. I smile with gratitude before taking mine over to the sofa and grabbing the remote. My finger hovers over the button, about to change the channel, when the name of our town stops me in my tracks.

'*The Epping community has rallied together in search of a forty-five-year-old man who's been missing for ten days. Dexter Tanning disappeared on Thursday the ninth of June. Police have now released door camera footage, provided by Mr Tanning's wife, to show exactly what he was wearing when he was last seen. Police are appealing for witnesses.*'

Eyes glued to the screen, I watch the missing man leave his spacious suburban home, climb into his car – a bright yellow Lexus that's sporty and expensive-looking – and then pull out of his driveway, probably never to be seen again.

Dexter Tanning.

I know that name, but I have no idea where from. The car is striking; nobody I know drives a car like that.

Slowly, from the underground vault in my memory bank, the yellow fades and a wash of pink surfaces. I've never heard the name spoken. I've seen it...written down...on a piece of pink paper.

Then it hits me.

Paul's van. The invoices in his glovebox. All but one had Dexter Tanning's name on them.

I snap my head in Paul's direction and catch him staring at the screen with an expression I'm not expecting. His eyebrows are battened down in a deep frown and he's chewing on his bottom lip.

Unless he's playing a part – the helpful passer-by, the supportive friend, the romantic suitor – Paul's face is usually a blank canvas, as immovable as rock. So, in these rare moments when his guard is down, the change is so stark that he can be read like a book.

Guilt.

Watching him quizzically, I prepare myself to lie. I act as if I haven't rummaged through his van as well as his flat. Instead, hoping it will put him off-balance, I pretend I have him all figured out just from his unguarded expression.

'You knew that man, didn't you? Did you kill him too? What did he do to deserve it? Forget to pay his bill?'

Paul's head snaps in my direction. The guilt evaporates in the flash of a spark, and his eyes burn with contempt.

If I'd thought my remarks were clever, it takes less than ten seconds to realise their stupidity and the gravity of my mistake. Not only have I made it clear that I know Dexter Tanning owed Paul money, my slip-up could have devastating consequences. If there was ever the remotest chance that if I let Paul go free he'd leave me alone and not come back to kill me — I've just diminished my chances of survival.

I'm probably the only person who can link three murder victims back to Paul.

If the police find James's or Dexter's body, it could be my way out. But if they don't, and there's no way to connect Paul to any of their deaths, then knowing he's guilty only makes me a target.

[illegible]

CHAPTER FORTY-TWO

PAUL

Millie's up, moving around upstairs.

Dread creeps in.

On the nights I wasn't locked away in her room, I used to lie in bed and listen for movement. Not from my father – he'd rarely get up in the mornings, his body pickled and brain fogged until midday – he'd grunt and cough up phlegm as he moved clumsily around his bedroom, trying to put on yesterday's clothes.

It was her I listened for.

Skye.

Some mornings she was up early, woken by the pains of withdrawal – yesterday's crack high depleted to an agonising low – or by cocaine-induced insomnia. Sometimes, after prolonged periods of sleep deprivation, she wouldn't wake up for a whole day, and many of those I spent locked in her wardrobe for twenty-four hours.

Now, it's hard to recall which of those was more frightening: being trapped in the dark for a whole night and day, or those mornings when, suffering withdrawal, she was at her worst. Bitter and spiteful, full of self-loathing, she'd do whatever it took to find the next high to wipe it away. I'd get ready for school, go downstairs on edge and try to keep out of her way. The kitchen cupboards were always empty, but I'd rifle through them anyway. I'd try to make something for breakfast before picking green mould off stale bread to make sandwiches for a packed lunch.

I learned to be invisible.

If she saw me before she got high, that's when the punishments would start.

I won't suffer them again.

From Skye.

From Millie.

But the craving for her approval still gnaws away at me. My overwhelming hunger for it temporarily pushes the door shut on the fury, but it's always in there, fighting to break out. It twists the handle while hammering on the door's wooden surface. Somewhere deep inside me is the child who stands on the other side of it, feet planted on the floor, pushing his back against it for all he's worth. He waits for her in the dark, praying for some sign of love: a smile, a touch, a hug. She has the key. She *always* has the key.

Millie comes down the stairs and I sit up on the stone floor, resting against the grate. The lounge door opens and she walks in, grabs her keys from the side table. She's in a hurry, dressed in Lycra, trainers on, gym bag in hand. She's going out. Yoga class.

What day is it? Monday or Wednesday? I've lost track.

Without so much as a glance in my direction, she walks out, and her footsteps cross the hall to the kitchen. Cupboards open and close; she's looking for something.

A moment later, she's back. I smile at her, but all I get in return is hate and disgust. Millie spots her purse on the sofa, snatches it up and walks out again. I wait for her return, but then the heavy front door clunks shut.

The house is cold, the curtains closed, the wardrobe so dark, I can't see my own hand held right up to my face. Monstrous shapes form and fade against a pitch backdrop and I tell myself over and over they aren't real.

I have no idea how long I've been locked in here. At least one night and one day. I know that for sure, because I heard the neighbours' car engines start in the morning when they left for work then stop when they came home. Maybe it's night again. I don't know. I slept and lost track of time.

Usually the keyhole tells me if it's day or night: yellow sunlight means it's daytime, orange streetlights mean it's night. But this time it's all black and I don't know why.

If I stay one moment longer, the monsters will turn me raving mad.

I have to get out.

I bang on the door and scream Skye's name until my voice is hoarse. Then, out of desperation, I even scream for my father. When nobody comes, I slide down the door, put my head on my knees and sob. And when I wipe away the tears, I flinch from the pain of my forgotten black eye.

Still nobody comes.

I had to go to the toilet in one of Skye's fake-leather knee-high boots. Burning with shame, I stuffed an old sock in the top to keep in the smell. She used to wear the boots to the pub or to parties. She doesn't any more. But she'll still beat me when she finds out what I've done.

Feeling around in the dark, I find the door handle and, beneath it, the keyhole. I try to peer through, but something inside stops me seeing all the way into Skye's bedroom.

The key.

That's why there's no light. Skye always takes it out. She puts it in her pocket or in the dresser drawer so he can't unlock the wardrobe and find me in here. But this time she forgot.

One of the boys at school is always getting locked in his room for being naughty and he's always bragging that he can get out, but I don't know if it's a lie. He's always lying.

I grope around on the floor until I find a shoe box and pull out the paper inside. After pressing out the creases until it's completely flat, I slide it under the door until just a strip remains on my side. Then I pull one of Skye's short dresses off its wire hanger and cut my palm when I straighten out the hooked end. But I don't cry this time. I feel around until I find the keyhole and poke the end of the hanger inside.

It takes some jiggling but eventually I twist the key until it's straight in the lock, then I push. It drops to the floor, the paper crackles, and I pray it hasn't bounced. Then, on my hands and knees, I slowly pull the paper back under the door, hoping it doesn't tear.

It doesn't.

When I kneel upright, after so long in the dark, I'm blinded by yellow light beaming through the keyhole.

Sunlight.

A whole night. A day. Another whole night. Another day.

Skye left me. Forgot me. And *he* didn't even realise I was missing.

I look down at my palm and the key is gone, replaced by a Zippo lighter.

The key's in the lock, turning.

I flick the Zippo open, flick it shut.

Flick it open, flick it shut.

Then I flick it open, spin the flint wheel and stare into the yellow flame with my one eye that's not swollen shut. Before I can stop it, the handle twists and the door flies open with the force of an explosion.

The boy is blown into smoke, and this Paul stands in the doorway, a vision of murderous fury.

'Bitch-whore!'

I leap to my feet and shoot out of the fireplace, straining forward with all my might so I can watch Millie leave...leave me behind.

Just a few feet out of reach, the T-bars from the chains' collar bolts sit on the side table. They stare at me from beneath that new, fucking ugly oil lamp.

I swear she left them there to torture me.

To let me know escape is just out of reach.

As I relax my muscles and back up into the fireplace, one chain on my arm slips. The links on my right wrist are slightly looser than those on my left, so I shake them down to my hand. I pull at the chain until it wedges itself around my thumb joint which stops it from sliding any further.

If I had one hand free, how far out of this fireplace could I reach?

Far enough to get the T-bar?

Far enough to get the T-bar.

Gripping my right hand with my left, I try again, crushing my thumb inwards until I'm sure it will break and I'm shaking from exertion. The chain barely moves, and, no matter how hard I squeeze, I can't dislocate my thumb. With the pain at its peak, unable to stand it any longer, I let go and slide the chain back up to my wrist to recover.

Retreating to the hearth, I sit down, and, with the weight of the chains on the floor, rest my arms.

I need to think.

Five or ten minutes go by, and, although the throbbing in my hand has subsided and my arm muscles have recovered, my shoulder blades are stiff. So I let my head droop and stretch out my legs, staring at the hearth between them.

An idea forms.

Leaning forward, I place my right hand on the stone, palm up. I suck in air, fill my blood with oxygen and psych myself up to force my body to release adrenaline. Then I draw back my left arm, curl my hand into a tight fist and yell out as I slam it into my thumb joint. Pain sears as muscles tear and I grip my right wrist as if that will stop the spasms shooting up my arm. After breathing through it, I finally manage to uncurl my right hand.

The thumb still isn't dislocated.

'Fucking bastard!' Blind fury takes over and I scream out as I repeat the process again and again. 'Motherfucker!!' I'm past hurt now, a red mist blocks everything out.

After the fourth attempt, I quit, and agony washes in, screaming up my arm until sweat pours down my face. But my thumb remains in its socket, the weight and awkwardness of the chains stealing the power that's needed for a punch to dislocate it.

My pulse ticks down while I cradle my hand in my lap until the pain dies down to a steady throb.

There has to be a solution.

There's *always* a solution.

I don't know how long I've been sitting here; my bum's gone numb and the fire grate's digging into my back.

The fire grate!

I shuffle around to assess the gaps between its heavy wrought-iron bars. Tentatively, as if reaching through a letterbox, I slip my right hand through the centre gap. With my left, I force the chain link by link between the protruding bones of my hand and the bars until the whole chain sits inside the grate.

I smile.

Now, I have leverage.

After a few breaths, I ease my arm back until the chain locks against the back of the fire grate. Then I pull. But it isn't long before I'm forced to stop. Instead of my hand sliding out of the chain, the links rip the skin off. It's no use. I need lubricant.

I try snorting as much phlegm into my mouth as I can, but I've drunk all the water Millie left me and now my nose and throat are dry. All that comes out is a tiny bit of spittle, which isn't going to help me.

Turning my palm up, I stare at the damage from the broken lock-pick. The stab wounds have scabbed over but the cuts are still fresh and deep. Picking off the scabs, I wipe blood under the chains, but it quickly reacts with the air, turning sticky. I need more.

Leaning forward, I sift through the ashes in the firepit. Eventually I catch a glint of shiny metal and fish out the grip end of the broken pick. Holding it between my left thumb and forefinger, I scrape it back and forth across the stone hearth. I grind it faster and faster until I have to pause to let the red-hot metal cool down. After a few minutes, I press my thumb against its tip. Now razor-sharp, it slices the outer layer of skin.

This is the hard part.

Gripping the pick in my trapped hand, I push my free palm on to the makeshift blade until it bites into the flesh. Breathing fast to psych myself up again, I drag my skin across the sharpened metal, slicing ever deeper until I'm forced to stop.

Instinctively I stretch out my palm against the pain and the action opens the wound, making it bleed profusely. Not wanting to waste any lubricant, I squeeze my fist until blood trickles over the links. And I don't stop squeezing until both my trapped wrist and the chain are liberally covered.

With a foot on each corner of the cast-iron fire, and the chains crisscrossed in my lap, I stare up at the chimney. Sucking breaths rapidly in and out, I prepare myself mentally and physically.

Pumped up and ready, I push out from the hearth, pulling my arm back while crushing my hand between the links until they stop at the thumb knuckle. There's plenty of power in my thighs – I can squat a hundred and ninety kilos – and, as my legs increase the pressure pushing me further back, I'm so focused I don't notice the pain.

There's a tear and pop from the base of my thumb. My hand shoots out from the chain, and I'm thrown flat on my back outside of the fireplace. In a moment of shock and numbness, I lie there, breathing heavily. Then the pain shoots in waves up my arm.

Forcing myself upright, I stare at my thumb hanging awkwardly against my palm. I grit my teeth, wrap my left hand around it and yank it out and up. Electric shocks fire through my body as my thumb pops back into place and I yell out in an agonising release.

Flopping down on to my back, I don't move while my mind and body rest, waiting for the pain to subside to a level they can operate on.

With five minutes gone, I roll over. Clutching my injured hand to my chest, I get to my knees then stand up. My thumb's already swollen, and the slightest touch is agony.

Covered in ash, dirt, and blood, I emerge from the fireplace, only stopping when my left arm is fully extended behind me. With the heavy chain pulled tight, I stretch out until my bloody fingers slide over the edge of the table.

My entire focus is on the T-bars.

I touch the end of the nearest one.

My thumb is useless, so I have to pick it up by pinching my middle and index fingers together. Breathing slowly, I lift the end of the tiny rod off the table, only for it to slip out of my grip. Pulling back, I wipe sweat and blood on my trousers, wincing every time my thumb sends a new wave of electric shocks up my arm. Then I stretch out again, sliding my palm over the edge of the table.

The moment my fingertips touch the cold metal again, a car pulls up outside and I turn to the window.

Shit! No! Could that much time have passed? Is that her coming back?

I pinch the bar, lifting one end up.

A car door slams.

The bar's off the table's surface but it slips in my grip until its end points at the floor, ready to fall at any second. I stare at it, sweat trickling down my face as I try to bring it closer. I can't risk dropping it and having it roll out of reach. Pinch too loosely, and it'll fall. Pinch too tightly and it'll pop out of my grasp.

Outside, Millie's voice is faint. She's speaking to a neighbour.

Swivelling around, I drop the T-bar into my left hand.

A key turning in the front door makes me move faster. Dropping to my knees, I fumble as I slide the bar through the hole in the clamp's bolt. The front door opens as I curl my fingers around the bar and attempt the first twist. Millie has tightened the bolt so firmly, it takes all the strength I have to loosen it. Releasing my grip, I spin my hand a hundred and eighty degrees then grab the rod for another turn.

Millie walks into the room.

Our eyes meet.

She looks down and sees what I'm doing.

There's a frozen moment in time.

Dropping her gym bag, she runs towards me as I twist the bar again, freeing the bolt from the andiron. But its shaft widens at the top so I have to loosen the bolt even further before the collar will slide off.

I rotate my wrist again, ready for another turn, but as my fingers curl around the bolt Millie's on my back, one arm around my neck, yanking my head up. She grabs the chain with her free hand and pulls mine off the T-bar.

In defensive mode, there's no thought, just a violent reaction. Twisting, I throw myself backwards and smash Millie painfully into the side of the fireplace. Then I snap my elbow back into her ribs with such force it nearly breaks them. Bouncing off her, I spin around and power a left punch hard into her face.

The chain snaps tight, my fist an inch from her eye.

The sudden halting of power nearly rips my shoulder out of its socket, and I'm jerked backwards. Millie rolls across the rug out of reach. Incensed, I grab her with my free hand, but my damaged fingers only manage to rip off her trainer.

'Fucking bitch! I'll choke the fucking life out of you! Just like I did your boyfriend!' The shout is a release; the insane rage thrown out with my words allows a glimpse of rational thought to creep back in.

Escape.

Millie's gasping and groaning as I turn back to the fire. Throwing myself to my knees, I reach for the bolt.

The T-bar's gone.

Where the fuck's it gone?

CHAPTER FORTY-THREE

MILLIE

On my hands and knees, one trainer torn from my foot, I scrabble across the carpet away from the fireplace, as far away from Paul as I can get.

I estimate how far he'll be able to reach with one hand free of his chains, and only spring to my feet when I'm confident I'm well clear of his grasp. But then I retreat even further until my back slams into the far wall between the sofa and sideboard. The collision is a painful reminder of that punch to the ribs.

Paul's still on his hands and knees, scrabbling around for the T-bar.

That tiny rod of metal has kept me safe up until now.

A thin steel line between life and death.

If Paul breaks free of that second chain, I have no doubt that he will kill me. He might not mean to – his obsession with me could keep me alive – but his temper isn't something he has any control over. One false move on my part will end me.

*One...*false move.

Such as stabbing him in the leg. Knocking him unconscious. Chaining him to my fireplace. Drugging him.
Violating the privacy of his home and van. Treating him like
a caged animal. I have so much to pay for. And I have no
doubt he'll collect.

I'm out of time. In about fifteen seconds, he'll have found
that T-bar. He'll be sliding it inside the collar's bolt and
twisting his way to freedom. Thoughts rip through my mind:
a swarm of tornadoes where panic suppresses my ability to
process one before another crashes through. I've already
proved that I can't fight him. If that chain had been a single
link longer, that punch would have landed. And it was
powerful enough to kill me.

If Paul gets out, even if he doesn't beat me to death the
moment he's free, he will make me suffer for what I've done.

I glance from him to the lounge door.

I could run.

But then I'll be right back where I started: hoping the
police will catch him before he finds me. And, when they
inevitably release him, looking over my shoulder for the rest
of my life. That's what landed me here in the first place.

I stare at him on his hands and knees groping around in
the ash beneath the grate.

Nanny used to kneel right there on the rug making firelighters. In my mind's eye, she folds sheets of newspaper into
two-inch strips and wraps them around her palm. Then she
pushes the tail end through the centre to keep the firelighter's
shape. She'd pile kindling on top then take an extra-long
match from her pewter matchstick-holder and swipe the head
against the striker plate. With one eye on the fire and one on
the television, we'd snuggle under the same blanket, curled
into each other. We'd giggle like schoolgirls over repeats of

Monty Python, Some Mothers Do 'Ave 'Em, or Morecambe and Wise.

Now her hearth and rug are ruined. From this day forward, every time I stare into that fireplace, I won't see Nanny kneeling by the grate any more. I'll see that monster.

Paul finds the T-bar among the ashes.

I'm out of time.

Out of options.

After my failed attempt to wrestle him for that T-bar, I'm drenched in sweat, covered in ash and Paul's blood. It's all over my hands and in my hair. It's too much. I can't take this any more. Can't take him any more. He's destroyed my life and every sweet memory I had in this home.

He wipes the cinders from the metal rod on to his trousers.

Even if I make it out of this alive, even if I manage to scrub the hearth and rug free of his stench, and even if Paul never comes back to kill me, Nanny's cottage will be forever soiled by his presence, haunted by his memory. When I come home, I'll no longer step into my hallway and breathe in the scented memory of her lavender skin and sweet scones, still warm from the oven. That's gone. Now I'll choke on the stinking memory of Paul's blood, sweat and hate.

Since she died, this cottage has been my grandmother. My heart. My home.

Now it might as well burn.

Hunched over on his knees, Paul slides the T-bar into the hole of the collar's retaining bolt. As he twists his way to freedom, I walk slowly past the sofa to the side table, lift up the oil lamp and raise it aloft. Then, with all the strength I have, I smash it on the back of Paul's head.

The lamp's peacock-feather shade and mosaic body shatter against his skull. Glass tinkles around the grate as he crumples into the fireplace. Fuel soaks his honey-brown hair then runs down the back of his shirt, the fabric drinking it in. Splashes spread in dark patches across his trousers and the dry stone hearth reflects a river of gloss.

I don't know what the lamp was filled with – paraffin maybe, I'm not sure – but it's not thick like oil, it's fluid like cheap petrol. Its fumes shimmer on the air as it evaporates.

Paul groans and twists in the flammable puddle as I reach back to the side table and pick up Nanny's pewter match-stick-holder.

Slowly, deliberately, I remove a long match, then turn back to Paul as I press its red tip against the striker plate.

Paul opens his eyes.

CHAPTER FORTY-FOUR

PAUL

Fumes burn my nose and the liquid stings my watering eyes. I ignore the pain that stabs in waves at the back of my head, blinking away my blurry vision to focus. I look down at my hand and frown. The T-bar was ripped from my fingers.

It's gone.

My thoughts stall, the blow to my head disrupting my all-consuming quest to free myself. Millie stands in front of me. She's picked up the metal pot, taken a match from within, and is holding the tip against the striker. My attention falls on the glass pieces scattered around me.

What *is* that?

What am I covered in?

As if I've been punched in the ribs, the answer rips the air from my lungs. Fear and panic grip every inch of me as the fumes from the slowly evaporating fuel take on the smell of Balkan vodka.

I look up and there's Skye.

She's not holding a match; she's holding a lighter.

She flicks the Zippo open, flicks it shut.

Flicks it open, flicks it shut.

'Please,' I beg her. 'Please don't. I'm sorry. I'm so so sorry.' The words tumble from my mouth over and over as I wait for flames to engulf me. 'You weren't supposed to be there.'

Looking back over my shoulder at the door to the bedroom, I hear my father moving around downstairs and a shiver of cold sweat runs down my spine.

I'm not supposed to be in here. I don't *want* to be in here.

This morning, I crept past her bedroom so quietly that Skye didn't hear me. If she had, she would have called me inside. 'Make me feel good, Pauley. Like I showed you.'

And I would have protested as I always do. 'No. I don't want to. I'm going to be late for school.' When I was young, it felt like love. But now I'm twelve and I hear the other boys talking about their mothers, I know it's not right and I don't want to do it any more.

Skye left for work a few minutes ago and Dad turning on the TV downstairs triggers a sigh of relief that he's not coming up here. So I turn back to rummaging through the top drawer of her chest looking for batteries for my Game Boy. They don't know I've got it. Apart from a few charity shop things, most of which are broken, I don't have toys. I stole this off a boy at school but now the batteries are flat and I don't have any money to buy more.

I pocket two AA batteries from an old remote and search the rest of the chest. Lifting out a stack of papers from the bottom drawer, I find two more in an old torch. I stuff them in the front pocket of my jeans and grin with satisfaction when they rattle against the others.

As I'm putting the papers back, three sheets fall out along with a photograph. As they float to the floor, I scrabble to pick them up while listening out for the sound of the television.

I study the photograph first. It's me and Skye. I remember that day at the fair, how happy we both were. Hand in hand, holding sticks of candyfloss, we're poking our pink-stained tongues at the camera, laughing.

So much love.

We don't have days like that any more.

I slide the photograph into my back pocket and, as I'm returning the papers, the one on top catches my eye because it has my name on it. I study it first out of mild curiosity then in more detail before leafing through the others. The bottom sheet is a death certificate for my grandmother, Christine. I never knew her; she died soon after I was born.

Heart slamming in my chest, I walk out of the room and down the stairs, reading each piece of paper over and over again as I try to make sense of them.

The top sheet is my birth certificate with Skye Cooper listed as my mother and Lester Ray Cooper listed as my father. Dad always hated the name Lester, so everyone calls him Ray. But it's not my birth certificate that's bugging me. It's Skye's.

Her birth certificate has Christine Cooper listed as her mother. I frown, puzzled: I always thought Christine was my dad's mum. And why wouldn't I assume that, since her surname was Cooper, same as his?

But although Skye's mother's name confuses me, it's her father's that completely destroys me.

Stepping into the lounge, I look between the papers and the drunk piece of shit on the sofa, unable to decide what to do or say. My father glances my way without acknowledge-ment, leans forward and grabs the bottle of Balkan 176 vodka from the coffee table. Spinning the lid off, he pours it into a chipped coffee cup then sinks back into sofa, gulping it down as if it's water, spilling half of it on to his grubby white vest. With heavy eyelids, he puts another cigarette between his nicotine-stained fingers. Lighting it up, he sucks in a drag, its end glowing red as he throws the lighter on the coffee table. Standing at the door, I watch him exhale a cloud of rancid smoke before his eyes close and the cigarette droops between his lips.

Moving to the coffee table, I pick up his lighter.

In my other hand, I read his name on Skye's birth certificate over and over while I flick the Zippo open, flick it shut.

Flick it open.

Flick it shut.

As the still-lit cigarette falls from my father's lips and smoulders on his vodka-soaked shirt, everything I thought I knew evaporates in the alcohol fumes.

She lied to me.

They both lied to me.

Snatching up the bottle, I slosh the remaining contents of the vodka over his face, his shirt and the sofa. He snorts and mutters something incoherent, but he's so out of it, he doesn't even realise he's soaked.

I stare at the certificate one last time, at her name, then at his, and remember every night I watched them through the keyhole, Skye whimpering in her cocaine-induced escape.

I flick the Zippo open, spin the flint wheel and stare into the amber flame with my one eye that's not swollen shut. A smile curls the corners of my mouth as I drop the papers on the floor and toss the lighter in his lap.

The Balkan 176 vodka with its 88% alcohol content ignites in a whoomph of blue flame that spreads in an instant across my father's clothes and the sofa.

His eyes snap open.

His pain receptors scream, sending agony at the speed of light to his brain. Then he looks at me, shock and confusion etched on the old bastard's face as his hair catches light.

The heat intensifies and I step away.

He tries to scream, but nothing comes out. He shakes and thrashes as the skin melts off his face. And as I back out of the room it ignites, consuming his body.

I walk out of the house, slam the door and stand on the kerb staring. I watch as the fire spreads from room to room. I'm wide awake now. Alive. Powerful. No longer afraid of his beatings, I'm finally the one in control.

Neighbours come out and move around me. They talk, shout, panic, but it's just noise.

Then above it all comes a muffled scream.

I look up and Skye is banging on the upstairs window. The window of my bedroom.

No, no, no! Why is she in there? She left for work; I saw her go.

She's pulling on the handle, but the window won't open. We weren't allowed to open the windows; he always kept them locked to keep the shouts and abuse inside. Private, invisible.

I run back the front door and throw it open, but a wave of heat rolls out from inside, searing my skin and forcing me back.

Back on the lawn, I look up at my window but she's no longer there, only thick black smoke and orange flame.

She's gone.

Skye's gone.

CHAPTER FORTY-FIVE

MILLIE

Still holding the match to the striker plate, the tension in my wrist relaxes. The urge to destroy this monster has evaporated as quickly as the monster vaporised before my eyes.

The man of few words is suddenly a man of many, and all I can do is listen.

With the floodgates open, Paul just keeps rambling. Vivid memories spill from his lips as he relives each painful moment: the years of abuse, being locked in a wardrobe sometimes for days while his father raped his mother night after night, and the things she made Paul do as soon as he was old enough to do them.

As his words sink in, I close my eyes and swallow bile while struggling to remain calm and in control. The memory of having Paul in my bed and my body's reaction to his intimacy burns like a scab that remembers a wound. The experienced lover who taught Paul how to get a woman's body to respond *to* his touch the way mine did...that wasn't a lover. It was his mother.

I retch.

I'm going to be sick.

But, as if my match has already lit the fuel, the fire's still raging in Paul. There's no putting it out. It burns away layer after layer of scar tissue, raw flesh exposed, until all that remains of him is a frightened child recounting a decade of abuse, and the belt beatings that left those terrible marks on his back.

I believe him. Of course I do. But he has fooled me before, several times. My fingers, tight around the matchstick, tremble. Is this a trick?

Only, if this is another of Paul's skilled performances, *I'm* not his audience. I'm not sure he even sees me. It's as if I'm not in the room with him but spying through a window on his past. He's not talking to me; he's talking to her: Skye.

Trapped in memories he can't escape from, he's begging for my forgiveness as if I'm the woman standing up at that window, a fire raging behind me.

Although I'm too scared to let go of the match – too jaded from meeting both sides of Paul's nature – when he describes standing over his father it's not Paul I see, it's me.

The vodka is lamp oil.

The lighter is a match.

Paul acted as judge, jury and executioner for his father's crimes and there's no question that he deserved to pay for the things he did. But to be burned alive? Perhaps Lester Ray Cooper had a story of his own, a history of abuse that turned *him* from a frightened child into the man he became. Now Paul has become the very thing he despised enough to destroy.

A little boy died that night in the fire with Skye, and from the ashes *this* Paul arose.

A monster.

Will the same thing happen to me if I strike this match? Will Millie die in this fire and a different woman arise? One who's cruel and hardened from taking a life in the worst possible way?

Paul is sobbing now, still looking at me as if I'm trapped behind glass, dying in front of his eyes, consumed by the fire he made. 'You weren't supposed to be there,' he says. 'I tried to get to you. I tried to get back inside, but the house went up so quickly.' Then he just keeps saying, 'I'm sorry,' over and over and I wonder how much of that is for her and how much of it is for me.

I place a hand on his shoulder and become the woman he's been searching for all along. 'You were just a little boy. You didn't know I was home. You couldn't have known what would happen. It wasn't your fault. And I don't blame you.'

His eyes clear and he looks right at me. I catch a flicker of evil. I flinch and step back. It's as if, way down in the depths of his mind, the monster that's been in command since the day of that fire is fighting to regain control. I imagine it raging from the shadows of his subconscious, telling Paul to stop snivelling and grab me while he has a chance. Kill me. Escape.

My fingers tighten around the match again.

'Do it,' Paul says. 'I wouldn't blame you. I deserve it.'

Does he?

Is a monster born or made?

If Paul hadn't endured a childhood of abuse, would he have grown into a man who never learned that you get what you want by taking it – by force if necessary – and that any resistance should be met with violence? Or would he have been carefree, adjusted, and capable of love?

I can't answer that.

But it all makes sense now. When Paul saw me in Starbucks that day, he came face to face with Skye. For him the love was instant, already there. Whether I wanted it or not, he would love me in the same twisted way she loved him. And if I resisted he would take me by force, because it was all he knew.

But look what I've done to him.

Isn't this abuse too?

Instead of locking him in a dark wardrobe for days, I've chained him up for days, and now I'm threatening to burn him alive.

Paul isn't just a perpetrator; he's a victim.

And I can't burn one without the other.

CHAPTER FORTY-SIX

PAUL

The flames don't come.

Skye doesn't strike the match. Her face is a picture of conflict, the outcome of which I cannot read, but eventually her features soften ever so slightly.

'If I let you go, you have to swear to me that you'll leave here and never come back.'

Millie's voice – so different from Skye's – finally snaps me back to the present. She falters as she asks the question. She's strong, but there's a tremor in her voice when she says the words, 'come back'.

Avoiding her gaze, I roll over on to my back. I drag my wretched, bleeding body up into a sitting position against the fireplace.

'Let me go, and you'll never see me again.'

I mean it this time. Yet at the back of my mind the other Paul is going ballistic, screaming and shouting, his face red and distorted with rage.

Millie doesn't move for ages.

She must be replaying my words over in her mind as she tries to decide whether or not I'm telling the truth. Then she speaks again, her voice firm.

'You have to swear it, Paul. Swear on your life – if that even means anything to you – that, if I let you go, you'll never go anywhere near my clients, my friends, or anyone I care about. And I'll never see you again. If you see me on the street, you'll turn and walk the other way.'

'I swear on my life.'

Slowly, very slowly, she turns away and walks out of the room.

My head droops, my vow fallen on deaf ears.

Then suddenly, unexpectedly, a hand curls around the chain on my wrist and the jaws of a wrench slide around the jammed-tight quick link. A jerking movement loosens the thread, followed by Millie's fingers spinning the nut down far enough to unhook the carabiner. She hesitates, just for a moment, before freeing the chain from my wrist and letting it drop to the floor.

I look up at her as she backs away.

Unwilling to risk eye contact for more than a second, I stare down at my free arm before slowly drawing my legs in and pushing myself upright. Even though I can't look her in the eye, I know she's staring at me.

Her strength has grown as mine has disappeared.

Without so much as another glance in her direction, I shuffle through the lounge door and down the hallway. My filthy, sweat- and blood-covered hand slips on the front door latch, but then I pull it open and step into the fresh air. Not daring to look back, I walk away, my pace quickening.

But something inside me knows Millie's at the front door, watching me go.

I don't stop until I reach my van. My hands shake as I fumble around in my pockets, then I almost collapse to the ground when I realise I don't have the keys. A few minutes go by, and I pull myself together, leave the van and head towards the high street on the long walk home.

The other Paul's shouting has turned to a low growl.

He's not as far away as he was.

Keeping my head down, I walk past a bus stop where a group of youths are waiting.

'Jesus, man! Look at the state of that sad fuck!'

'Probably a piss-head. Skanky tramp.'

'Is he fucking *crying*?'

'Yeah, he is. Sobbing his girly heart out. Fucking loser!'

Like a lightning bolt I'm propelled back into my rightful place. Cutting through the guilt and self-loathing, I shove the old Paul back in the wardrobe and lock the door. Then I fill the space and grow. My posture straightens, my chest expands and my head lifts to look dead ahead.

'Oi, keep walking, piss-head! There's an offie on the high street. Jog on before I make ya.'

The group tightens, pack mentality focusing their aggression while they feed off the conviction that they're safe in their numbers.

I turn slowly to face them. My eyes burn with a new-found excitement and my mouth curls. The pack fidgets as I take a step towards them. But they keep up their bravado.

'Go on, fuck off, piss-head, I don't wanna get my hands dirty beating on your shitty arse.'

I've already assessed the threat. I'll take out the big mouthy one first, followed by his mate next to him. The one at the back will try to run, but I won't let him.

I smile, step closer and hold out my blood-smeared hand as if to beg. 'Spare a quid for someone down on their luck?' The move confuses them. As I expected, the big guy steps forward while his mate hangs back and running boy shuffles from foot to foot behind.

In a flash I move in, kicking the big guy in the balls so hard his feet leave the ground. Then I twist and punch his mate in the throat. Pushing through them as they go down – one holding his groin, the other holding his throat as he struggles to breathe – I grab running boy's jacket. Pulling him close, I throw my forehead in, headbutting the bridge of his nose with all my body weight. The cartilage collapses, his eyes roll back in his head, and I let go of his jacket as he slumps to the ground.

Adrenaline surging through my veins, I grab big guy's hair and ram his face into the glass screen of the bus shelter. The boom of the impact fuels my excitement into a frenzy, so I yank his head back and drive it into the screen again and again. I only let him drop to the floor when the glass explodes into a million crystals.

Breathing heavily, I walk away.

I'm back. Alive.

And my thoughts are immediately on Millie.

She needs to be punished for what she did, taught who's in control.

Broken down until I'm all she needs.

CHAPTER FORTY-SEVEN

MILLIE

Standing in the doorway, I watch Paul go.

I need to see him leave.

As he lurches along the pavement on the other side of my garden fence, I'm convinced he won't come back. Paul's no longer the person he was, and neither am I. The power balance has shifted: his confidence has been crushed while mine has been wrought from brass dogs, steel chains and lamp fuel. He won't risk coming back here to lose again. If the monster does manage to subdue that frightened boy and return to the surface, he'll find an easier target than me. Someone he can control.

He disappears behind the hedge and is gone.

With a broken Paul out of sight, my heart flutters then pounds. Bile rises from my stomach and I'm suddenly light-headed, sick. I have to sit down. Closing the door, I make my way gingerly along the hallway into the lounge. I take a seat on the sofa and stare at the ruins on the hearth. The room stinks. Everything is spoiled.

The stench of blood and sweat mixed with lamp fuel overwhelms my nostrils, and when I swallow it's as if I'm gulping it down. It roils in my stomach as I stare at the chains still hanging from the andirons.

Suddenly, it's as if I'm the one imprisoned by them.

It hits me then, a blow to the chest so powerful, I lean over, grab the rim of the coffee table and vomit on the rug.

I've just made a deadly mistake.

CHAPTER FORTY-EIGHT

MILLIE

The shower brought me to my senses.

All it took was Paul's broken form disappearing behind that hedge for reality to come barrelling through my conviction that I'd never see him again. I only saw that frightened boy for a few moments – just long enough to convince me I was safe and to set him free – but the second he disappeared I was hit by a flashback so powerful, I saw clearly again.

Only a fool would believe that that frightened boy would remain on the surface. The real Paul – the monster beneath – will always rise to the top. He'll always have true power and control. He's had it for decades. It's what he thrives on.

But I'm no fool. Not any more. Paul has seen to that.

Clean clothes are the armour I've donned to face the mistake I've made. I should have struck that match. The creeping dread that he's already back, breaking in through my conservatory door, chokes me.

Fear is suffocating.

I'll never be able to live like this. Never knowing where he is. Never knowing if – when – he's coming back for me.

I think fast.

When Paul left this cottage, he had no money, no keys, no phone. He'll have to walk back to his apartment and break in before he can collect the spares I found in his drawer that day. As I roll my wet hair into a bun and pin it in place, I work out how long it will take to walk from here to Loughton. At least an hour and a half. Then, once he's got his hands on the keys and cash he has stored there, a ten-minute taxi ride back to his van.

It's not a lot of time, but it's enough.

In the hallway, I scrabble around in the drawer for my car keys and take them into the office nook at the front of the gym. Unless I know where Paul is at all times, I'll never know if and when he's coming for me. I don't have time to buy and fit a tracker to his van, but there's one thing I do have: an AirTag. The problem is that the moment an AirTag loses its Bluetooth connection to the owner's phone, it starts beeping.

At my desk, I power up my laptop and Google: *How to remove a speaker from an Apple AirTag*. It's easy, and within minutes the tag is silenced. I also put in a new battery just to be safe.

Using Apple's network – billions of customers – an AirTag reports its location to its owner via any iPhone it comes within Bluetooth range of. Paul's phone is still here, broken. But along with the spare keys and cash, he has a spare iPhone in his desk drawer. I'm banking on him using that. As long as he has it with him it will report my AirTag's location whenever Paul is online. Fortunately, older iPhones don't inform the user that there's an AirTag nearby – that's a newer safety feature. Apple added it later to stop women being inadvertently stalked by an AirTag dropped into their handbag. With its speaker missing, Paul will have no idea that mine is tracking him.

Pulling up behind his van, I check the street. It's lunchtime. Industrial estate workers mill around the buildings smoking cigarettes and there's a regular flow of traffic up and down the road. The timing isn't ideal, I'd rather there was nobody around, but my window is closing fast. It's now or never.

Luckily, Paul has parked his van alongside a railing fence that has a tall hedge behind. Once I'm on the passenger side, nobody can see me. I pop the key fob and linger by the van, pretending I'm another worker on my lunch break while making sure nobody is walking towards me from either direction. Confident the coast is clear, I hop into the passenger seat and quickly force my AirTag between the windscreen and roof upholstery. The gap is tight and the device only just fits, but that's good: it's unlikely to slide out, even if Paul brakes hard.

Back in my own car, I take a moment to regain my composure before driving away. The relief that I won't have to look over my shoulder every moment, terrified he's behind me, comes out in one long breath. If he ever he parks within walking distance of my house again, I'll know to be on my guard.

[illegible]

CHAPTER FORTY-NINE

MILLIE

It's been two weeks since I planted the AirTag in Paul's van. The Find My app stays permanently open on my phone, and I monitor it as if my life depends on it.

Because it does.

So far, he's kept his vow and hasn't been anywhere near the house, the leisure centre or even the industrial estate. I thank God every day I don't see him.

He's taken a job in Colchester and has been there all day, every day for the past fortnight. I drove up there at the weekend while he was at his flat to make sure it was a genuine job. It is. A huge barn conversion that will take at least another month or two to complete. Knowing he's there, and will be for some time, has given me some breathing space, time to think.

However, something he does makes my Spidey-sense tingle. Every morning before he drives to Colchester, Paul makes a trip to a nearby DIY store. Then, every evening when he comes back, he makes his way deep into Epping forest. I need to know why.

At the point where his van always takes a sharp turn, I slow to a crawl on the Epping Road. I almost drive past the barely discernible gravel track between overgrown trees and shrubs on either side.

I take the turn.

When the screeching branches finally stop clawing my paintwork and the track opens up, it's impossible to ignore the large white signpost that cautions me against going any further. Although time-worn, its bold red lettering is no less menacing.

PRIVATE PROPERTY
TRESPASSERS WILL BE PROSECUTED

The threat, albeit probably empty, stops me in my tracks. After a moment of pause, I ignore its injunction and push the accelerator, the crunching of gravel exacerbated by the slow crawl of my tyres.

The house that greets me at the end of the track is like something from a horror film. It must have been abandoned for a decade or more, the windows are all boarded up, the roof crawls with vines and the grounds are completely over-grown. Pressing in on all sides, the forest plunges the house into darkness, even though it's the middle of the day. I can't even imagine what it must be like at night. I doubt you could see a hand in front of your face.

Scared to get out of my car, I scan the trees through the passenger's and driver's side windows. I'm half expecting a madman to come running out of the trees wearing a Leatherface mask and wielding a chainsaw.

But there's no movement at all; the tree branches are deathly still. Not even a breeze makes it this deep into the forest, let alone people. It's like an island in a desolate sea where ships would never risk venturing, and the sign at the head of the track is the lighthouse that warns of rocks ahead.

Despite that, I open my car door and dare to step out. The dank smell of aged trees – long deprived of fresh air and sunlight – fills the grounds. I could be trapped in a room rather than outside.

I check my phone again. The Find My app tells me Paul's still in Colchester, but that doesn't stop me from peering back along the gravel path for a long minute. I'm constantly plagued by the worry that the app isn't accurate, or that he's found the AirTag and left it in Colchester to trick me into thinking he's still there.

Paul has visited this derelict house so many times over the past two weeks that no matter how hard my blood is pumping, and how desperately I want to hightail it out of here and leave this shack to eat my dirt, I can't leave without knowing why.

So, heart in my ears, palms sweating, I approach.

I have to watch my footing as I climb four rotten wood steps to a deck that stretches along the front of the property. It's surrounded by railings but most of the spindles are either missing or broken.

I check the front door first, although that's a generous description for the entrance. If the house ever had a proper front door – perhaps with pretty glass panes, a brass knocker, an ornate key lock – it's been replaced by a thick plywood panel and a padlock. Even though I'm sure it's a fruitless exercise, I pull at the padlock in the hope it's broken. It's not. I'm not getting in this way, that's for sure.

Dodging gaping holes in the decking, I tiptoe to the left-hand front window and peer through the wooden boards screwed into its frame. Inside, the room is largely empty apart from dead leaves on the floor and a decayed, upturned armchair.

I make my way back past the front door to the window on the right. Inside, the room is similarly empty. The gap in the boarded-up window reveals wallpaper peeling back on itself to betray black mould on the plaster beneath. If Paul is renovating this property for someone, even if he's only working on it in the evenings, I would have expected there to be some signs: the floors swept, perhaps a few tools lying around.

Gripping tight to the rotted railing, I descend the steps and fight my way through overgrown weeds and stinging nettles to the side of the house. The windows here are boarded up, as well, but too tightly to see through the gaps between the planks.

At the back of the house, I find another door. Just like the front, it's been replaced with plywood and a padlock. However, back here, the trees are planted further away from what must have been a lawned garden before it ran wild. Here, the house is more exposed to the elements, and some of the window boards have warped in the sunlight and rain to create wide openings between.

I peer inside.

The hairs on the back of my neck stand up.

Paul has renovated one solitary room in the house: this one.

It's almost empty apart from a bedside table and a double bed against the wall, iron-framed with a tall headboard, just like mine. The damp and mould has been covered up with new wallpaper and its design sends a shiver down my spine. It's a carbon copy of the lilac-flowered pattern in my bedroom. I can just make out curtains partially blocking the gaps on either side of the boards. They're lilac too. My favourite colour.

But it's not the décor and bed that truly shake me to my core, it's the other items in the room. At the foot of the bed, there's a velvet ottoman almost identical to the one we had sex on. On the floor, there's a lidded metal bedpan, and attached to the bed posts there are two steel chains.

Weightlifting chains.

On the bedside table sits a photograph of me and Nanny, a photograph I hadn't realised was missing. It was tucked behind the others on the mantelpiece. Seeing it here sends a chill up my spine; Paul must have taken it the day he strangled James...with my scarf...in my house.

The last thing I notice in the room is a side table just out of reach of the bed. On its surface lie two tiny metal rods.

The metal T-bars that Paul has cut from the chains' collar bolts.

CHAPTER FIFTY

MILLIE

It's been almost a month since I found the house in the woods. Four weeks of checking my phone, praying he'll keep his vow and stay away.

Knowing he won't.

After realising what Paul has in store for me, any number of solutions ran through my mind. At first, I resolved that calling the police was finally my best and only real option. Imagining myself on the stand being cross-examined, the accusation *Why didn't you call the police?* kept looping around my mind. But every time I punched 999 into my phone and once again found my finger hovering over the call button, Nanny's ever-present voice in my head told me not to.

If I was going to press that button, I had to know what I was letting myself in for. So I spent three hours at my computer reading case histories of victims of false imprisonment, sexual assault and rape.

What I read shook me to my core.

Even when brave survivors subject themselves to six hours of rape-kit testing to provide irrefutable proof, backlogs in crime labs and crown courts mean that thousands of rapists like Paul are out on bail while their victims wait more than two years for justice.

A government statistics website wrote that only one in six victims even reports the crime. And the stats for men, people of colour and LGBTQ+ victims are significantly lower. Almost fifty per cent of those pull out before a verdict is reached. They do that to protect themselves from the emotional trauma of the British justice system – the very system that is supposed to provide protection. With another forty per cent of cases still awaiting trial, the resulting rate of conviction is a staggeringly low 1.5 per cent. And with those few cases, prisons at a hundred and seventy per cent capacity encourage judges to grant bail, suspended sentences and early releases. Previously convicted murderers accused of rape have been let out on bail with devastating consequences.

On her website, a barrister who described herself as 'jury-friendly' listed among her successes rapists she had kept out of jail with acquittals and suspended sentences, then achieved an identical result for the same offender a few years later, one of which was taking part in the multiple rape of a fifteen-year-old girl.

Among the worst cases I read about was a serial rapist who was released eight times following short prison sentences. After telling his parole officer that he *would* do it again, he went on to rape and murder a woman in her thirties while leaving her mother barely alive.

I sat back in my chair and cried.

It never again crossed my mind to dial 999.

It sounds insane, but at that moment I considered hiring a contract killer. But I wouldn't know where to start finding one, and couldn't afford it if I did know. Plus, the money trail undoubtedly leads back to the person who hires them, and that's a risk I'm not willing to take.

I thought of all manner of ways to kill him myself, but I learned something about Millie Holland the day I released Paul: she's no cold-blooded killer. I don't know if he will see his plans through, and I can't carry out a premeditated murder on the chance that he might. I'd forever wonder – probably from jail – if I'd committed the ultimate sin while he had had every intention of keeping his vow. I don't know if not taking pre-emptive action is a mistake that will prove fatal, but I've made my decision.

Only Paul can set the wheels in motion now.

When they stop – if they ever stop – I'll have to come to terms with the choices I've made. One way or another, over the days to come, I'll either be here in this cottage, waiting for Paul to end my nightmare, or living with him in that house in the woods.

It's dark tonight. Cloudy. Occasional moonlight breaks through a gap in the dense clouds.

A sickle moon.

It's supposed to symbolise the divine feminine, empowerment, intuition. But it also symbolises life and death.

As I have so many times over the previous weeks, I unlock my phone and re-read the last text that Shawn sent me, back in June.

> Sure. Working from home today. Come whenever.

If only I could.

. . .

With every door and window locked, I open the Find My app and stare at my pulsing AirTag for a few moments as it travels along the map on my screen. In my bedroom, with the lights on behind me, I'll be seen from a distance, from the track that runs along the back of the house. I stare out across the garden, the lawn black as the night, the shrubs that surround it even blacker.

As I do every night, I draw the curtains, leaving a gap just wide enough for the sun to stream through in the morning and wake me. Only, tonight, I say a prayer that the sun *will* wake me.

I suspect it won't.

The air shivers with anticipation.

He's out there.

CHAPTER FIFTY-ONE

PAUL

I walk the last ten metres along the track that runs behind Millie's cottage. Separating the low tree branches, I look across her back garden. The house is in darkness apart from the bedroom.

She walks up to the window and glances in my direction. I know she can't see me in the dark, but I feel the connection. She's mine, and, once I have her alone at Dexter's house in the woods, she'll learn to respect and obey me.

Then, in time, she'll learn to love me again.

Millie closes the curtains, leaving just a silhouette that shrinks into the room as she backs away. I stand motionless, eyes never moving from the window, even when the light goes out.

I can wait.

Twenty minutes have gone by. No sound, no movement, no lights.

I move towards the doors to the sunroom and kneel by the lock. The hood, cable ties, and ball gag dig into my thighs pulling the pockets of my jeans tight against my legs.

As a matter of habit, I reach up and pull the door handle down; it's locked. Taking care not to tear my latex gloves, I tug a new pouch of lock-picks out of my back pocket and get to work. I lift the pins by touch until the last one is up and I can turn the barrel.

With a smooth movement, I push the handle down and ease the door inward, anticipating the grind of hinges or wood.

Moving into the sunroom, I stand motionless between the two old armchairs and listen to the house: the ticks from the cooling pipes of her recently turned-off heating and the occasional soft creaks as the cottage settles for the night.

Slowly, I enter the living room. Rolling my feet from heel to toe, never transferring all my weight in one go, I avoid any groans from the old floorboards. From the streetlights out front, an orange glow bleeds through the edges of the curtains, providing just enough light to outline the furniture in the room: dark grey shapes against a darker grey background.

My thigh catches the corner of the side table near the fireplace and with lightning reflexes I shoot out both hands. I grab the top of another antique oil lamp – no doubt as ugly as the last – and that bastard brass bulldog before they both slide off the edge.

I pause for a breath then head towards the hall.

Three paces on, I stop, turn back and stare into the dark lounge. Why does this feel off – the table, the brass dog? Millie has replaced the lamp she smashed but something else is different. I scan the room for answers: the sofas, coffee table, rug and pictures on the wall are all familiar shapes in their familiar places, but something...

The faintest creak from the floorboards above snaps my eyes upwards.

Thoughts move back to her.

I move to the base of the stairs. The ascent takes an age, my movements painfully slow. I tread lightly on the edges of the steps where the joints are solid and the wood flexes the least.

Now I'm at the top, stealth doesn't matter. There is no escape.

I'm blocking the only way out.

A primal excitement builds as I pull the zip ties, ball gag and hood out of my pockets. But my eyes never leave the open bedroom door as I approach.

As I step inside, the air is overpoweringly thick with scent, like flowers and spice and...something else. It's darker up here than in the living room. There are no streetlamps at the back of the house. The only light comes from a silver slice of moonlight cutting its way through the gap in the curtains.

I can see her outline and advance towards her. She's sleeping on her side, not moving. As I slide my knee on to the mattress, it sinks, crushing down to the base as I reach over to grab the sheet. Again, something isn't right. We've had sex on this bed. Its memory-foam-topped luxury mattress held its form as I took her.

I whip the covers back.

Bolster pillows.

I grab one and throttle it as if it's Millie's neck. It's heavy, soaking wet. As I drop the pillow and step off the bed, the scent of flowers and spice fades beneath rising fumes. Balkan vodka sears my nostrils, and I don't know if it's in this room or my imagination.

There's a low creak behind me. I snap my head around. On the landing, the cupboard door opposite Millie's bedroom opens. I back up into the metal bed frame as the boy with the key emerges from the shadows, staring with black, lifeless eyes.

He steps across the landing carpet, carrying something. At the door, he leans in and dumps a container on the bedroom floor. The lid's off and its contents glug readily on to the rug.

I look down at his palm and the key is gone, replaced by a Zippo lighter.

He flicks the Zippo open, flicks it shut.

Flicks it open, flicks it shut.

An alien sense of fear overpowers everything.

When he straightens up, his shadowy outline morphs into a figure taller than the boy.

Millie.

The softness in her features is gone, replace by hard determination. Pure hate. My fear evaporates, and insane rage takes over. 'No, no! I'm in control. Me, not you, you hear me, bitch? I'm in fucking control!'

My eyes drop to her latex gloves...to the matchbox in one hand, to the bunch of matches in the other.

Everything moves in slow motion.

Millie strikes.

Our eyes lock.

'You swore on your life.' She flicks the matches over the threshold and slams the door.

On the rug, the dipped ends flare and the room lights up. My legs tense, flex, then release as I bolt after her. Seconds later, I grab the doorknob and pull but the door doesn't open so I pound its wooden surface with my fist.

Fumes from the thinners flash blue flames around my feet that change to yellow as the liquid ignites.

I grab the handle with both hands and pull with all my might, but it won't budge so I thrust my shoulder into it again and again until the latch gives way. The door opens a millimetre: just enough for me to realise that she's switched the hinges and latch around to open outwards on to the landing. I take a step back and slam my body into the wood, but something heavy blocks the door.

Pain sears around my ankles, forcing me to back away to the other side of the burning rug. The realisation that I'm trapped hits me like a lightning bolt. As I spin in the room, the flames rising from the rug chase across the carpet and ignite a chest of drawers to the right of the door. It must be soaked in fuel to go up so quickly.

On the other side of the wall, Millie's footsteps thud down the stairs.

Fucking bitch.

There's too much fire, too much heat. Moving to the far side of the bed, I squat down and grab the frame. The duvet is already burning and I have to turn my face away from the flames as I yank the bed on to its side. Fury and adrenaline charge my muscles as I slide it towards the chest of drawers in an attempt to smother the blaze. As the mattress slams into the dresser, the surge of expelled air sends a geyser of flame upwards and across the ceiling. Its rippling orange beauty singes my hair as it recedes.

I step back into the centre of the room. The shunted bed has bought me some time, but flames still whip around its edges. I glance at the door then back at the bed. One end of a metal slat on the underside is broken. Rushing forward, I grab it with both hands and, using its length as leverage, pull it down with all my body weight. The superhuman strength driven from self-preservation snaps the head off the bolt holding it in the bed.

Stamping out the flames that lick up around my feet, I dig the slat into the gap between the door and its frame. Desperately, I try to push the end in far enough to lever off the jamb so I can open the door inwards.

The slat breaks. I curse this fucking old house, built in an era where walls were solid and doorframes were made from oak, so aged and dense it might as well be steel. Roaring with frustration, I slam my shoulder into the door over and over in a last-ditch effort to shift whatever Millie has used to barricade it. It doesn't move.

Intense pain from my melting trainers and smouldering jeans forces me back to the centre of the room. I turn to the window: my only means of escape. Running to it, I yank the curtains back, pull the latches up and push on the glass.

It won't open.

I pound the wooden surround; the casement is stuck in the frame. But it's a diamond leadlight, the metal soft and pliable. Stepping back, I punch the glass hard and fast, but, instead of breaking, it flexes and booms as the pane absorbs the blow.

She's changed the window.

Below me, Millie emerges from the sunroom and runs across the lawn. Then she stops, turns and looks up at me.

Rage consumes everything.

There's a whoosh behind me, then intense heat as a flickering amber glow dances around me. I punch the window again and again, blood smearing the glass as my knuckles split on the rock-hard reinforced pane.

It refuses to shatter.

Through the blood, I see Millie's face.

Her expression is devoid of emotion, but her eyes display enough contempt and hate to make up for the lack of it.

She'll pay for this. Millie's a fool to believe that whatever furniture she's used to barricade the door will be completely destroyed by the fire; nothing ever is, even if it's soaked in fuel. The accelerant she used will be uncovered by forensics and she'll spend an eternity behind bars for arson and premeditated murder.

Even in death, I still have ultimate control over her life. I've still won.

The skin on the back of my neck crinkles.

The window's surface mirrors the image behind me. The growing inferno blends with the image of Millie outside. My focus flicks from her to the reflection, where a shaft of white flame shoots up by the door.

Its outline shifts into the burning body of my father. The drunk bastard who raped his own daughter while his wife, Christine, lay dying of cancer in the hospital. Raped Skye and got her pregnant with me.

I smell the hair burning on the back of my head as he vanishes in the fire. Then a second shaft of white flame shoots up in his place and Skye steps out towards me. Her reflected face sits perfectly over the top of Millie's outside.

Fused together as one.

There's searing pain as Skye appears over my shoulder and embraces me with the love I've always craved. My skin blisters from the touch of her lips on my cheek.

My mother, Skye.

My sister, Skye.

I look down at Millie and smile.

CHAPTER FIFTY-TWO

MILLIE

Ten minutes earlier

'You swore on your life.' I flick the matches over the threshold and slam the bedroom door so hard it shakes.

Five seconds. That's all the time it'll take Paul to make it from the bed to the door and figure out that it no longer opens inwards, but outwards. It's all the time I have to execute a perfect power-clean lift.

One slip and I'm dead.

I set my stance: grab the handles, flatten my back and engage my core. In one explosive movement, I lift the weight from floor to shoulder-height and drop it on to the shelves on either side of the architrave.

The second I let go of the handles, the door slams into the barricade with a thunderous boom and I stumble backwards. Falling to the floor, I pray it won't break. The knob turns frantically left and right and the door reverberates again. But, with no more than a few millimetres between it and the barricade, Paul can't get the momentum he needs to break through.

I have to be absolutely sure it will hold, so I wait until the banging stops. When flames lick the landing carpet beneath the threshold, I know that the burning rug has forced him to back away. Tendrils of smoke crawl through the gap around the doorframe and, as if their ghostly fingers are Paul's reaching out to grab me, I turn on my heels and bolt down the stairs two at a time.

At the back of the kitchen, in the utility room, I lift the wooden crate and carry it through the lounge to the sunroom. Even though it's not heavy, it's over a metre long and bulky. With my muscles spent from executing that power lift upstairs, my arms tremble beneath its weight.

As I pass the side table, I misjudge the narrow gap between it and the fireplace. My thigh bruises as it has many times over the previous weeks. The replacement antique lamp rocks on its base and the brass spaniel falls to the floor but I don't stop to pick it up.

Out in the garden, the pummelling above my head tells me that Paul is fighting to get out. He's just realised that the casement window no longer opens.

Working quickly, I set the wooden crate on the sunroom's window sill. Then I fill it with the potting soil that's waited patiently by the wall for its box planter to arrive. The soil is heavy, and my exhausted arms burn, but I empty each bag, until the crate is full. Then I thrust four bedding plants into the earth before running to the shed, where I toss the plant pots and empty soil bags. Finally, I stumble across the patio on to the lawn and run until I reach the gate at the foot of the garden.

Only then do I stop and turn around.

Paul is a dark shape illuminated from behind by a wall of fire. But, as the flames draw closer, his face flickers in the blaze to reveal the rage in his eyes. He punches a fist into the leadlight window and my heart stops for a beat.

It flexes, booms, but doesn't break.

The fire has taken hold, and it won't be long before it reaches the thatched roof. In the far distance, sirens wail. The fire brigade is on its way, and I can't be here for that. It's time to go.

Much as I hoped Paul would keep his vow, I never truly believed he would. I knew this night would come. I thought I'd be forever changed by it, but I'm not.

I was already changed.

Paul may not have been the one to commit premeditated, cold-blooded murder this time, but he killed the old Millie when he broke into my cottage that awful night.

Behind the red smears on the diamond window panes from Paul's bloodied and broken fist there's a sudden flash. The whole bedroom fills with amber light and I hold a hand up to protect my face as – even from this distance – the searing heat singes my exposed skin.

He's still at the window.

We lock eyes.

I must be mistaken, but I could almost swear that, as the flames engulf Paul, he's smiling.

I'm not.

The thatched roof catches and Nanny's cottage – my heart, my home – is engulfed by flames.

All I can do is stand here and watch it burn.

MILLIE

Eight months later

When the removal men leave, Shawn and I don't speak while we work. We cut the masking tape off the plastic wrapping that protects Nanny's rugs and roll them out, one by one, until each is back in its rightful place.

Shawn comes into the lounge as I'm unpacking the very last box. I place Nanny's brass bulldog – to whom I owe my life – back on the side table in his familiar home next to the unfamiliar antique table lamp: the fourth that Charlie has sat beside. The decoy was destroyed by water damage and this is the closest to Nanny's I could find.

Flopping down on the sofa, clearly tired from a full day of moving and unpacking furniture and boxes, Shawn is silent for a long time. Of course he has questions; the difficult ones I have resisted answering. I can almost hear the cogs turning when he says, 'Wasn't it lucky that, when the house burned, all of your nan's furniture was at the antiques store being cleaned and repaired?'

'Mmm.' I nod. 'That was lucky.'

He knows it's a lie. But I don't tell him that Nanny's furniture wasn't at the antiques store. It was in storage with Budge-It Removals, the company that took everything away and brought it back today. I lied to them, too. I told them that the fictional purchase of my new home in Cambridge had fallen through.

I did visit the antiques store again, though, several times before the fire. The first time I went back, while the dealer lowered each copper cauldron into its box he said, 'They're beautiful, aren't they?' before filling it with packing chips.

Behind me, a woman holding a pair of candlesticks hopped from foot to foot, impatiently waiting her turn. I glanced at the dealer and, when our eyes met, gave him a wink and a smile. Then I stole one of the packing chips, turned around to the woman and popped it in my mouth. Seeing the shocked expression on her face as I chewed and swallowed was a brief moment of joy. The dealer and I both laughed at the shared prank, but she didn't find it at all amusing.

I wasn't in the mood for humour back then, but it served its purpose. I needed him on side.

While he was wrapping her candlesticks, I hung back, feigning interest in a shelf of carriage clocks to the right of the till. The moment the door closed behind impatient-woman I returned to the dealer. 'Have you got a minute?'

We struck a bargain. He loaned this budding antiques dealer a houseful of pieces to get my business up and running. The agreement was that I would pay for or return anything that hadn't sold within the year, and, with anything that did, we would split the profit down the middle.

It was a risk. I gambled on Paul coming at night and not turning on the lights to discover that every item of furniture, every rug and every painting, while similar in size, was a slightly different design from Nanny's. The only item I couldn't match closely was the side table. It was noticeably bigger and I bumped into it every time I walked past. And although the brass spaniel was wearing a necktie instead of Charlie's bow tie, the top hat they both wore was enough to fool any casual viewer. Especially in the dark.

Once the house insurance came through, I was able to pay the dealer in full. I didn't tell him that all his pieces had burned in a fire – nor that the insurance payout for Nanny's furniture and antiques was ten times the value I paid him for his.

When he offered me more of his pieces to sell, I told him that sales wasn't my thing after all and had proved harder than I thought it would be. He accepted that with a measure of disappointment and condescension, saying that selling antiques wasn't everyone's forte.

I suppose that means that, along with premeditated murder, I've committed insurance fraud as well, but not making the claim would have been suspicious. Besides, I had no other way of paying him back for his torched antiques.

I had to change every window in the house so that the alterations to the bedroom one wouldn't raise suspicion. And I had to trust John and Linda from Cutting Edge Stained Glass that their zinc-coated steel rebars – used to stop church windows from sagging due to gravity over time – were strong enough to take a punch.

Thank God, they were.

Of course I didn't tell them that I wanted to keep intruders *in*, not out. And I waited until they left to paint the casements into their frames to seal them shut.

'Are you ever going to tell me what happened that night?' Shawn asks. 'Where you really were? Why I lied to the police and said you were with me all night?'

'It's best you don't know.'

I twist Charlie so he's looking towards the door, as if he's a guard dog against intruders, and Shawn watches me, frowning.

'What *did* he do to you?'

I think back to everything Paul did to me.

He tried to rape me, almost killed me, and had plans to make me his prisoner, but he was also my unwitting accomplice. He set himself up in so many ways.

Janet across the road shared her front door camera footage with the police. It didn't catch him arriving that final night because he came in from the back. But it did show Paul's van at my house the day James disappeared and his breaking into my house that dreadful night in June. He never noticed the camera hidden behind the wing of one of her butterfly sculptures hanging on the front wall.

For the police interviews, all I had to do was channel the old Millie, the scared and naïve Millie. She told them he was nothing but a two-night stand who stalked her for weeks afterwards. A psychopath who threatened to torch her house with her inside if she didn't agree to continue the relationship.

Todd Markham corroborated this tale. He told the police about Paul's seething jealousy the day they crossed paths in my hallway. It helped that Todd was in no doubt that Paul had slashed his tyre.

And, much as it turned my stomach to do it, I called the man from Courante's who'd slipped his business card into my pocket. He testified that I'd said it was just a date, nothing more, yet Paul had been disproportionately possessive and had threatened to cut his balls off just for speaking to me. I hadn't seen the knife Paul had apparently pulled on him, but it was one more nail that he hammered into his own coffin.

I told the police I was absolutely certain that he'd killed Brooke Fletcher to get my address, and James Buckley to remove him from my life. James's body hasn't been found but he never showed up for the Antarctica trip and the police are convinced that Paul fabricated the Facebook post.

In Paul's van, along with the invoices evidencing his long-term relationship with Dexter Tanning, they found a half-empty tub of paint thinners I'd deliberately left behind. The same brand that had apparently been used to start the fire in my bedroom.

I didn't need to direct the police to the run-down house in the woods; they found it in the search for Dexter. With the chains attached to the bed frame and the stolen photograph of me and Nanny on the bedside table, they quickly pieced together what Paul had had in store for his innocent victim.

The investigating officer did ask why I hadn't taken out a restraining order, but it wasn't difficult to convince her that a protection order was as useful as the paper it was written on. I told her I'd read somewhere that restraining orders often made matters worse. That obsessed stalkers often escalated to violence when their rights of access were removed, which was when their victims usually ended up dead. All protection orders really did was offer the victim a sense of peace that wasn't real, making them believe they could let their guard down. As if a piece of paper signed by a charming old man in a curly wig would have ever stopped a psycho like Paul.

She couldn't argue with *that* truth.

In reality, I'm not sure it would have been possible to escalate the violence. Other than killing me, what could Paul have done that he hadn't already? He would have just repeated the same horrors over and over in that run-down house.

You would think that protecting myself from such atrocities would have been enough to justify murder. It wasn't. I knew Paul wouldn't keep his vow and would eventually come for me. But that – the threat to my welfare and liberty – wasn't what turned me into a cold-blooded killer.

Paul did that himself.

He did it the same day I found the house. After returning from Colchester that evening, Paul made a journey that would cost him his life.

The shock of opening the Find My app and seeing my AirTag pulsing right outside Shawn's house ignited a blaze in me that I had no idea existed. I don't know how Paul found him, but protecting the man I love finally brought out the murderer in me.

Like Paul's boyhood persona, she was hiding just beneath the skin.

I called Shawn that very moment.

The night we kissed, I had struggled to convince him that Paul had killed Brooke and James. Paul changed his mind. Seeing that white van parked outside his house was enough to convince Shawn he was in danger.

Almost three weeks had passed since he'd shown up at my door only to be sent away, and although he didn't understand, he wasn't a man to bear a grudge and heard me out. I explained how Paul had been there that morning, that I'd forced Shawn to leave to save his life.

He believed me.

I left out the part where Paul was chained to my fireplace. Another lie by omission, like the many I'd told him in my gym when he was benching less than he thought he was.

Shawn left by the back door and went to stay with a friend whose email address I could contact when the coast was clear. Knowing he was safe meant I could concentrate on keeping myself alive. I made him swear not return to his house under any circumstances. He wasn't to contact me or anyone, and he wasn't to use his credit card, mobile phone or anything that could reveal his location. He took some convincing that those measures weren't overkill, but in the end he did as I asked. I had no doubt that Paul would have either killed Shawn or used him as a pawn to keep me under control.

If I hadn't stopped him.

Now, we're both free.

'Millie,' Shawn presses. 'Please tell me... What did he do?'

'It's best you don't know that either.'

I take the seat next to him and shuffle up close. Lifting his arm, I wrap it around my shoulders as if it's an old winter scarf, well-worn and much cherished.

We sit like that for a while until I say, 'I should have told you this that night on the phone but there wasn't time. I've been wanting to say it for ages, but with the rebuild, the police, the fire investigations, it's all been so crazy.'

I twist around to face him because I need to look him in the eye when I say this.

'I'll be forever sorry for how I treated you that morning after we kissed. I *really* wanted you to call in sick, stay with me. I wanted it more than anything in the world. I just... I couldn't involve you. Not after Brooke...and James.'

'You should have told me you were in trouble. I would have helped you.'

'No. You would have tried. And Paul would have killed you.'

'He could have killed *you*.'

'I can take care of myself.'

'Clearly. But I could have done *something*. What if things had gone a different way? I could have lost you. You could have died in that fire. He could have—'

'Paul didn't want me dead, he wanted me alive. You, on the other hand...' That thought lingers. 'I knew what I was doing. And I did what had to be done.'

Shawn goes to speak again but I interrupt him.

'It's over now. And honestly, all I want is to forget I ever met him. I don't want to talk about it any more.' I spin around and kiss him softly on the lips before pulling away to look him in the eye. 'Can you do that for me? Can you let it go?'

He kisses me back, gentle at first but then with more urgency, and I know then that it's really over. Shawn won't ask me again.

Maybe one day I will tell him about all the horrors that took place in here...and that the woman he loves is a cold-blooded killer.

Maybe.

In the meantime, the murder investigations are still ongoing but all the evidence – much of which Paul left behind himself – corroborates my testimony of a psycho stalker who set himself on fire with his own paint thinners. The police are running with the theory of a murder-suicide gone wrong. After all, as the fire investigators concluded, Paul could have easily opened the bedroom door and walked straight out.

So why didn't he?

The only person who knows the answer to that is me.

Many times, over the years, I had inwardly despaired at my more obsessive clients for wasting so much of their lives in my gym. It never crossed my mind that, in the end, it would save my life.

Even at the peak of my performance I could only power-clean sixty-five kilos. So throughout July, never knowing when Paul might come for me, I trained every hour I could. I perfected my execution and acceleration, each day shaving off valuable seconds. Eventually, I made it to seventy-five kilos. But it still wasn't enough. I needed to reach elite level for my body weight.

The carpenter who built and installed the shelves on either side of my bedroom door never questioned why I refused to let him glue or screw on their lipped fronts. Or why I insisted they be carved from a single block of Brazilian walnut.

He never noticed that the internal depth of the window box planter he custom-made for me precisely matched the depth of the shelves. And he never asked why they needed to hold so much weight.

Every day, I trained in the gym. And every night, I meticulously rehearsed each step of my plan, again shaving off valuable seconds. The only step I had never been able to complete was that final power-clean lift.

I'd run out of time and that almost cost me my life.

With the AirTag in Paul's van just minutes from my house, I executed each step knowing that if my strength failed me at the end, Paul would probably kill me.

I couldn't lift the barricade up the stairs, it was far too heavy. I had to drag it from the utility room to the landing, then into the cupboard opposite my bedroom, on polythene sheeting that enabled it to slide.

Once I'd shut the door on Paul, I set my stance and grabbed each handle of the two copper cauldrons buried inside the precision-moulded barricade. I flattened my back, engaged my core and prayed to God to give me the power I needed.

Pushed to hysterical strengths by fear and adrenaline, in one explosive movement I executed an eighty-five-kilo power-clean lift that would save my life.

With the barricade in place, I knew the door wouldn't open more than a few millimetres, and the strong lips on the front of each shelf would lock it in position.

Then it was just a matter of time.

While Paul was trying to escape through the window, the intense heat from the bedroom melted that one-and-a-half-metre-long block of ice. And as it disappeared, it slowly lowered the two antique cauldrons – frozen deep inside up to their handles – perfectly on to their display shelves on either side of the door.

Knowing Paul couldn't come after me, I stashed the polythene sheeting in the landing cupboard and ran downstairs to execute the final steps of my plan.

During rehearsals, the window box planter I'd used as an ice mould had been lifted in and out of Nanny's chest freezer dozens of times over the previous weeks. Not by me, obviously – I'd never have been able to lean in and lift it out. So, above the freezer, I'd fitted an electric hoist to the ceiling. It was only ninety quid on Amazon.

That night, back in the utility room, I quickly disconnected the planter's handles from the hoist hook and lugged it outside into the garden. On the conservatory window sill, with earth and plants inside, there was no reason to suspect it had ever been used to kill a man.

Even if the resulting pool of water – which would have soaked the landing carpet – didn't have time to evaporate before the fire was extinguished, it would have blended with the rain of firemen's hoses that poured in through the thatched roof.

There was no evidence that *anything* had prevented Paul from walking out of that bedroom.

As far as the police are concerned, whether it was suicide or an arson attempt gone wrong, a murderer had paid for his crimes with his life. And once they'd settled on that conclusion, they stopped looking in any other direction.

Especially mine.

It was cut and dried.

Holding tight to Shawn, I stare into the cold hearth.

When Paul was here, when this lounge was filled with the stench of his presence, I had been convinced I would never again feel the same about Nanny's cottage. I'd felt sure he'd irretrievably violated her memory. But when the fire ravaged through this house it burned every cell of his existence in its wake. It scorched every place he'd ever stood, and scrubbed clean everything he'd ever touched. And once what remained of him – and my memories of him – was nothing but dust, the builders swept it all up and tossed it in a skip, flecks of ash floating away on the breeze.

The cottage is no longer haunted by him because everything is slightly different – especially my new gym and yoga studio out back – and yet, at the same time, everything is just as it was.

Except me.

I take Shawn's hand and lead him from the sofa, through the lounge door and up the stairs. But, when I reach the landing, something stops me in my tracks.

Every hair on my body stands up as I sense the presence of someone in this house. I stare down into the hallway below, scanning every door, waiting for one to open.

With my own eyes I watched Paul burn in that fire, and yet, sometimes, my mind still plays tricks on me.

I can't catch my breath.

Then Nanny walks out of the kitchen carrying a tray, and as she passes the bottom stair she looks up at me and winks. 'Well done, my girl,' she says. 'Bloody well done.'

'Is everything alright?' Shawn asks.

I breathe her in.

The sweet warmth of freshly baked scones wafts up the staircase carried on the scent of lavender talcum powder.

'Yes,' I say. 'Everything's perfect.'

PLEASE, PLEASE, PLEASE

Leave a review for Watch It Burn

As independent authors, we can't stress enough how import-ant your Amazon reviews are to getting our work out there.

We love writing these books for you; it takes months of hard work to create each one. So please, please take a few minutes to scan the QR code with your phone camera and leave a short review or just star rate it.

Thank you so much
Carrie and Stephen

SLY TRAP FOR A **FOX**

Four years ago, a near-fatal car crash left Diane with crippling agoraphobia. When another car goes over the embankment at Cruickshank's Fell, she suspects her own brush with death was no accident.

Unless Diane confronts her fears and escapes before it's too late, the next woman will die...

WHEN **HE'S** NOT **HERE**

When Eva finds a secret safe, hidden in her husband's study, her world is turned upside down. The three things inside make her question everything she held true.

Who is the man she married? Was her patient's death even her fault? And are her nightmares the key that unlocks the truth?

STONE THE **DEAD** CROWS

All Rose wants is for her sister Daisy to wake up. Now, Daisy's psychologist has taken an unnatural interest in Rose, and has made a shocking accusation: that Rose's husband is a psychopath.

As the psychologist's interest turns to obsession, Rose is torn between the two men. Who should she believe?

YOU'RE RIGHT **NEXT** DOOR

If you'd told me four months ago that I'd be lying on damp grass, clutching a bullet wound to the stomach, while the love of my life lies dead from a bullet wound to the head, I'm not sure I would have believed you.

If you'd said it was all because of an argument over a metre of land, I might have even laughed.

This is nothing to laugh about...

BUY NOW ON AMAZON

Sport of Kings

When Danny's old SAS buddy goes missing, Danny's unit reunites to find him. When they follow Smudge's trail they find themselves on the wrong side of an international drug-smuggling operation and the Sport of Kings, an exclusive hunt of a deadly nature...

Blood Runs Deep

Five years ago (*Vodka Over London Ice*) the London mob clashed with the Russian mafia. Death and violence escalate, putting Danny's family in danger. Danny Pearson ended the war, or so he thought...

Command To Kill

When Australian billionaire Theodore Blazer takes advantage of today's plugged-in world with sinister intentions, Danny travels to the far side of the globe to stop the world falling apart...

No Upper Limit

Journalist David Wallace is killed when he tries to find out the identity of an arms dealer known as the Wolf. Danny Pearson's SAS unit is also trying to stop the Wolf selling arms to the Taliban. When they get close the Wolf disappears forever, or so they think...

Leave Nothing To Chance

When Danny's best friend Scott goes missing from his hotel room in Brazil, Danny pulls out all the stops to find him. The search takes him into the heart of Colombia and the clutches of a drugs baron known as El Diablo...

Won't Stay Dead

Snipe's back, awoken from his coma and with no recollection of the past few years. When the facility recondition him and put him to work, everything is fine until his memory and insanity return...

Till Death Do Us Part

Danny, his best friend Scott and his old SAS buddies travel to Benidorm for his stag do. What could possibly go wrong?

Enemy At The Door

Disillusioned with the government, the state of the planet, and their future prospects, a group of the country's elite university students take matters into their own hands...

With money, power and connections, they kick off their campaign of terror by blowing up The Red Lion on Parliament Street, a pub where well-known Members of Parliament drink. A pub that Danny Pearson and Scott Miller have just stepped out of...

BUY NOW ON AMAZON

ACKNOWLEDGEMENTS

First, as always, you, dear reader, for buying and reading this book. It's your imagination that breathes life into our stories and we're nothing without you.

Darrell and Emma, our wonderfully supportive spouses, with a special shout-out to Emma for coming up with a great title.

Linda McQueen who tied up all the loose ends that naturally occurred when writing a book over WhatsApp without Carrie or Stephen having any idea what the other would do next. And Charley Chapman for another tireless proofread. These lovely ladies don't make mistakes, they just do their best to catch ours.

Tim Barber at Dissect Designs for your beautiful cover.

Willie Grundy, retired firefighter at Cumbria Fire & Rescue Service, Kendall, for for shooting down in flames all of Carrie's initial ideas for how Millie could get away with murder.

John and Linda from Cutting Edge Stained Glass for coming up with a window that would take a punch and keep our intruder in instead of out.

SarahKate Abercrombie for beta-reading the first draft in one sitting on an aeroplane to Atlanta when there were plenty of movies to watch instead.

All our friends and fans who lift us up every day with wonderful support and reviews.

And finally, as always, from Carrie to Nick: your hand is in mine every day, if not in flesh then in spirit. Love you, sweet girl xxx.

ABOUT THE AUTHORS

Carrie Magillen and Stephen Taylor are both successful authors in their respective genres – psychological thriller and action thriller – with series that have sold hundreds of thousands of copies.

In 2020, they met in a Facebook group and quickly became fast friends. Jump forward several years and they decided to write a thriller over WhatsApp without telling each other what they were going to do next.

It made for very exciting writing since they had to respond in real time, rapidly and creatively, to situations they didn't invent. For the first time, neither of them knew what their antagonist was capable of or how far they would go.

On many occasions, Carrie and Stephen read what the other had written and thought, *How the hell am I going to get out of this?* It was both great fun and super chilling.

They hope you loved reading *Watch It Burn* as much as they loved writing it.